Film Blue

Film Blue

a novel

Patricia Leavy

Paper Stars Press

For Kip Jones

Praise for *Film Blue*

"*Film Blue* is a joyful, inspiring and painfully beautiful novel written by gifted scholar and writer, Patricia Leavy. *Film Blue* shows all of us how to move forward through times of pain, crisis or complacency with hope and love."

Norman Denzin, Ph.D.,
University of Illinois at Urbana-Champaign

"I love it. I just love it. *Film Blue* is a page-turner, but also dives deep beneath the surface. This is Leavy's greatest skill, along with her ability to write characters with whom we empathize. The people in this novel bring with them their familial histories, their #MeToo experiences, and their desire to make it in the world. They have 'big' dreams, and we root for them as they overcome their obstacles and discover what really matters. *Film Blue* takes you inside yourself, and outside, too. It inspires a belief in *possibility*. It's absolutely gorgeous. In the accolades of the 1980s, it's uniquely cool. It would be fantastic in any number of college courses. Young adults should read this. Brava!"

Laurel Richardson, Ph.D., author of *Lone Twin*

"An engaging piece of public scholarship, *Film Blue* provides rich food for thought about the pop culture landscape and how its shapes our own stories. With a subtext about privilege, opportunity, sexual assault and gender, this would be a useful and fun teaching tool."

Sut Jhally, Ph.D., University of Massachusetts at Amherst;
Founder & Executive Director, Media Education Foundation

"One of my favorite authors, Patricia Leavy, has done it again. With her novel, *Film Blue*, she covers a lot of ground: following your dreams, the magic of serendipity, and the importance of pop culture in life (as well as in teaching). *Film Blue* is the quintessential novel of young adults in NYC and LA– exploring friendships, jobs, life, relationships, and finding themselves. This book is set in current times with a love of the 1980s and it's eminently readable, thoughtful, and satisfying. It can – and should – be used in university classrooms for a variety of subjects (and includes further engagement), but it is also meant to be read outside of the university – for yourself, or with your book club. There's much to ponder, and discuss, but also much to ingest, reflect upon, and relate to your own life. I couldn't put it down, absolutely loved it, and can't stop thinking about it. *Film Blue* is a treasure. Highly recommended."

Jessie Voigts, Ph.D., Wandering Educators

"*Film Blue* reminds me of what it meant to live through the *blue* of young adulthood, a time spent working through the complexities of a life that's constantly changing like the sky while struggling toward self-love, spiritual balance and happiness. I was immediately pulled in by Leavy's refreshing use of language, her descriptions helping me see the world she's creating, a world that feels as familiar as one I remember as if it were yesterday."

Mary E. Weems, Ph.D.,
author of *Blackeyed: Plays and Monologues*
and Cleveland Arts Prize winner

"Placing women's experiences in the forefront, *Film Blue* tells a powerful story of women who overcome obstacles in pursuit of their dreams. With a subtext of sexual harassment and inequality especially relevant in the #MeToo era, this timely novel illustrates the cultural context in which girls and women live their lives. An engaging read, *Film Blue* is sure to stimulate reflection, both personally and more broadly in book clubs and courses on media and gender."

Jean Kilbourne, Ed.D., author, feminist activist,
and creator of the *Killing Us Softly:*
***Advertising's Image of Women* film series**

"An engaging reminder of the struggles that come and go in the course of a life, *Film Blue* captures the experiences of multiple characters at transformational times in their lives and demonstrates the importance of persistence, creativity, and support for the achievement of one's dreams. The novel swims at a beautiful pace with an undercurrent of sexual and gender tension and conflict especially fitting for talking and teaching about our current social world."

J. E. Sumerau, Ph.D.,
author of *Scarecrow*

"*Friends* meets *Girls* meets *The Perks of being a Wallflower*, all with its own 1980s vibe. *Film Blue* is a novel I had no idea I was waiting for until I started to read it. At the core, it explores the pursuit of a 'big life.' How do we get in our own way? How do unaddressed past traumas leak into our present and prevent us from moving forward? There are so many elements that demonstrate Leavy's expertise in explicitly and implicitly drawing out the truths at the heart of humanity in today's world in ways we can all relate to, while creating a story that feels incredibly intimate. This is a brave novel, dealing with issues sparked by the #MeToo Movement, in a sensitive yet direct way that will resonate with any reader. Her characters help us all realize that we only really see shades of people, tips of icebergs that often hide deep wells of pain. I could write a thousand pages of reasons to consume this novel on a lazy afternoon, since once you start you won't be able to put it down. I could even write a long list of reasons to use this novel in your college courses. It's light and fun reading, with messages that linger."

U. Melissa Anyiwo, Ph.D., editor of *Gender Warriors*

"This novel is written for anyone who has ever confronted the shadow side of their life to find the courage to light their own fire. *Film Blue* provides inspirational fuel for forging the life, work, and art we need by watching the characters realize their own passions

in a sexist culture. *Film Blue* is a feminist fist bump and a gorgeous visual of what women helping women and being your own muse looks like on the big screen of our lives."
Sandra L. Faulkner, Ph.D., author of *Real Women Run*

"Once you pick up this book, you won't be able to put it down. Like Leavy's previous novels, *Film Blue* shows us how beautiful our lives can be when we embrace possibilities. It's a powerful commentary on living your best life, one that will leave you inspired."
Jessica Smartt Gullion, Ph.D., Texas Woman's University

"*Film Blue* is a love letter to popular culture, and in particular, illustrates how art may sustain us through life's challenges when those around us may not. Leavy's voice is palpable and inviting as she draws vivid and knowable, strong and complex characters, to whom many can relate in their struggles for success and desire. Leavy's refreshing and authentic dialogue and relatable plotting defy the complexity of the work and its subtexts about opportunity, creativity, and privilege, as well as feminism, equity, and sexuality. Leavy has delivered another title in her original and unique voice, yet again demonstrating her mettle as a masterful writer of fiction."
Alexandra Lasczik, Ph.D., Southern Cross University

Selected Fiction by Patricia Leavy

Celestial Bodies: The Tess Lee and Jack Miller Novels

Low-Fat Love: 10th Anniversary Edition

American Circumstance: Anniversary Edition

Low-Fat Love Stories (with Victoria Scotti)

Spark

North Star

Supernova

Constellations

Twinkle

Shooting Stars

For more information, visit the author's website
www.patricialeavy.com

Contents

Acknowledgments

There are so many people to thank for their generosity along the journey of writing this novel. From the bottom of my heart, thank you to the reviewers for your incredibly kind endorsements. Sincere appreciation to Shalen Lowell, the best assistant, spiritual bodyguard, and friend. Heartfelt thanks to Celine Boyle, the world's greatest writing buddy, for your invaluable feedback. Thank you to Clear Voice Editing for the always phenomenal copyediting services on earlier versions of this work. Liza Talusan and the Saturday Writing Team—thank you for building such a supportive community and allowing me to be a part of it. To my social media community and colleagues, thank you boundlessly for your support. My deep gratitude to my friends, mentors, and colleagues, especially Vanessa Alssid, Renita Davis, Pamela DeSantis, Sandra Faulkner, Ally Field, Jessica Smartt Gullion, Alexandra Lasczik, Linda Leavy, Laurel Richardson, Xan Nowakowski, Mr. Barry Shuman, Eve Spangler, and J. E. Sumerau. Mark Robins, you're the best spouse in the world. Thank you for all that words cannot capture. This novel is dedicated in loving memory of my friend and fearless creative, Kip Jones.

We are possibilities.

PART ONE

Chapter 1

That can't be right, Tash thought, squinting again to look at the time. "Shit. Damn thing never works," she mumbled as she reached for the alarm clock. *I'm gonna be late again. I should hurry.* She rolled over before slowly stretching her arms and lazily dragging herself out of bed. Stumbling to her dresser and opening the top drawer, she rifled around for underwear before heading to the bathroom.

Twenty minutes later, wrapped in a towel after showering, she used her palm to wipe the steam from the mirror. *I look like crap. God, I hope I can cover those bags under my eyes*, she thought as she started to apply her signature black liquid eyeliner. *I'll use gray eyeshadow and make them smoky.* Realizing it must be getting late, she dried and straightened her long, dirty-blonde hair but skipped curling the ends to save time. Returning to her bedroom, she scoured her closet wondering what to wear before deciding on an off-the-shoulder, loose white tunic, a pair of skinny black jeans, and high-heeled black leather booties. Staring at herself in the mirror, she tried on four pairs of earrings, posing left and then right to fully view each option, before deciding on gold hoops. To match, she threw on her favorite gold, turquoise, and red evil-eye bracelet. *Coffee. I need coffee.*

En route to the galley kitchen, Tash stomped past her room-mates' closed bedroom doors, clomping her heels without concern as to whether they were asleep. She got a bag of coffee and the nearly empty carton of milk out of the refrigerator, placed them on the counter, and opened the cupboard to get a coffee filter and her to-go tumbler, neither of which were there. She found her tumbler in the sink, dirty from the day before. *Fuck.* Turning back to focus on the coffee pot, she spotted a note sitting beside it. *There's nothing I dread first thing in the freaking morning more than these notes.*

Morning, Tash. Hope you didn't forget to turn the volume up on your alarm again and oversleep. I didn't want to wake you in case you had the day off. We're out of coffee filters and it's your turn to go to the store. I left my list on the back of this note. I can't cover for you this time so please go. Thanks. Have a nice day. Penelope

Tash flipped over the note and rolled her eyes. She started to leave the kitchen when she turned back, remembering to put the milk away. *Don't want the Gestapo after me for that again.* She headed into the common room, sans coffee, and looked around. *Where did I leave my bag?* The small love seat was overflowing with random clothing, topped with her black blazer. *Hmm. Two pairs of men's shoes under the coffee table. Jason must have met someone. Good for him, but where's my stupid bag? Ah, there you are,* she thought, spotting her black bag hiding in the corner, with her keys and sunglasses conveniently lying on top of it. She scooped them up, put her dark glasses on, and headed out, double locking the door behind her.

"Hi, Mr. Collier," she said, passing her neighbor on the stairs.

"Good morning, Miss," he replied.

Despite the morning rush, she was able to hail a cab quickly. As the cab passed Washington Square Park, she glanced at the chess players, already at it for the day. Soon she drifted into thoughts of the drama the day before. *Ray was a jerk, Jason was so right. He didn't deserve me. I'm glad I ended it.* As they pulled up to Alice & Olivia, Tash rummaged through her bag for cash before giving up and surrendering her credit card to the driver.

She flew into the store, quickly heading to the backroom before Catherine could open her mouth. Tash threw her arm up and hollered, "I know, and I'm sorry. My alarm didn't go off and blah, blah, blah."

"You're half an hour late, again," Catherine called after her.

"I know, I know, and I'm sorry," Tash said, rolling her eyes. As she hung her bag and blazer on a coat hook, Catherine continued to reprimand her.

"You need to get a new alarm clock then, because I…"

"I'll close for you tonight, okay? You can leave early; it's fine."

"You know if you left on time you could walk here and save yourself the cab fare. You probably lose at least an hour's wages by creating a situation in which you need to take a taxi. And is it even faster with the morning traffic?"

As Catherine continued, Tash muttered under her breath, "Get off my ass, you bitch," if only to make herself feel better. She took a deep breath and headed to the Keurig machine to make some much-needed coffee. She plugged it in and flipped the switch, but Catherine announced, "Don't bother. It broke yesterday." Tash squeezed her eyes shut, shook her head, and took another deep breath before forcing a smile onto her face. "Great, that's just great."

"I'm going to head out now, since you're closing tonight."

"Uh huh, fine Catherine. Have a good night," Tash said while leaning on the store counter and checking her phone. She was exchanging texts with Jason, reminding him to get them on the club list that weekend.

"Make sure you change the shoes and handbags in the window display. Last season's accessories go on sale tomorrow, so the newer items should be featured in the window," Catherine reminded her.

"Uh huh," Tash replied, without looking up from her phone.

"Okay, well, good night."

"Night, Catherine."

An hour later, after ringing up the final customers, Tash retrieved the new handbags and shoes from the backroom. She liked working on window displays because it was a chance to be creative and put things together in unexpected ways that were sure to perplex Catherine. Tash imagined the windows as still images from film, designed to convey a feeling as much as to display clothes. While there was a limit to what she could get away with, she pushed the bounds as much as possible. She didn't mind her job and loved working in SoHo, but window displays and the employee discount were the only aspects from which she derived genuine pleasure.

After putting accessories from the window onto the sale table, Tash gathered her things and locked up. With only a blazer on, she felt a chill. These early spring days were unusually warm but the evenings were still cold. *I should really walk home. I can't blow more money on a cab.* Desperate for a scarf, she stood on Greene Street rummaging through her slouchy leather hobo bag, which she carried everywhere despite its tendency to become a black hole in which she couldn't find anything. "Ah, there we go," she whispered as she pulled out a periwinkle scarf, which she double wrapped around her neck.

As the sky darkened, the SoHo lights seemed to shine at their brightest. Store windows screamed with flashing light bulbs, a frenetic attempt to command notice. Tash looked in the windows as she passed by, tempted by sale signs even though she was accustomed to them. These days, even New York City itself was on sale. Street vendors yearning to end their days well tried to her entice her with sunglasses and other trinkets. When she smiled and shook her head, one guy screamed, "You look like Lindsay Lohan. You're dope."

"I get that a lot," she replied with a mischievous smile.

As she crossed over into the Village, the restaurants and corner cafés were already bustling with people clamoring to sit outside. After a brutal winter, New Yorkers were ready to enjoy outdoor dining again. Waiters turned on heat lamps and uncorked wine bottles amid casual conversation and bubbling laughter.

Her feet sore, she slowed her pace as she passed Washington Square Park. As day turned to night, the park was the center of the world around her. People from all walks of life appeared. The parade of artists, writers, students, homeless people, drug dealers, professors, tourists, and countless others made it the perfect microcosm of the city itself, the dream and its shadow side. She overheard a group of preppy college students talking about social justice as they passed Harold, actively trying not to notice as he set up his sleeping bag on a bench. *Jerks*, she thought. *They're such posers.*

A year earlier, Tash had twisted her ankle racing to work one morning. A barrage of f-bombs flew out of her mouth. Harold, a witness to the accident, helped her to a bench and told her not to curse.

"Are you for real?" she asked.

"It's undignified," he replied. "Do you think you can walk?"

"Uh, yeah, but not in these shoes."

They spoke for a few more minutes before she decided to stumble back to her apartment to ice her ankle and change shoes. Since that day, she'd say hi to Harold when she saw him and stopped to talk with him at least once every couple of weeks, usually bringing him a cup of coffee and sometimes a doughnut. Powdered sugar was his favorite.

He once started to tell his life story and she interrupted saying, "It's cool, Harold. We don't have to do this. I don't need you to explain." He seemed relieved. Since then, their conversations were usually about how they were each doing that particular day.

Although routinely chased away by the police, he always returned. On this night, she just waved as she passed him.

Only half a block from her apartment, she had the horrible realization that she was supposed to get groceries. Not willing to endure a lecture from Penelope, she passed her apartment building and headed to the corner grocer. After grabbing a hand basket and making a beeline to the freezer for some ice cream, she started searching for the items on Penelope's list. As she fumbled for the note, mumbling, "Ah, where is that stupid thing?" she heard a voice say, "Maybe you'd have better luck if you shut your eyes and put your hand in."

"Huh?" she queried, looking up at the six-foot-tall guy standing before her, dressed from head to toe in black. He had bleached blonde spiky hair, high cheekbones, a strong jawline, and a piercing through his right eyebrow that she thought was simultaneously cool and disgusting.

"You know, sometimes if you're looking too hard, you can't find anything."

"Uh, yeah," she said, staring into his evergreen eyes. *Oh my God, he's seriously hot.*

"Here, tell me what you're looking for and I'll shut my eyes and stick my hand in for you."

Raising her eyebrows, she said, "How stupid do you think I am? Maybe I should just go outside and scream, 'Somebody rob me!'"

He laughed. "Fair enough, but you try it."

Tash smirked and stuck her hand into her bag without looking. "Uh huh, here it is!" she exclaimed as she pulled out the small, crumpled paper. "That's uncanny."

"Sometimes you just have to concentrate less, you know? What's so important, anyway?"

"Oh, it's just my roommate's grocery list. She's pretty uptight so I can't screw it up. You wouldn't believe the things she writes, like 'two organic red apples and flax seed powder,' whatever the hell that is. Anyway, I should probably get back to shopping."

He smiled and waved his arm, to indicate she could pass by. With only a few aisles in the small store, Tash bumped into him again in the produce section.

"Should I even ask what that's about?" she remarked while giggling, looking at the twenty or more coconuts in his basket.

"Oh, these are for a party I'm deejaying for a couple of friends over at NYU."

"They're serving whole coconuts?" she asked, mystified.

He laughed. "People try to get them open. It's like a drinking game kind of thing. It's pretty funny."

"Gotcha. Do you go to NYU?"

"No, I went to school in Chicago and moved to New York after I graduated. I'm a professional deejay. I'm just doing this party as a favor."

"So, what kinds of clubs do you spin at?" she asked.

"Uh, well, tomorrow I'll be spinning at the Forever 21 store in Times Square."

She smiled. "Well, do you get a discount at least?"

He laughed. "Didn't think to ask for that. So, what's your name?"

"Natashya, but my friends call me Tash."

"I'm Aidan. Do you live around here?"

"Just a block away. I share a place with two roommates."

"Pretty awesome area, good for you."

"Yeah, well we're in like the only non-restored building in the neighborhood. Don't get me wrong, I love living here and it's pretty close to my work, but we're not in one of the swanky buildings with a marble entrance. It's more like splintery wood floors and a scary old-fashioned elevator that makes me want to take the stairs."

He smiled. "What's your work?"

"I work at a couple of stores in SoHo."

"For the discount, right?" he joked.

She laughed. "Well, nice to meet you but I've gotta finish up and get going."

"Sure, me too. Maybe I'll see you around. If you're not busy, stop by Forever 21 tomorrow."

"I have to work."

"Well, can I maybe get your number?" he asked.

"Why don't you give me yours instead?"

"Sure, that's cool." He put his coconut-filled basket on the ground and held out his hand. "Give me your phone and I'll put it in."

"You don't want me to have to search my bag again. Here," she said, handing him the note with Penelope's grocery list. "Do you have a pen?"

He smiled and pulled a red crayon out of his pocket. "Don't ask," he said as he wrote his number on the little paper. "Here," he said handing it to her. "See ya."

"See ya," she replied.

When she casually glanced around the store a few minutes later, he was gone. She brought her basket to the checkout. The cashier asked, "Did you find everything you needed?"

"Yeah, yeah I did."

Her feet aching and her arms overloaded, Tash felt like she was going to drop by the time she made it home. She dumped her handbag and keys on the entryway floor and swung the shopping bags onto the kitchen counter. She opened her new box of popcorn and stuck a packet in the microwave before putting the rest of the groceries away. She giggled to herself, thinking about the coconuts filling Aidan's basket. *I wonder if Jason is home.*

Tash met Jason Woo at a club a few years earlier. She was having trouble getting past the bouncers when Jason came to her rescue. His modeling career was just starting to take off thanks to landing a gig as Calvin Klein's first Asian male model. Both sarcastic and carefree, they bonded immediately and moved in together as soon as

Tash graduated from college. Though they had a hard time looking out for themselves, they did a remarkable job of looking out for each other.

Tash was so lost in thought about Aidan's coconuts that she didn't hear Jason approaching.

"Hey," Jason said from the doorway.

"Oh, hey." She tossed him a bag of coffee. "Stick that in the fridge." As he put the coffee away, Tash said, "This too," and flung the loaf of bread.

"I can't believe you actually went shopping. Did Pen leave you one of her famous notes?"

"Yup," she replied just when the microwave beeped. "Is she in her room studying?"

"She's not here. I think she had dinner plans with her study group or something."

"Seriously? She's unbelievable, making me do all this when she's not even here," she complained as she opened the popcorn bag. Steam burned her hand and caused her to drop the bag on the counter. "Fuck."

"How is it you never learn not to open it that way?" Jason asked facetiously. "Here, I got it." He grabbed a bowl from the cupboard and emptied the bag for her.

"You know if you leave it in the bag it's one less dish to wash. That's why I do that."

"Since when do you ever wash the dishes anyway?" he retorted, as he ate a handful of her popcorn.

"I don't know why she made me go to the store if she wasn't even gonna be home," Tash whined as she threw the two empty grocery bags in the garbage.

"I know you can't relate, but some people actually plan ahead. She probably wanted breakfast."

"Oh, right, like you plan ahead," Tash jabbed, tossing a jar of maraschino cherries.

"You're lucky I caught that. What is it with you and these things?" he asked, sticking the jar in the door of the refrigerator.

"You know I love them. I can't help it," she replied. "But listen, I kind of met a guy. I met him at the store while I was getting Pen's crap, so maybe it was meant to be."

"You met a guy? Ah, do tell," he prodded.

"From the looks of things this morning, I'm guessing you also met a guy, so you tell first." She opened the refrigerator and grabbed two cans of diet cola.

"Some lighting guy from the shoot. I kicked him out this morning."

"You're such a slut. Must be hard to be so irresistible," Tash bemused.

Jason smiled. "You would know. Come on, let's go curl up on my bed and you can tell me all about the guy you met. I hope he's better than Ray. I'm eating half this popcorn, by the way," he said, taking a fistful and heading to his room.

"Hey, that's my dinner!"

Chapter 2

Two afternoons a week, Tash worked at Anna Sui, which was directly across the street from Alice & Olivia. She was friends with one of the saleswomen, Isabelle, an aspiring actress who needed afternoons free for auditions and hooked her up with the job.

When the store was quiet, Tash was supposed to dust the glass display cases filled with jewelry and wallets or flatten old shoeboxes in preparation for the recycling company. Instead, she frequently used one of the tester nail polishes on the front counter to give herself a manicure. She loved how the bottles were shaped like a woman dressed in a black bustier. *The gold sparkle is definitely better than the silver,* Tash thought as she admired her glistening lacquer. She leaned her elbows on the counter, blowing gently to dry her newly polished nails.

Her nails were still tacky when her phone beeped on the counter beside her. She peered over to read the incoming text from Jason:

All set on the list tom night. But no shots for u tequila girl. Xx

She replied:

Hey, any chance u could add one more? Xx

Fuck, I smudged my nail, she muttered, scrutinizing her right hand as she waited for a response.

For Coconut Boy I presume? Who's the slut now? Yeah, can do. U owe me. U pain in the ass. Xx

Next, she texted Aidan, having saved his number the night before, just in case.

Hey. It's Tash from the store last night.

Before she could put the phone down it beeped. *That's eager*, she thought.

Hey. So now I have your #. Setting up at 4ever21. Times Sq. = insanity. Can you swing by?

She waited a minute before responding.

Gonna pass on the neon signs + mobs of tweens. Must be good 4 your self-esteem 2 spin Katy Perry's greatest hits 4 the kiddies. Bet the girls looove u.

Only a moment passed before her phone beeped again.

Ah, so I see we're already up to the mockery part of this relationship. Ok smart ass, u tell me. What's next?

As she started to laugh, she heard the annoying bell on the store door and the chatter of customers. "Please let me know if I can be of any help," she said unenthusiastically as they passed by.

She texted her response to Aidan quickly, smudging another nail.

My roommate got us on the list at Y tom night. Can get u on 2. 10pm.

"Miss, can you open this case please?" one of the customers hollered from the back of the store.

"I'll be right there, ma'am."

Cool. C u there. A.

Smitten, she leaned on the counter to daydream when she remembered the customer in the back. "Shit," she mumbled as she jumped up and grabbed the shop keys from beside the register.

"On my way, ma'am."

Although she told Aidan to meet her outside the club at ten o'clock, Tash and Jason arrived at ten thirty. There were throngs of over- and underdressed bodies, fighting for their place behind the velvet rope, without realizing that even if they made it behind the rope there was little hope of actually getting into the club that night. Tash knew those souls didn't stand a chance and she loved blowing past them, pretending her privilege was so grand it even prevented her from recognizing her special status. Jason was her ticket to that particular euphoria. Despite the mob scene, Tash spotted Aidan immediately, nonchalantly standing slightly outside of the crowd. With Jason in tow, she grabbed him and without a word spoken, the three waltzed into the club, with a mere nod exchanged between Jason and the bouncer.

They reached the main bar on the far side of the club before Tash stopped. With the music blaring, they stood close together and she shouted, "Aidan, this is Jason. Jason, Aidan."

"Hey man, thanks for hooking me up," Aidan said with an out-stretched hand.

Jason shook his hand. "No worries." He then turned to Tash and asked, "You all good?"

"Yeah, thanks sweetie," she said as she leaned in and pecked his cheek. "Go do your thing and I'll see you at home, or not."

"Later. Be good!" With that, Jason disappeared into the crowd.

Before Aidan could say anything, Tash asked, "So, do you want a drink?"

"Hello to you too," he said with a chuckle. "I'll get them. What do you want?"

"Tequila sunrise."

"That makes sense."

"What does that mean?"

"Tequila sunrise: hardcore but flirty. Totally you."

Tash smirked.

"Forgive me, I've bartended. You start to see patterns."

"So if I hadn't told you what I wanted, what would you have guessed?"

"Tequila sunrise."

She smiled. "Okay, very cute smart boy. Now go get my drink."

"You got it. And by the way, you look amazing." When Aidan returned with her drink, he said, "Cheers," and clinked his glass to hers.

"Cheers," she said before taking a gulp. "Wow, that's strong. What's that?" she asked, gesturing to his glass.

"Club soda."

"Club soda? Just club soda?"

"Club soda with lime. I don't drink."

"Alcoholic?" she asked with a hint of hopefulness.

He shook his head. "Nope, just don't drink."

"You don't look like a straight edge."

"Well, then I'm already surprising you. That's good, right? I mean, for a girl who I bet gets bored easily."

She couldn't help but smile. "So when you're spinning at parties and coming up with crazy drinking games, you're stone-cold sober?"

"That's why my games are so good."

Tash nearly finished her drink as they looked around. There was a lot to take in. The club boasted a mammoth dance floor with platforms that people could jump up on when they wanted to be noticed, as well as bars on every side. Dozens of strobe lights and black iron chandeliers draped with crystals and purple light bulbs pulsed in sync with the techno music. Like Tash and Aidan, most people were dressed in black. Drag queens in long, sequined, jewel-colored gowns stood at the edges of the bars passing out cheap feather boas for twenty bucks a pop.

Aidan leaned over to Tash as she took another swig of her drink. "Is this a gay club? It's cool, I'm just curious."

"No, it's just gay-friendly," she replied.

"Do you want to dance?"

"Sure." She grabbed his glass and said, "I'll ditch these. Be right back." She returned a moment later and soon they were on the corner of the dance floor, jumping, spinning, and swaying along with everyone. Aidan never took his eyes off her and every once in a while she smirked. They danced for hours, only taking breaks to use the restroom or when Tash wanted another drink.

Late in the evening, when Tash returned from a trip to the restroom, Aidan draped a white boa around her neck. She smiled and he said, "It gets better. Come here. Working in the deejay circuit has its advantages. And by the way, if you ever want to get onto a club list, I can hook you up."

He pulled her onto the dance floor, and within moments, a remix of ABBA's "Dancing Queen" came on. She finally broke down and laughed hysterically. Everyone around them jumped and cheered as loose feathers from all the boas flew in the air, falling around them like the sparkles in the snow globes she loved as a child. Tash pulled Aidan to her and leaned into him. They held each other and swayed as feathers landed in their hair.

The next morning, wearing black palazzo pants and a bra as she searched for a top, Tash heard a gentle tap on her bedroom door. She threw the clothes in her hands onto her bed and opened the door to find Jason holding two mugs of coffee.

"You're the best," she said as she snagged one.

Jason stood in the open doorway, scanning the room with a mischievous look on his face. "No Coconut Boy?" he queried.

"Oh shush. Come help me choose an outfit."

Jason plopped himself on her bed.

"What do you think of this?" she asked, holding up a sparkly top.

He shook his head, took a sip of coffee, and said, "I think I drank too much for that. The one over there is better."

She slipped on the simple white tank top he pointed to and stood in front of her dresser holding various hoop earrings to each ear. After she settled on the larger pair, Jason said, "Seriously, I expected you to steal my coffee for Coconut Boy. No sleepover? He was hot. Very Billy Idol in his heyday, but taller."

"I'm meeting him later."

"Wow, you didn't give it up on the first night. I'm impressed. You must like him."

"Oh shut up. I'm just not a slut like you."

"Yes you are," he quipped, sipping his coffee. "Ooh, speaking of sluts, Pen didn't come home last night."

"Oh please, she probably fell asleep at the library," Tash said as she applied her lip gloss.

He laughed.

She sat on the edge of the bed, zipping up her black platform booties.

"So where are you meeting him?"

"I'm working a half-day and then meeting him at the MoMA."

"Wow!" he exclaimed, his eyes widening. "You must really like him to take him to your special place. Good for Coconut Boy."

"Please stop calling him that."

"Ooh, you reeeally like him."

"We just needed a place to meet, drama queen."

"Uh huh, sure."

"Oh screw you," she said as she leaned over and kissed his head.

"Screw you too, bitch."

She grabbed her purse, threw her hand up, and said, "Later, sweetie."

18

"Hey, I know. I'm sorry. I'm not always late, really," Tash blurted out, before Aidan could say anything.

"I already know that's not true," he said with a laugh. "No worries. Should we get tickets?"

"My membership will get us both in."

"Cool. Shall we?" he asked, putting his hand out.

"You're so corny, straight edge," she said as she took his hand.

They walked hand in hand. Aidan leaned over and whispered, "You know, your bullshit doesn't fool me, beauty queen."

She leered at him, but her eyes sparkled. As they headed up the escalator, she suggested, "Let's start at the top and work our way down. My favorite spot is on the second floor and I want to save it."

"If I'm worthy, right?"

"You're worthy."

The top floor boasted a special exhibit that paired the "blue" works of Picasso and Miró: paintings from Picasso's Blue Period and a sampling of Miró's greatest pieces, including his three-part masterpiece, Triptych Bleu I, II, III.

"Picasso is one of my favorites," Aidan said, "but the Blue Period is so dark. It isn't even just sad, you know, it's bleak. I'm not afraid of the dark side, but this is pretty far down the rabbit hole."

"Well, his friend offed himself and he was depressed."

"The people look like such sad souls, isolated and alone."

"I think it's their loneliness that makes them so wretched. I mean look at this one," Tash said, stopping in front of a portrait. "She's one of the prostitutes he painted. A rare moment of solitude. She probably wasn't alone much."

"But you don't need to be alone to be lonely, right?" Aidan remarked.

"True." They continued their tour, and when they reached the room devoted to Miró's Triptych Bleu, they stopped to take it in.

"It's amazing how one color can convey so many different emotions. Is there anything more cheerful than this? He was so playful," Tash observed.

"I have to admit, I don't necessarily understand what he was doing, but I think it's awesome," Aidan replied.

"Yeah, it makes sense to me, but not in a way I can explain with words."

Aidan nodded, and then walked to the corner of the room to read the curator's notes. When he returned he said, "It says that Miró thought blue was the color of the unconscious and the surreal, like a dream state."

"That's probably why it makes sense even though it like doesn't. You know? It taps into something that we get deep down."

"Totally," Aidan agreed.

"You know I never do that, look at what they write."

"Why?" he asked.

"It clouds how you see it. This might sound strange, but when I look at a painting and I start to get it, the images move, you know like a little film. It's like the film shows me what it means."

"That's not strange; it's awesome and I get it. I sort of have that with music. I see things, like objects or people doing something from a distance, and then I start to hear them."

She smiled. "Even as a kid, before I studied film, I did that."

"So if you don't read in museums, how do you know that Picasso's Blue Period was inspired by his friend's suicide?"

"I said I don't read the curator shit. I didn't say I don't read at all, genius."

He blushed and looked down. "Fair enough, beauty queen."

"Okay, let's move it along," she said, taking his hand. He chuckled and they continued through the exhibit.

"I know a few things too," he said. "Did you know that Cézanne supposedly had at least sixteen shades of blue on his palette when he painted?"

"The guy who painted fruit?" she asked.

"Uh huh."

"Yeah, I knew that."

Aidan blushed and looked down again.

"But how about when he started painting skulls instead of apples and pears? Talk about dark. Maybe all that blue got to him after all," she said with a wry laugh.

"Yeah, maybe. Nothing gets past you. You know who should be known for his blue stuff? Chagall."

"I was never really into him. Did he use a lot of blue?"

"At the Art Institute in Chicago there are these amazing stained glass windows that Chagall created, cobalt blue with all sorts of symbols about America. They're pretty cool and there's always a flock of people standing in front of them."

"Aren't those in *Ferris Bueller's Day Off*? You know, in the museum scene?"

"Leave it to you to turn visual art into a movie," he said.

"I'm obsessed with all things eighties these days, especially movies."

"Cool. They kiss in front of the Chagall windows, Ferris and Sloane."

"She was so pretty. I wanted to be her in that time. I wonder what happened to that actress."

"She's got nothing on you. Funny how that kissing scene casually comes up in conversation, and we just happen to be in a museum and all."

"Okay, smart boy. Let's move it along."

By the time they reached the next floor, talk of art faded and they shared the details of their lives. Painting by painting, floor by floor, they talked about their childhoods, families, and what brought them to New York.

Tash learned that Aidan grew up in a small, middle-class suburb in the Midwest, in a home that his lower-middle-class parents struggled to afford. Although he clearly had a loving family, he was a misfit from an early age in a town that "prioritized football and God, in that order." In grade school he often found himself alone, lost in graphic novels and music, "imagining the beats of the music were footsteps, marching me away from that place."

He told her he was always the kid wearing headphones because they provided a protective bubble that no one could puncture. He lived in a sonic world when the real world let him down. Thanks to his height, which had him towering over many of the jocks, he was rarely bullied. Things changed in high school when his good looks and charisma propelled him into popularity with the girls. On several occasions when he was walking home alone at night after studying in the library, he was jumped by a group of jocks. They did little damage but always left a mark, like a fat lip or black eye. Despite his attempts to conceal his injuries or lie about their origin, his mother worried terribly and became critical of his gothic dress and "attention-getting" piercings. It put stress on his home life.

"Suddenly, who I was became a problem," he explained.

"If they only attacked you when you walked home at night, why didn't you just study at home or get a friend to walk with you?" Tash asked.

"Acquiescing to fear is a dangerous road. I guess I wasn't going to walk down it and give them that kind of control over me. I knew it would never be that bad. But you know what really got me? Every time they'd come after me, they'd call me gay. I know that it was a catch-all insult for those misogynist fucks, but come on. They're beating me up for fucking their girlfriends while they call me gay? Even as they hit me, I was laughing on the inside."

"They weren't very creative, that's for sure. Pathetic dicks."

"They said it so frequently that sometimes I wondered if they really believed it and they were just confused about why they hated me. Getting into the world of deejaying in Chicago was my way out of that small-minded crap. New York was the next stop. I'm making a name for myself on the circuit."

"Yeah, I kinda gathered that last night," she said, looking down sheepishly.

He smiled.

"Wanna hear something really messed up?"

He nodded.

"When I was in college, I studied abroad in Amsterdam."

"Don't tell me, you picked Amsterdam for the pot?"

"No, to work in the Red Light District," she said with a straight face.

He just looked at her.

"I'm kidding, God. I went to The University of Amsterdam for a semester because they have a kickass film studies program. Plus, you know, the pot."

He laughed.

"So I'm in Amsterdam during orientation and they set up all of these activities to help us get to know each other and the city and stuff. I signed up for a boat tour. A big-time feminist, Gender in Film professor took us. So we're on the boat and the automated guide is blaring out information like, 'look left to see whatever.' We all turn to see the famous thing, and there is this chick up against a wall, like my age, and this guy is screwing her. I mean, his pants are around his ankles and he's got her pinned against the wall, holding her wrists."

"Oh my God."

"But here's the messed up part: everyone just watches and the professor shouts, 'He's fucking her! He's totally fucking her!' And we all just watched until the boat was too far away to see them anymore. To this day, I don't know if they were having public sex or if he was raping her. I can picture it clear as day and still don't know what to think. How could they all be so sure it was consensual, or did they just not care? Voyeuristic fucks. Sick. It was never mentioned again, not by the professor or anyone."

Aidan stopped walking, turned to Tash, and said, "That's really horrible."

"My point is that sometimes people don't know what to think about what they're seeing or feeling. They pick a reaction and go with it, even if it really doesn't make sense. It's all they're capable of. Even when they're right in the middle of it, sometimes they don't know. Like with those assholes who beat on you for screwing their girls while they called you gay."

He leaned in and gave her a soft, quick kiss on her lips. They continued walking, loosely holding hands, as if entirely natural.

As the escalator reached the second floor, Tash pulled Aidan along. "Come on."

"Wow, this is cool," he said as they entered a large space with eight different parts of a film being projected onto the walls.

"Shh," Tash cautioned, as she tugged him.

Cushions lined the edges of the room and large bean bags and pillows filled the center of the space. People were sitting all over the place watching the moving images.

Tash spotted an empty cushion in the far corner of the room and led Aidan there. From that vantage point, they could see most of the installments.

She leaned over and whispered, "It's this genius Japanese filmmaker. She won an international competition and got a huge grant when she was still in grad school. It was supposed run as a special exhibit, but that was over a year ago. It's like temporarily permanently here. It's about energy, about nature and humans. She filmed it in at least four Asian countries, and the images are incredible. It's the cinematography that I really love. Just watch. You'll get it."

People came and went, but an hour later, Tash and Aidan were still sitting there, leaning on the wall and each other.

Eventually Aidan whispered, "It's mesmerizing. I could stay here forever."

"Yeah, me too."

They looked at each other and he leaned in and kissed her. With his hand cupping her cheek and beautiful images floating all around them, she felt entirely content.

The next morning, Tash awoke to realize she was cradled in Aidan's arms. She tried to wriggle her way out without disturbing him, but as soon as she moved, he sighed.

"Good morning," he said groggily.

She sat up and said, "Hey, sorry. I didn't mean to wake you."

"That's okay. What are you doing?"

"I need to shower."

"So you got what you want and now you're done with me. Is that it?" he joked.

Expressionless, she turned to face him. "Yup, that's it."

"Come on, beauty queen," he whispered as he rubbed her arm. "Don't run away. Get back over here." He pulled her down and started tickling her while taunting, "Can you take it? Can you keep a straight face?"

Soon she was laughing hysterically. "I give in. I give in!"

He stopped tickling her and gently brushed her hair away from her eyes. "You're beautiful. Last night, well…"

Before he could finish, she leapt up and said, "Yeah, yeah, yeah, but without a shower and coffee, I'm gonna be a mega bitch."

He looked down and smiled coyly. "Coffee would be good."

Tash wrapped herself in her robe while Aidan threw on his T-shirt and boxers.

"Come on. Let's see if Jason's up and then you can meet my other roommate."

They passed Jason's bedroom and saw the door was wide open. "Looks like someone didn't come home last night," Tash muttered.

Just when they approached the kitchen, Penelope was catching her bagel as it popped up from the toaster. She fumbled a bit and dropped it on the counter. Tash wasn't sure if the bagel was hot or if they had startled her.

"Good morning, Tash."

"Hey. This is Aidan."

"Hey," Aidan said.

Penelope brushed her long, loose curls away from her face, adjusted her glasses, and nodded in acknowledgment.

"We were just gonna make coffee. Do you want some?" Tash asked.

"Oh, no thanks. I made this to take with me. I have plans and I'm already late."

Tash was no longer paying attention. She loaded a filter with coffee grounds as Aidan waited in the doorway.

Penelope wrapped her bagel in a napkin and scooted past Aidan.

"Nice to meet you," he called after her.

"You too."

Tash turned to Aidan and gave him an exaggerated eye roll. She opened her mouth but he put his finger against his lips and turned his head to watch Penelope leave the apartment.

The door clicked shut and Tash opened her mouth, but was again derailed when Jason came in.

"Hey," Aidan said.

"Oh, hey Aidan."

"I'm in here," Tash called. "We're making coffee. Want some?"

"No, I'm gonna crash for a while," he replied as he made his way through the small, crowded space.

"I need to go text my friend about something. I'll be right back," Aidan said before making himself scarce.

"See ya man," Jason said.

As soon as Aidan was out of earshot, Jason turned to Tash. "So, you and Coconut Boy must have had a good time yesterday."

"Oh, shut up you slut. What boy's heart did you break when you abandoned him this morning?"

"Well, at least I stayed until the morning," he replied, opening the refrigerator.

"Yeah, what's up with that?" Tash asked.

"I had one too many shots and staying over just seemed easier." She laughed.

Empty-handed, he shut the refrigerator and said, "Pen passed by me without even taking a beat for a hello. Where's she running off to?"

"Who the hell knows? Probably the library. You should have seen her face when she saw Aidan. It was so funny."

"He does look pretty fine in his skivvies."

"How much do you want to bet that Pen leaves me a note asking me to cover him up better? Little miss propriety."

"She's not that bad. Just remember, without her, you and I would need to be the grown-ups."

Tash smiled.

"I'm going to crash. Say goodbye to Coconut Boy for me."

"His name is Aidan."

He smirked. "Say goodbye to Aidan for me."

Chapter 3

Later that night as Tash lay in bed, Aidan's scent still on her sheets, images from the night before swirled in her mind. His eyes locked onto hers, his soft lips, and the firm press of his flesh, their bodies entangled. It was so good she could hardly remember it all, just a jumble of flickering moments and sensations etched in her memory. Over and over again, she imagined the feel of his touch and the look in his eyes. *Fuck. What's wrong with me? It was just good sex. Really good sex. Don't be one of those idiots who loses it because of an orgasm. Get a grip.* But no matter how hard she tried, whenever her mind quieted it was flooded with memories of how she felt lost in his eyes. Lost and found. Then, she had a surprising realization. *Shit, I don't usually open my eyes with guys. Why did we do that? What was that? New cardinal rule: no orgasms with open eyes. Messes with your brain.* She rolled over to go to sleep. As she drifted off, she pulled the sheets up high, clinging to the faint smell of him.

The next morning, she woke up to a text from Aidan.

Hey beautiful. When can I see u?

Not wanting to appear overly available, she showered, flipped through a magazine, and ate breakfast before responding.

No plans today.

Spinning at the H&M on 5th until 6. Meet me?

She laughed and thought, *I could use some tights anyway.*

Sure. Will be fun to see your groupies.

Tash arrived at H&M at five thirty. Aidan was set up just inside the store's entrance. Although he was wearing large black headphones and was engrossed in the music, he acknowledged her immediately with a wide smile. She made a funny face and he looked down, blushing. She pointed to the accessories on the far wall and he nodded, continuing with his work. No matter where she was in the store, whenever she looked back at Aidan, he had his eyes on her. Twenty minutes later, she returned with a small plastic bag containing her new tights and a belt. She walked over to Aidan, pecked him on the cheek, and sat on the edge of the display case near him. She sat back among the mannequins and watched nearly everyone checking Aidan out, girls and guys alike. While some women might feel insecure that a stream of people were admiring and even flirting with the person they're seeing, Tash reveled in it. *He can hold his own*, she thought.

Aidan gestured that he was shutting it down after one last tune. He transitioned from techno to a remix of "Dancing Queen." She put her hand on her chest, bowed her head, and laughed, overjoyed. When the song was over, he took his headphones off, turned to her and said, "I planned that one for you."

"Yeah, I sorta got that," she replied, blushing.

"Want to make sure I keep surprising you."

You are, she thought.

Tash fiddled with her phone while Aidan packed up. Soon, he threw his backpack on and announced, "Ready if you are."

As they headed out onto a bustling Fifth Avenue, Tash asked, "Where do you want to go?"

"Have you seen *Kinky Boots*, the musical?"

She shook her head. "But I do have a secret Cyndi Lauper girl crush."

He smiled. "I don't want you to think it's always gonna be like this because there's no way I can usually afford this kind of thing. A buddy of mine works on the show; he's been promising me tickets for ages and finally came through."

"Is he an actor?"

"Lighting guy. Nothing glamorous but it comes with perks. He called earlier and said if we get there fifteen minutes before the show, he has a couple of balcony seats for us. You in?"

"Fuck yeah."

"You know you have a real potty mouth," he said jokingly.

"Oh fuck, your Midwestern upbringing?"

He laughed. "No, I dig it. They say cursing is a sign of honesty."

"Well, don't believe everything you fucking hear."

"I'll keep that in mind, beauty queen. Come on, let's head down fifty-second to cut over," he said, grabbing her hand and guiding her.

On the way to Times Square, Tash teased Aidan about his "groupies." When they passed the MoMA, he gently squeezed her hand. They decided to stop at Aidan's favorite sandwich shop for a quick bite before the show, but as they got closer to the neon signs and Broadway lights, Aidan stopped against a building and handed his backpack to Tash.

"Hold this for a sec," he said as he unzipped it and pulled out his iPod and large headphones. "Put these on."

She looked at him quizzically.

"It's a new remix I'm working on. It's inspired by something I saw on the Times Square Midnight Moment – you know, the big arts campaign that uses the billboard space for digital art."

She nodded. "I've seen it."

"I want you to listen to it as you walk into Times Square."

She put the headphones on and Aidan pressed play before tucking the iPod into her pocket. He put his backpack on, grabbed her hand, and zipped towards the epicenter. Her heart raced as the music kicked in. Everything was vibrating: the ground, her skin, the neon signs begging for attention. She felt like she was racing through a film. Suddenly Aidan made a sharp right turn and pulled her into an old-fashioned sandwich shop. He took the headphones off her head and the clamor of human sounds in mundane conversation returned.

"You look flushed," he said. "What did you think?"

"Incredible rush. It was like you created the soundtrack for my energy mixing with the city's energy."

He leaned over and kissed her. "Come on, there are a couple of seats at the end of the counter."

They snagged the seats and Tash looked up at the menu board.

An older waitress with dyed red hair came over. "What can I get you?"

"You first," Tash said.

"Steak and cheese, no peppers please."

"Something to drink?"

"I'm good with water. Thanks."

"I'll have a grilled cheese and tomato on the challah bread and just water. Thanks," Tash said.

"I discovered this place when I had my first gig in the area. Killer sandwiches. We were lucky to get a couple of stools; it's usually packed so I have to eat on the go."

"Your music is really amazing. After that first drop, I felt like I took off. I don't know how else to describe it. It was like it injected me into the cityscape."

He blushed. "Thanks. After seeing that film installation at the MoMA, I knew you'd get it."

"Jason's the only other person I've taken to see that. Most people I know wouldn't appreciate it."

"You two must be really close."

"Yeah, he's my person, you know?"

"He seems chill. What's he like?"

"He's a really good guy, very smart. People see that he's hot and funny and miss out on all of his best qualities. He's so often the center of attention that people don't realize he holds back most of who he is. He's careful about what he chooses to let people in on."

The waitress returned and slid their plates in front of them.

"Always super fast here," Aidan said as he took a couple of napkins from the dispenser and handed one to Tash.

She picked up her sandwich and pulled apart the two halves, watching the cheese ooze. "This was my favorite when I was a kid. But I didn't know about challah bread until I came to New York." She took a big, uninhibited bite. "That's so good," she gushed as she chewed, the gooey cheese mixing with the buttery toast.

Aidan smiled and dug into his sandwich.

When they finished eating, the waitress dropped off the bill and Tash quickly took it. "I got this," she said and threw down some money. He thanked her and they headed to the show.

When they arrived at the theater, Tash stood in line while Aidan picked up their tickets at Will Call. They found their second-row balcony seats and marveled at their good fortune. Aidan offered Tash a program and she shook her head.

"Of course, you don't want to spoil it."

"Exactly."

They stood up to let an elderly couple pass by. The couple sat beside Tash, and the man asked his wife, "What's this about?" She replied, "It's about the gays, but it's supposed to be excellent." Tash shot a sideways glance at Aidan and they giggled discreetly at each other. Moments later, the lights went out. A wave of anticipatory energy flooded the room and the show began, instantly captivating Tash. By the final number, they were standing and clapping along with everyone else, including the older couple next to them.

"That was brilliant," Aidan raved as they slowly made their way out.

"I knew from the opening number. Anything that starts with coveting shoes has to be good."

He raised his eyebrows.

"Kidding. I loved it."

When they stepped into the cool night air, Aidan asked, "What now?"

"Come to my place."

They walked to the subway station, still talking about the play.

"What was so beautiful about that was the message of accepting others as they are. So simple," Aidan said.

"Yet so hard," Tash replied.

"Especially when we can't accept ourselves as we are. That's the real challenge, right?"

"I guess."

Soon they were back in Tash's bed, making love with their eyes wide open. They never spoke about their relationship, but after that night they became inseparable.

Chapter 4

Jason's life was a series of late night see-and-be-seen parties. Suddenly the "it" guy of New York, the city was his playground. He went to club openings, enjoyed backroom VIP treatment at his regular haunts, and was the person every guy and sexually confused girl wanted to take home. His lucrative and exclusive modeling contract made his time his own, other than occasional photo shoots, public appearances, and international trips for fashion shows.

Most days he slept in, ran a few miles, practiced yoga, and hung around the apartment reading until it was time to head out for the night. When Tash had time off, they snuggled in his bed, watching movies or marathons of their favorite talk shows. Sometimes they bummed around the city, shopping and checking out art galleries. When he suspected Tash's credit card bills were out of control, which was most of the time, he'd treat her to new shoes or accessories to discourage her from overspending.

Over the last six weeks, he spent many days hanging out with Aidan, who had basically moved in. Aidan worked at night so they had plenty of time together when Tash was at work during the day. They bonded quickly, sharing a love of *Monty Python*, sarcastic humor, and gently teasing Tash. Aidan was sensitive to Jason and Tash's close relationship; he knew when to pick up food or grab something from his apartment so they could have their alone time.

On this Friday, Jason woke up at seven thirty for a nine o'clock call time. It was his first solo commercial shoot and he stayed in the night before to get a good night's rest. Tash left him a note by the coffee pot that read, "You got this, rock star. xoxo"

Unfortunately, the subway was delayed. He arrived at the sound-stage at nine thirty and was rushed into hair styling. After more than half an hour getting his hair to look naturally tousled, he plopped down in his makeup chair.

A short man with dark hair greeted him. "Hi, I'm Sam, and I'll be doing your makeup today."

"Hey," Jason replied, so busy texting that he didn't even look up from his phone.

"We're going to do a matte look, nothing iridescent for commercial shoots."

"Uh, huh. Whatever, dude," Jason mumbled.

Sam pursed his lips in annoyance at the very moment Jason looked up to see himself in the mirror. Sam blushed, clearly embarrassed.

"I'm sorry I was running late," Jason said, trying to smooth things over.

"The talent is always late."

"There was a problem on the subway. I'm usually on time."

"Uh huh. That's fine. Please turn to your right," Sam instructed.

Twenty minutes later, Sam sprayed a finishing shield on Jason's face and said, "You're all set. I'll go see if they're ready."

"Thanks, man."

When Sam returned, he said, "Wardrobe is waiting for you."

Jason stood up, slipped his phone into his pocket, and said, "You know, I'm a little nervous."

"Haven't you done this before?"

"Group shoots. Sometimes I was like the lead, but I've never shot solo."

Sam sneered. "You just have to stand there with your hands in your pockets and gaze off into the distance while a voiceover guy sells cologne. You'll be fine."

Jason was taken aback. It had been a long time since anyone had spoken to him that way. Surprise flashed across his face, and Sam looked mortified, his cheeks reddening. Before either broke the awkward silence, a frazzled-looking woman stormed over.

"Come on, come on. Let's get you in some jeans," she barked.

Jason followed her, but not without a glance back at Sam.

Throughout the day, Sam retouched Jason's makeup on set. With a crowd of people around, the bright lights burning and cameras rolling, neither said a word, despite the palpable tension between them. As Jason was leaving the shoot five hours later, Sam ran up to him.

"Listen, I wanted to apologize to you. I didn't mean to be so rude. I'm very sorry."

"No worries, dude. I actually wanted to apologize to you."

"What for?" Sam asked.

"For not seeing you. When I first sat down, I was so preoccupied I didn't really meet you properly. I got us off on the wrong foot. I'm sorry."

"Uh, okay. Wow, uh thanks," Sam stammered.

Jason looked confused.

"I'm sorry. I don't mean to be, well, so incoherent. It's just that most people don't surprise me."

"Yeah, me either," Jason said before walking away.

"I can't believe you have to spend this long on the subway just to get anywhere. That sucks," Tash said, as the train roared into their stop.

Aidan smiled. "I use it as a chance to read or put my headphones on and get lost in new music. The subway has its own sound too, like the rest of the city. Sometimes I shut my eyes and feel the sound."

"I guess. You have a better attitude than me."

He laughed. "It's all I can afford, and as you'll see, it's not much. It's actually way better than my first crash pad in the city. I never would have brought a girl there, not even once."

"No offense, but I hate the subway. This would drive me nuts," Tash said as they exited the station.

"You do what you have to do. I'd kill for an apartment like yours. I still don't know how you manage to afford such a sweet place in that part of the city."

Tash took in the sights and smells of the neighborhood. Many of the buildings were in decline but she admired the vibrant graffiti. Aidan greeted a few guys standing in line at a food truck.

"Who are they?" Tash asked.

"They live in my old building. Nice guys. Met them when I couldn't get my futon up the stairs. They helped. The little guy did some of the subversive street art you were checking out."

"Cool." They continued walking, but moments later Tash complained, "I can't believe you have such a long walk on top of that subway ride."

"We're almost there, beauty queen. The truth is, I would sacrifice anything to be in a major city – Chicago, New York, whatever. I just can't go back to the 'burbs and bullshit."

"Yeah, I still can't picture you in a place like that."

"Neither can I. I'd rather scrape to get by and be here in the middle of it all. Here I can just *be*. I'm not really into material stuff anyway, just people, places, and music. The deejay thing has its benefits too. I never pay cover charges."

"And you don't drink so you go out to the best places for free."

"Exactly."

"Pretty sweet."

"Okay, here we are," he announced as he unlocked the door to a dilapidated walk-up.

Tash smiled half-heartedly.

"Don't worry; you don't have to start hanging out here. Thanks for coming with me. I just want to grab some clothes for tonight."

"Sure, but I don't know if I'm up to going to Brooklyn with you tonight. You'll be there late and I need to catch up on some sleep. You know I have to go to the store tomorrow morning."

"No worries. We can go for a bite and I can get you a cab before I head to the subway."

They entered the rancid-smelling building, and Tash followed Aidan to the stairwell. She put her foot on the first stair heading up, but he pulled her hand.

"This way," he said, leading her downstairs.

"You live in the basement?"

"Think of it as the ground floor."

She followed him into the tiny studio apartment, which was about the size of the small common room in her apartment, and she wondered if the bars on the windows made him feel more or less safe.

"Can you believe I have a weekend roommate?" he asked.

"Uh no, I literally don't understand how that even works," she said, noticing one couch and no other places to sit.

"It was a bigger problem before I started seeing you. Couldn't swing this place on my own and my friend needed a place to crash on weekends because he's got a part-time job in the city. He pitches in a little rent and it's enough for me to get by. He used to sleep in a sleeping bag on the floor and I'd take the futon."

"Fuck," she said.

"When I have good gigs on the weekends I'm out all night anyway. Do you want a glass of water or something?"

"No thanks," she replied, rifling through his shelves. "Wow! I can't believe you have all of these VHS tapes. I mean, that's crazy."

"When I first moved to the city, I went to this charity place to score some furniture and they had a working VCR for five bucks. You can still buy old VHS tapes for like a dollar online and at stores all over the Village, so I figured why not."

"How can you have the most modern laptop, headphones, and deejay setup and be watching freaking VHS tapes?"

"I spend my money on the things that matter. Plus the 'be kind, rewind' stickers are hilarious. The retro thing is kind of rad."

"Oh my God, you have *Staying Alive*," she said. "Finola Hughes was so beautiful in this. I remember when Travolta's character, uh…"

"Tony."

"Yeah! He said that watching her dance was like watching smoke move. Brilliant line. Totally captures what lust feels like. But God, the rest of the thing was so cheesy."

"Come on, that was Travolta at his best. The soundtrack was killer for the time too."

She shrugged and continued flipping through movies. "Is this any good?" she asked, holding up a tape.

"*Heathers*? Don't tell me you haven't seen it."

"Nope."

"It's great. Completely dated but great. It's the original *Mean Girls*, only darker. Total cult classic. With your eighties fascination I would have guessed that you knew it by heart."

"Wanna watch?" she asked.

He looked at the clock on the microwave before saying, "Sure. I could run to the takeout truck down the street and pick up dinner. We can watch it before I head to work."

"Cool. I'll wait here."

"What do you want, beef or chicken?"

"Just get me whatever the veggie option is. I never warmed to the idea of meat from a truck."

He smiled. "Yes, your majesty."

"Hardy har har."

Aidan returned twenty minutes later. The couch was set up with pillows and a blanket, and the small coffee table was cleared to make room for their food. Aidan smiled and said, "I see that my place brings out the domestic goddess in you. Very unexpected."

"Oh please," she said casually.

"Nah, it's cute. You wanted to make things nice. I dig it," he said with a sly smile.

She rolled her eyes and tried to blow him off but was given away by the ever-so-slight upward turn in the corners of her mouth.

While Aidan cracked open the soda cans, Tash opened the food containers and released the smells of the Middle East into the small space. "Oh no, they put peppers on yours," she noted.

"Ah, you remembered I don't like 'em. No worries. I'll pick them out."

"I'll get it," she said as she scooped the peppers out of his container and into hers.

"Thanks for looking out for me," he said.

"More for me."

Aidan put the tape in the VCR and warned, "The one bad thing about buying this thing used is that it didn't come with a remote. But hey, I'd probably lose it anyway."

"Not in this tiny place," she quipped.

"Touché, beauty queen."

"Wow, this is really good," she remarked as she took a forkful of her rice and veggie mixture. "Thanks for dinner."

"Sure thing. There's some pita in the bag."

"Cool," she said, reaching for it.

"Okay, so here we go," he said as the opening credits rolled.

Tash placed her food container on her lap and leaned into Aidan's shoulder. As the movie began, she nestled into him, her eyes lit up, and she declared, "Oh my God. The colors are brilliant!"

Chapter 5

As Tash spooned coffee grounds into the filter, Jason crept into the doorway and said, "You're up early."

She dumped the grounds all over the kitchen counter. "Jeez, you startled me."

"Sorry."

"Do you want some coffee?" she asked as she wiped the grounds into the palm of her hand and threw them in the kitchen sink.

He shook his head. "No thanks. I'm going to try to catch a yoga class. Why are you up so early on a Saturday, and where's Aidan?"

"He was spinning at a club in Brooklyn last night. I was too beat to go and didn't want him to wake me up at like four in the morning, so he crashed at his place. Oh my God, I went to his apartment yesterday."

"It's about time."

"Oh, shut up."

"He said it's tiny. Is it awful?"

"Yeah, it's pretty heinous but we had a good time. He has an old VCR and all of these great movies. We watched *Heathers*, which was totally disturbed."

"Never saw it."

"See, he thought I was a freak for not seeing it before. I'll have to tell him that you've never seen it either."

"Well, you are the movie maven."

"True. Anyway, I needed sleep last night. I have to go into the store for a couple of hours to deal with a shipment; Isabelle has a callback. He's meeting me there and then we're going out for a bite with Kyle."

"Ooh, that's big! Introducing him to the one relative you actually like. What's next, a little walk down the aisle?"

"Oh shut up," she said with a roll of her eyes. "It's just lunch, drama queen."

Jason smiled. "You know I think Aidan is the bomb. I'm just teasing you."

Tash opened the cabinets in search of a travel mug. "So, rock star, how did your shoot go yesterday? And why weren't you out partying all night?"

"Um, it was okay."

"Uh, hold up," she said, giving her full attention to Jason. "Just okay? What happened?"

"It was fine. It's just that I was late because of a problem on the damn subway and some guy sort of said something to me about it."

"Who?" she asked.

"The makeup guy, Sam."

"Who gives a shit what the makeup guy said? He was probably jealous of you. I bet you could have gotten him in trouble."

"It wasn't like that. It was more of a misunderstanding. I was kind of rude to him but I didn't mean to be."

"I think the pressing question is: why are you still thinking about this? Who cares?"

Jason didn't respond.

As she poured her coffee, Tash pronounced, "Ooh, I seeeeee. This is about a boy. Shall we call him Makeup Boy? Will you be going down the Clinique aisle? Or going down…."

"Ha, ha, ha. Very funny. It's not like that at all. If you had seen this guy, you wouldn't be saying that. He was *so* not my type."

"Say what you want, but you're the one still talking about Makeup Boy." She grabbed her coffee and breezed past Jason, stopping to kiss him on the cheek.

Tash looked up from the large cardboard box she was unpacking and noticed Aidan wandering around the store.

"Aidan, come here and help," she called from the door of the backroom.

"Hey, babe. Love the space of this store. The whole purple and black thing against the glossy cherry wood floors is badass."

"Hey. Hold this open," she instructed, handing him a large garbage bag.

Aidan sat on a small stool and held the bag as Tash stuffed it full of discarded Styrofoam packing materials. "Why do they pack the shipments in this non-recyclable crap?" he asked. "It's so retro, and not in a good way."

Tash sat on the floor, collecting errant Styrofoam bits. She looked up at him, clearly annoyed. "Think I know? Let's just finish so we can get the hell out of here. What time is it, anyway?"

He looked at his phone. "Twelve fifteen."

"Shit, we're late. Let me just go to the bathroom," she said, tossing the full garbage bag aside.

They finished up at the store and headed to Café Borgia. The little SoHo staple was busting at the seams. Tash spotted her cousin sitting in the far right-hand corner. She slid into the booth next to Kyle, and Aidan took the opposite seat.

"I'm so sorry we're late," she said as she leaned over and hugged him.

He laughed. "I would expect nothing less. I know how you like to make a grand entrance."

"That's why it sucks; I was planning to be on time for once, but I got held up at work."

"It's good to know some things haven't changed."

She rolled her eyes. Noticing Aidan sitting there silently smiling, she said, "Oh sorry, Aidan, this troublemaker is my little cousin, Kyle."

"As usual, Tash forgot *she's* the troublemaker," Kyle retorted as he extended his hand.

"Nice to meet you," Aidan said, still smiling.

"What's so amusing?" Tash asked.

"It's just fun to see someone else mocking you. Plus I think it's adorable that you always seem surprised you're late," Aidan replied.

"I like this guy already," Kyle declared as Tash shook her head.

They all laughed. A moment later, the waitress came over to take their lunch orders.

"The ham and cheese sandwich and a coffee, please," Kyle said.

"And for you?" the waitress asked Tash.

"A slice of today's quiche with salad and coffee, please."

"Same for me," Aidan said.

"It's not as good as the blintzes, is it?" Kyle asked Tash.

She shook her head.

"What's that?" Aidan asked.

"There's a diner Kyle and I go to. We always share a platter of cheese blueberry blintzes. They're outrageous. The coffee sucks, but they give you a plate of bagel chips and spread while you're waiting."

"Except Tash eats the nasty cinnamon raisin bagel chips."

"I like them. Shut up."

Aidan smiled. "So, are you ever gonna take me for blintzes?"

"I don't know. We'll see," she replied coyly.

After some small talk, their food was served. Kyle and Aidan scarfed theirs down. Tash teased them, saying, "What is it about guys and food? I mean, breathe!" While she leisurely nibbled on her meal, Aidan filled Kyle in on how they met. Tash interjected from time to time, insisting that Aidan was "infatuated the second he saw me."

They talked about Kyle's life as a political science major at Columbia. When Aidan asked if he was seeing anyone, Tash proceeded to give him unsolicited dating advice. He was having none of it. "Listen you, with those freaky exes; you are so not giving me advice," he said. Aidan jumped in and insisted that he dish on her past beaus, and soon they were both teasing her mercilessly. Tash shook her head and smiled, giving in to the humor of it all. When the laughter died down, the conversation moved to shared interests in music and movies.

An hour later, they all threw down some cash and Aidan excused himself to use the restroom. With only a one-person restroom available, they saw Aidan waiting in line across the café and knew they had a little time alone.

Tash opened her mouth, but before she could say anything, Kyle said, "Aidan is great."

She was surprised. "You never like the guys I date."

"First of all, they've hardly been guys – more like trolls," he said with a laugh.

She playfully punched his arm.

"None of the guys you've dated have been even remotely good enough for you. You deserve someone who gets you."

She smiled.

"Anyway, he's great. So here's hoping he doesn't dump you," he joked as he burst into hysterics.

"Hey!" she said, again punching him in the arm. "You know me – I don't take things too seriously anyway."

"Maybe you should this time. What does Jason think of him?"

"He's in love with Aidan, but in a brother kind of way. You should see them together."

"Maybe Aidan is the roommate he always wanted," Kyle teased.

"Hey! I'm gonna punch you harder next time."

"Okay, I surrender," he said, putting his hands up. "But seriously, if Jason and I both think he's good for you, maybe you should lean into it a bit."

"Let's worry about getting you a date before worrying about my boyfriend."

"Oh my God, you called him your boyfriend!"

"That's it, smarty," she said as she walloped him.

"Okay, okay, I'm moving on. How are your folks?"

"Fine I guess. I haven't visited in a while. What about yours?"

"Um, I guess they're all right."

"What is it Kye?"

"Probably nothing. They just seem, I don't know, like something's up."

"Well, didn't your mom leave her job in publishing to become an agent or something? She's probably just really busy."

"Yeah, maybe. Anyway, they're fine. What about Jason, is his star still rising?"

Aidan returned and plopped down, not wanting to interrupt.

"He just had his first solo shoot in a commercial. It's freaking crazy. I'm so happy for him. And I think he met a boy, although he says he didn't."

"When does he not have a new dude on his arm? That guy has game," Aidan chimed in.

"Don't say anything to him. It might be nothing and I don't want him to be mad at me."

"What about Penelope, how's she?" Kyle asked.

"She's had a low profile lately, hardly ever home. No annoying notes."

"Low profile? I'd say more like downright mysterious," Aidan said. "I've probably seen her two or three times and I've barely left your place for weeks."

"She must be there more often than that," Tash said.

Aidan shrugged.

"Is she dating someone?" Kyle asked.

"I doubt it. I think she's just really busy with school and she visits her dad a lot and stuff. She's most likely spending her nights curled up to a library book. You know, the dusty, big-word kind she likes so much."

"You used to be good friends."

"Yeah, that was before we lived together."

"You lived together in college."

"I was abroad like for half of that year. She didn't have enough time to get on my nerves."

"She's a sweetheart; you should be nicer to her. Grad school is probably stressful too," Kyle said.

"You see sweet, I see uptight," Tash rebuffed.

Kyle shot her a stern look.

"Yeah, yeah, yeah. I'll make an effort. Okay gentlemen, ready to go?"

They left the café, hugging each other on the street outside before Kyle took off in one direction and Tash and Aidan in the other.

Tash and Aidan spent the next few hours wandering from SoHo back to the Village. They looked in store windows and stopped in art galleries.

"Come here," she said, pulling him into a gallery featuring Andy Warhol prints.

"Warhol was ahead of his time," Aidan remarked as they walked through the gallery.

"I know. Can you imagine what he would say about reality television?"

"He predicted it. I don't think he'd be surprised in the least."

"Uh huh. I love the Marilyns," she said, stopping in front of one of Warhol's most iconic pieces.

"Of course you do, beauty queen."

"Shut up," she said, playfully punching his arm. "I saw a documentary about her in college. Did you know when she talked to reporters she used to say, 'Would you like me to be her for you?' or something like that. She was in complete control. Marilyn was a character she created."

"Or one side of her personality," Aidan suggested.

"Exactly. It was like she was able to hold on to both Norma and Marilyn."

"But kind of fucked up if she never integrated them, right? I mean, living as two people instead of one whole person can't be easy. Maybe that's why she…"

"Oh don't even say it. I never believed she killed herself."

He smiled. "Neither did I, but that doesn't mean she was happy."

Tash shrugged.

"That's what was so brilliant about Warhol. He captured the lie and shoved it in everyone's face, decorated in bright, psychotically happy colors."

"Can I tell you something?" she asked, turning toward him.

"Of course."

"You know how some people have this romantic notion of New York in the 1920s?"

"Uh, rich white people might."

"Shut up," she said, punching his arm harder this time.

"I'm just kidding. Yeah, I know what you're talking about. People who read a lot of Edith Wharton or whatever."

"Well, I have this romantic notion of New York in the 1980s. I think that's why I've been so obsessed with the movies lately. My medium has always been film; it's how I connect with different times and ideas."

He smiled. "You always light up when you talk about film."

She shrugged. "Anyway, I have this love of New York in the 1980s, you know when the Mary Boone Gallery was the hottest place in SoHo, not a freaking H&M or whatever. The time of Warhol and all of those pop visionaries."

"You know who I love from back then? Jean-Michel Basquiat. Nobody blurred graffiti and art like that before he did. He was exposing the lie too, I think, but in his own way. I think the bullshit is really what killed him."

"Totally. I'm telling you, when Mary Boone closed her SoHo gallery and opened on Fifth Avenue, something died forever."

They smiled at each other and finished their tour of the gallery.

Once outside, Tash bought a black fedora from a street vendor. "How do I look?"

"Too cool for school, beauty queen."

"You're so lame," she teased, before grabbing his hand and continuing their stroll.

They were a few blocks from Tash's apartment when Aidan received a text message.

"Hey, a couple of my friends are in the neighborhood and they invited us for a drink. You up for it?"

"Sure."

A few minutes later, they sat down on the patio of a local Italian restaurant with Aidan's friends Jaime and Stu, both of whom Tash liked instantly. Jaime's black hair, black sundress, combat boots, and row of silver-studded earrings gave her a gothic look. Tash knew her appearance was just one facet of her personality when she greeted them ironically with, "Hello, happy shiny people." Jaime grabbed Aidan's arm. "Did you see the cover of *The Economist*, with the belly flop? Hysterical. Reminded me of what you said about Republicans." Not only did her outgoing personality contrast her gothic look, but Tash suspected she was wickedly smart. *I like her*, she thought. Tash pegged her as late twenties, maybe early thirties.

"Jaime works as a satirist for an art and culture magazine and freelances on the side, so we're always talking about art and politics," Aidan explained. "She got her master's in journalism at NYU, actually."

"Oh, Jaime, there's something on that seat. Let me get a napkin for you," Stu said as he raised his hand to get the attention of a waiter.

He's a sweetheart. And God, he's even taller than Aidan. He could be a basketball player, Tash thought.

"Stu works as a personal assistant, so he's used to taking care of people," Jaime explained.

"Who do you work for?" Tash asked Stu as he wiped Jaime's seat.

"I work for a New York celebrity," he replied.

"But due to a confidentiality agreement, he's not allowed to reveal any details," Jaime added.

Tash's eyes lit up.

"Oh, don't be impressed," Jaime said. "He's basically a man-servant."

Stu winced. "I can't even disagree. It's true. It's sad and true."

Everyone laughed.

"You guys seem like an old married couple," Tash remarked.

"Oh he wishes, but we're just roommates," Jaime said.

"Yeah, if only she had a penis," Stu said.

"And if only you had boobs!" Jaime added. They all dissolved into laughter.

Tash fit in as if she'd known them for years. Before long, they were on their second carafe of the house red, sharing fried calamari and a bread basket. Aidan couldn't stop smiling, and Tash was having a great time.

"So Tash, Aidan tells me you studied film at NYU," Jaime said.

"Yup."

"Did you ever have Professor Mercer?"

"Oh, I totally did. I signed up for some semiotics class, having no idea what it was. God, that was so boring."

"I took a class with him too; it was awful. It sucked because it was the only class I took in the film department but I didn't realize what it really was either. It killed my elective space."

"Did you like NYU?" Tash asked.

"Loved it. Of course, I'll still be paying off my student loans when I'm in the retirement home. I love my job but my salary is truly pathetic. That's why I have to share a place with this one," she said smirking at Stu. "What about you? Did you like NYU?"

"Yeah. I partied too much the first couple of years, so my folks didn't get their money's worth. Once I settled in, I loved the classes for my major. I'm really into avant-garde film studies and there were some amazing professors. I was constantly going to hear speakers outside of class and going to film screenings, especially senior year. You know, the perks that aren't for your grade. I just loved it all and couldn't get enough."

"You should think about going to grad school and doing something with it," Jaime suggested.

"I thought about going for an MFA in cinematography. Maybe. I don't know if I could do the school schedule thing again."

Aidan chimed in, "I know you could do it and I think it would be awesome. You have an amazing eye and it's obviously your passion."

She shrugged and changed the topic.

Before they left, Tash and Jaime went to the restroom together.

"It's so great to finally you meet you," Jaime said as they fixed their lipstick.

"You too."

"He talks about you all the time."

"Really?"

"Oh yeah. He won't shut up about you. He told us he met a beautiful girl who was smart as hell, and that we'd like her because she doesn't let him get away with anything."

Tash blushed.

Soon they were all standing in the street, saying their goodbyes and making plans to attend an animated short film festival the following month. Aidan took Tash's hand and they headed in the direction of her apartment.

"Your friends are pretty cool," she said.

He squeezed her hand. "Yeah, they're good eggs."

She giggled.

"They're sharp too. You know, Jaime was on point. You should do something in film. Is it a money thing, not going to grad school?"

"No, my parents can pay to send me."

"Damn. You're so lucky."

"I guess," she said dismissively.

As they approached Washington Square Park, Tash noticed Harold sitting on his favorite bench. A man walking past him flicked a cigarette butt, nearly hitting Harold's foot. *Jackass*, she thought.

"Follow me," she said, leading Aidan over. "Hey there, Harold."

"Hello, Natashya. Isn't dusk extraordinary tonight?"

Tash smiled. "Harold, this is Aidan."

Aidan put his hand out and Harold nodded, avoiding the physical contact. "Nice to meet you, young man. I've noticed you around."

Tash looked at Aidan, "Harold is my buddy. Sometimes we have coffee together in the mornings."

Aidan smiled.

"We gotta go, but I'll try to bring doughnuts on Monday if it's not raining."

"That would be lovely."

"Good night," Tash said.

"Nice to meet you," Aidan said.

Harold tilted his head down and blinked his eyes tightly.

As they walked away, Aidan asked, "What's his deal?"

"I don't know his story. Told him he didn't have to tell me. He's just my friend, sort of. I don't like people mistreating him. Sometimes I bring him coffee and stuff on my way to work. That's all."

Aidan stopped in his tracks, looked Tash in the eyes, and said, "I love you."

"Don't be so dramatic," she blithely said.

"I love you, beauty queen. You know I do."

She smiled. "Let's get out of here, you big sap."

He took her hand and they headed down the street.

After washing her face and slipping into an oversized T-shirt, Tash jumped on the bed next to Aidan, who was reading a novel.

"Uh, well hello there, beautiful."

"Listen, it's no big deal or anything, but do you want to see my final film project from college? It's experimental and I couldn't really achieve what I wanted to, but…"

"I would absolutely love to see it," he said softly.

Aidan beamed and Tash fidgeted as they watched it on her laptop. At one point Aidan said, "I love what you did there, with the swirling colors."

"Thanks. See, I had this idea that since cinematography is basically defined as painting with light, that I would mirror that here. I couldn't fully realize the idea, but…"

"But I totally see where you were going. I can actually hear it, like music."

She smiled.

When the short film was over, Aidan said, "You're talented. Truly. I'm so impressed."

"It's kind of my thing I guess. It's the only thing I've ever really been into," she said as she put her laptop away.

"What's your vision? I mean, if you could create something in the film world, what would it be?"

"I always wanted to bring the true pop art sensibility to contemporary film, but not in a cheesy or expected way. You know, something fresh and cutting edge."

He nodded. "Come here."

He put his arm out and pulled her to him. He wrapped his arms around her and whispered, "Thank you for sharing that with me."

She had never felt so close to anyone, and just for a moment, she leaned into the feeling and his embrace.

The next morning, Aidan was pouring some orange juice when Penelope came into the kitchen.

"Oh, hey," Aidan said.

"Hi," she replied as she set the coffee pot.

"I finally get to see the invisible roommate," he said jokingly.

"I'm not that exciting I guess. Not like Tash and Jason."

"Not at all. I didn't mean it that way. You're just out a lot."

Penelope continued tinkering with the coffee pot.

"I hope you don't mind that I'm here so much," Aidan added.

She shook her head.

"Tash said that you're in graduate school. What are you studying?"

"Art history."

"Oh, wow. Cool. Is that how you and Tash became friends?"

"Uh huh. I think she would say that even in art, she's all about the beautiful and fun parts. I like the boring history. Someone has to, I guess. It's not exciting to most people." Before he could respond, Penelope said, "I'm going to get ready while the coffee is brewing."

"Oh, sure," Aidan said.

She stopped and turned around. "I forgot to let Tash know the monthly bills are on the mail table. I broke everything down so she can just leave me a check. Would you please let her know?"

"Sure."

Tash was busy trying on possible outfits for the day when Aidan returned with two glasses of juice.

"Hey, what do you think of this?" Tash asked as she spun around causing the fringe running down the seams of her white shirt to sway.

"Cute. Very *Urban Cowboy*," he replied as he plopped down on her bed. "Oh, before I forget, Penelope said she left your bills on the mail table."

"You talked to her about the bills?"

"All she said was that she divided them up."

"Oh," Tash said as she searched her drawer for matching socks.

"It's kinda nice that she takes care of the accounting stuff for you guys."

"Yeah. She lives for that stuff."

"I still don't know how you can afford this place."

Tash, now more serious, turned to face him. "Jason and Pen pay more than I do. Obviously Jason can afford it and Pen has money from her family. I'm not a mooch. I pay, just less than them."

"That's cool. I didn't mean to make you feel bad. I guess I'm two for two and it's not even noon."

"What?" she asked.

"I think I kind of put my foot in my mouth with Penelope."

"Whatever. Don't stress. She's hard to talk to these days."

"Maybe the universe is telling me to close my mouth today. Come here, beauty queen."

"No way. I just got ready and you'll mess me up."

"You're such a girl."

"Yeah, I am."

"Come on," he pressed. "Just come sit with me. I won't mess you up."

She pursed her lips and conceded. He put his hands out, and when she leaned in to take them, he pulled her down, flipped her onto her back, and started tickling her.

"I knew you would mess me up," she squealed through laughter.

He stopped tickling her, brushed her hair from her forehead, and said, "Nothing could mess you up. To me, you are extraordinary."

He kissed her gently. All the while her mind was haunted by a single thought: *You don't really know me.*

PART TWO

Chapter 6

Penelope Waters was born in Boston. Her father, Ted, came from an affluent family with deep New England roots and became a corporate attorney because it was "expected." Her mother, Mallory, held a bachelor's degree in finance from Harvard, but pursued a career as a pastry chef because, "Living life means following your dreams." As a child, Penelope was overjoyed to see her mother on the cover of *Boston Magazine*, noted as the most revered pastry chef in the area.

Penelope inherited her father's gravitas. Both were reserved, studious, and above all, serious. Mallory was the opposite. For instance, when she whipped up Penelope's favorite cream puffs, she glazed the tops and smooshed them in rainbow sprinkles.

"Mom, aren't cream puffs supposed to be plain?" Penelope asked.

"There is no such thing as 'supposed to be.' Besides, everything is better covered in sprinkles," she replied.

"Dad, she's being silly again," Penelope complained.

Ted smiled. "She can't help it. Her spirit is as light and airy as those little pastry clouds," he said before popping one in his mouth.

When Penelope spent too much time hunched over her desk, Mallory barged into her room and dragged her outside to look up at the stars. She didn't let her return to her studies until, with pinky fingers hooked, they made a wish together. Secretly, Penelope wished to be more like her mother; despite her ambivalence about "frills," she always kept her hair in long brown spirals, like Mallory's.

When Penelope was seventeen years old, her mother was killed in a car crash. She died instantly, as did the driver responsible, who had been texting. The lightness left their house that day. Although she and her father believed Mallory was in heaven, their shoulders permanently slumped and they never once looked up at the stars.

At Penelope's high school graduation, her father told her that he'd quit his job, sold their Beacon Hill brownstone, and was moving to Vermont to open a bed and breakfast. *He's given up on life*, she surmised. While packing her room, half in boxes for storage and half bags for NYU, she was overcome by waves of guilt. *How can I abandon my dad? He seems irreparably damaged.* As guilt shook her confidence in her decision to forge her own path, she found the old *Boston Magazine* with her mother on the cover and remembered how Mallory always encouraged her to be braver and to find herself. *I need to be more like my mother, more fearless.* Mustering all her strength, she lifted herself from the gravity of grief and headed to New York City.

With a major in art history and minor in French, she excelled academically, but was less successful socially. During the first few weeks of freshman year, almost everyone left their doors wide open, popping into each other's rooms, jumping on each other's beds, and quickly forming friendships to carry them through their college years. Grief-stricken and out of her comfort zone, Penelope smiled politely as she walked through the dormitory corridors, but rarely spoke to anyone other than an occasional "excuse me" as she passed groups of friends overtaking the narrow space.

Her roommate was from New York. She spent most nights in her boyfriend's room, also an NYU student, and weekends at home, leaving Penelope on her own. When she saw groups of friends crammed in someone's room, laughing loudly, she wished she could start over again. She berated herself over the time a few girls invited her into their room for a horror movie marathon. With an assignment due the next day, she had hesitated. One girl said, "Don't worry if it's not your thing," and all Penelope could do was smile and walk away. *What's wrong with me?* she wondered as she shuffled back to her empty dorm room, locking the door behind her as usual.

During her junior year, she took an elective in French cinema. Each Thursday night, students were required to attend a film screening. One night, at a screening of *Betty Blue*, Penelope noticed Tash arriving ten minutes late. As Tash scanned the dark room for an empty seat, Penelope moved over, gesturing for her to take the aisle seat.

"Thanks," Tash whispered.

Penelope smiled. "Do you want me to fill you in?" she whispered back.

"Nah, it's one of my favorite movies."

At the end of the screening, Tash turned to Penelope. "So, what did you think?"

"The score was beautiful."

"Is that all?"

"Betty was so self-destructive. Do you think they ever had a chance?" Penelope asked.

"No one in love has a chance," Tash replied with a smirk.

Penelope looked at her blankly.

"I mean, we're each alone, right?" she added. "The love illusion just makes people lose their shit." As Penelope wondered if that was true, Tash followed up with, "I'm meeting some friends for a drink. Do you want to come?"

"Oh, it's already pretty late and..."

"You can't be that lame. Come on, live a little."

Remembering the price of hesitation, she responded, "Okay. Just for a little while."

Once at Jelly Belly, a local bar, Tash introduced her classmate to a group of girlfriends who were busy rating all the guys in the bar. Penelope sipped a soda while the others slammed the bar's famous Jell-O shots. Supporting a staggering Tash, Penelope got back to her dorm at three in the morning and she didn't care. When Tash slurred, "Thanks. I should really party less and do more of the school thing," Penelope thought, *And I should do the opposite.* They became fast friends, sharing class notes, attending film screenings together, and offering each other honest advice. Penelope became Tash's excuse when she wanted to forgo the party scene for a quiet night in, and Tash became Penelope's passport to the American college experience she had only seen in movies. They roomed together senior year.

One night, Tash met Jason at a club when she was having trouble getting in.

"Screw you! I'm on the damn list. Maybe you should look again," she was yelling at the bouncer. Out of the blue, with a wink from Jason, she was in.

"Thanks! My friend was supposed to get me on the list but I guess she fucked up," she said once they were inside.

He smiled. "No sweat. You're gorgeous – you would have better luck flirting than screaming."

"Yeah, I tried that. Asshole said he had a girlfriend. Like I care. I just wanted to get in."

Jason laughed.

"So, you're pretty connected to just waltz in here like that," she said with a coy smile.

"Honey, I don't play for your team. But nice work with the flirting. I totally want to buy you a drink."

They loved each other immediately. Tash introduced Jason and Penelope and they all became friends. When Tash was getting ready to graduate, she and Jason made a plan to live together.

"Come on, Pen, move in with us," Tash cajoled.

"Yeah, we need a grown-up," Jason added.

"Grad school is going to be hard. I'll need a quiet place to study and I don't want to cramp your style."

"We need you, Pen. Don't worry, we'll behave," Tash promised.

At first, the three spent a lot of time together hanging out in their apartment, watching movies or reality show marathons. They all squeezed onto Jason's bed with Tash in the middle, and laughed for hours at corny rom-coms. Tash threw her arms up and melodramatically reenacted the ridiculous "you're the one" speeches, as she called them. Jason mused that if they only had more gay storylines, it wouldn't be so cliché. Then he and Tash stood up, created new characters, and played out the climax scene. They didn't stop until Penelope's giggle morphed into a hearty laugh. Over time, such instances were fewer and farther between. As Jason's star rose, he spent more time going to clubs. Tash loved tagging along, but Penelope studied during the week and often traveled to Vermont on weekends. Tash and Jason's bond grew and Penelope felt increasingly lonely.

By the end of their second year in the apartment, Jason was famous throughout the city, Tash was spending every free moment with Aidan, and Penelope was quietly trying to finish graduate school.

Having completed her last semester of classes, Penelope planned to use the summer to finish her thesis. She had uncharacteristically fallen behind. She claimed to have gotten held up trying to pick the perfect topic, something intellectually interesting that her committee would approve. Everyone accepted this excuse as it affirmed their assumptions about her. The truth was something no one would expect.

I'll deal with it today, once and for all, Penelope thought as she stared in the bathroom mirror, searching for herself. *This can't continue. I wasn't thinking. I have to get out before anyone gets hurt. How could things get so complicated?*

She finished getting ready and jammed a few overdue library books into her backpack. Noticing the cover of one book about the Greek goddesses, she wondered, *Why did I pick this of all topics for my thesis? I miss being smart.*

Tash and Jason were cuddling on his bed as she passed his bedroom. Without meaning to, she stopped outside the partially open door and listened.

"Meet us there at ten. There's a bigwig club promoter coming to meet with Aidan and he needs good energy."

"You're relentless. I told you I should stay in tonight. We're shooting at a bunch of outdoor locations tomorrow and there's an early call time."

"Sleep during the day and just come for one drink. I'm not relentless, I'm restless. It's not just Aidan, I need you there. He's being really clingy and I need a..."

"You don't need me. He's not clingy, T. Come on, what gives?"

"His 'I love you' stuff freaks me out. What does he even know about me?"

"He knows what matters. Stop letting the past mess with your head."

"What if..."

Penelope caught herself eavesdropping and quickly scampered out of the apartment. The warm air caressed her face as she stepped onto the street. *It's a beautiful day. Too bad I'll be stuck inside.*

Soon she was at her regular haunt, the library, where she planned to spend the day working on her thesis. As soon as she sat down and opened her laptop, her phone beeped with an incoming text.

Meet me?

After inhaling slowly, she responded.

Tonight. At the library now. Need to concentrate on work.

She slipped her phone into her backpack and started reading. Stopping only once to go next door for a veggie wrap and smoothie, Penelope worked all day, taking such copious notes that her fingers hurt from typing. While her thesis focused on representations of Persephone, she became increasingly tired and began running searches on some of the other Greek goddesses. An amateur blog about Penelope, her namesake, captured her attention. The blogger described Penelope as faithful and loyal, suggesting she not only married a hero, but was herself a hero. It was no wonder she was her father's favorite. *That's it. I can't take it anymore. My dad would be so disappointed.*

As she switched her computer off, a librarian passed by. "Can I return those books to the stacks for you?"

"Yes, thank you," she replied. She pulled her phone out of her bag and sent a text.

Leaving the library now. Meet me.

The response was almost instantaneous.

On my way.

The library seemed to stop time, concealing the day from the night. By the time she left, the sky was dark. *I wonder if Tash convinced Jason to go out with her. They always have so much fun.* She hailed a cab and was on her way, with all of her thoughts redirected to the impossible task ahead.

As the driver pulled up to The Plaza, she remembered the first time she saw it. *Just like in the movies*, she thought. Although not materialistic or interested in the city's ever-changing hotspots, this New York landmark had once taken on a mythic quality in her imagination. She could still hear her mother reading the *Eloise* books to her, and their family movie nights often featured scenes at The Plaza. Suddenly feeling ashamed for having denigrated her childhood memories, she climbed out of the cab and marched into the hotel with conviction. *I will end it.*

Tash arrived at the club at ten thirty, half an hour late to meet Aidan who was already waiting inside. Wearing a sparkling black mini-dress and matching high heels, she looked like a movie star. Her hair was pimped out in perfect loose curls and her severe makeup was capped off with cherry red lipstick. Her style was all at once soft and hard, just like the dreamy trip-hop music swirling in the industrial club.

She made her way through the large space featuring exposed pipes contrasted with a perimeter of lush black leather sofas. The blaring trip-hop music and soft blue lighting around the bars set the mood. As she scanned the room both for Aidan and random celebrities, a tall, dark-haired guy dressed head to toe in Gucci offered to buy her a drink. Before she could respond, Aidan was beside her.

"Another time," she said to the guy as she turned to Aidan.

"Fending off your suitors already? Not surprised. You look amazing," he said.

"Well, that'll teach you not to wait for me outside."

"This place is pretty sick, isn't it?"

She nodded. "I guess. It's kind of nineties wannabe."

"The music is sexy. And see that roped off area over there?" he said, pointing to a mezzanine level.

"Uh huh."

"That's the VIP section. We have a private table waiting for when Tony and his crew arrive. It's pretty sweet."

"Not bad," she conceded.

"I heard there are some reality stars hanging around, so that should make it worth your while."

"Really? Who's here?"

Aidan laughed. "Don't know. But when you see them you can tell me all about it."

"Okay, smarty. How about you buy me a drink already?"

After a strong cocktail and half an hour of dancing, Tash pulled Aidan close to her and said, "I have to go to the restroom."

"Sure. I'm going to wait at the table. Tony should be here any minute. Meet me there. You're on the list."

He leaned in to kiss her on the cheek, but she pulled away too quickly.

It's too crowded, Tash thought as she entered one of the gender-neutral restrooms. After relieving herself, she waited for a sink and mirror.

"Damn girl, you're hot," said a young guy who reeked of beer.

When she raised her eyebrow in response, he adopted a more hostile tone. "Can't you take a compliment?"

She turned to face him and said, "Thank you. All right?"

"You don't have to be a bitch. You're not all that, you just look easy. Thought you might do me in a stall. Fucking cunt," he ranted before stumbling out of the restroom.

"That guy's just a dick," a nearby woman said. "Don't let him get to you. Girls have been turning him down all night and he's not taking it well."

"Thanks," Tash replied as she slipped her lipstick into her purse.

As she turned to walk away, the woman called after her. "Hey, come here."

"Yeah?"

The woman pulled a tiny plastic bag filled with white powder out of her Jimmy Choo clutch. "Do you need something to take the edge off?"

Tash stared at the little bag. At first, she was offended. *What the hell? Do I give off junky whore vibes?* But her outrage morphed into temptation. As she contemplated her choices, the woman pulled out another little bag.

"I also have some X if that's more your thing."

A chill went up her spine. Flashes of a horrible night from years earlier surfaced – she had woken up in a boyfriend's bed with him and his creepy roommate, fearing what happened to her while she was unconscious, feeling the violation to her core, blaming herself for acting like the cool party girl.

"I haven't done that shit since college and I don't plan to start again," she said firmly before leaving the room.

Despite her swagger, she was rattled. She leaned against a wall for a moment before heading to the bar and downing a shot of tequila to calm her nerves.

By the time she got up to the VIP section, Aidan was having an intense conversation with a group of people. When he didn't notice her approaching the table, her mind spiraled. *Fucking great. Maybe if he were a gentleman he would have met me downstairs. Now I have to chat it up with these tools. Can't believe Jason didn't even come. If…*

Her thoughts trailed off as Aidan waved her over, scooting over on the semi-circle leather couch to make room.

"Everyone, this is my girlfriend, Tash," he said.

Everyone smiled and nodded. The man directly across from her extended his hand and said, "I'm Tony. Nice to meet you."

"You too," she replied.

As the group conversation resumed, Aidan whispered in her ear, "You were gone a while. I was getting worried you ditched me."

"I was dealing with a douchebag in the gross bathroom."

"What happened?"

"Maybe if you had come with me you would know." Aidan looked stunned. Tash softened her voice and said, "Whatever, don't worry about it. It's not a big deal."

Tony redirected Aidan's attention. "Aidan, tell me more about your ideas for themed party nights."

Aidan squeezed Tash's hand and resumed his conversation with Tony. A few minutes later, the waitress stopped by. Tash ordered a shot of tequila, which she slammed back the second it was served.

As the night progressed, Tash became increasingly bored listening to Aidan talk music with Tony and his entourage. Despite his promises, there were only a couple of D-list pseudo-celebrities there, but none of them interested her. Desperate to shake things up, she coyly looked over at Tony and gave him a half smile, catching his attention.

"Aidan, I think your lovely girlfriend might like to dance."

"Oh," Aidan said, jarred. "I'm sorry Tash, are you fed up with music talk?"

"No, but I would like to dance," she said as she rose.

Aidan started to slide toward the edge of the booth, but Tash looked at Tony, extended her arm, and said, "Shall we?"

"Well, how could I resist such a beautiful woman? Aidan, you don't mind do you?"

"No, man," he mumbled, clearly dumbfounded.

Aidan watched as Tash and Tony walked down to the main dance floor, where she led him to the center stage, pulled him close to her, and danced seductively with him for nearly half an hour to Hooverphonic remixes. She was so tipsy that he had to hold her up a few times but she refused to return to the booth. Aidan watched from the mezzanine. When they eventually came back to the table, Aidan jumped up and said, "I think I should probably get Tash home."

"I think Tash can decide when Tash should go home," she slurred.

"Are we good, Tony? Can we follow up by email?"

Tony nodded.

"See you, man," Aidan said as he took Tash's hand to leave.

When they reached the front door of the club, she pushed his hand aside and said, "I don't like being manhandled."

"What the hell is your problem?"

"I don't have a problem."

"The one time I need you to do something for me so that I can make a good impression and land a job, you get wasted and flirt with the club promoter? Are you kidding me?"

"This is just who I am."

"No, it's who you're afraid people think you are."

"Leave it alone," Tash muttered.

"It or you?"

"Same difference."

"No, it's not the same. What is *it* anyway? What's wrong with you? Just tell me," Aidan pleaded.

"I'm getting a cab. You can come with me or not," she said as she tottered outside.

"I want to make sure you get home safely," he said.

Neither said a word in the cab. At one point Tash thought he was going to say something so she opened her window and stuck her face into the breeze.

When they got to her apartment, Tash walked in but Aidan stood outside the door.

"Are you coming in or not?" she asked in an irritated tone.

"I don't know. We need to talk but I think you should sleep it off first."

"I'm not drunk."

"Yeah, right."

"We can't talk here. Jason is probably sleeping. He has a big day tomorrow. Come to my room."

He followed her in, locking the door behind them. When they got to her bedroom, she sat on her bed to take her shoes off. Aidan leaned against the bedroom door, arms crossed.

In a quiet and calm voice he asked, "What was that tonight, with Tony? Why did you do that?"

She shrugged. "I was bored."

"You were bored? Big freaking deal. You weren't the center of attention for all of five minutes, but that doesn't mean you have to go crazy. You're so damn narcissistic, but it's all bullshit. There's more to you behind this wall of crap."

She didn't respond.

"Fuck, that's it. I can't take it anymore," he said, wringing his hands.

"Then leave."

"Don't you get it? I don't want to leave. I want to be with you but you need to confront your stuff."

"I'm not your fucking project."

"Everyone has stuff to deal with. Stop pretending. Let me in."

"I'm fine the way I am," she insisted.

"Really? Let's examine things. You went to NYU to study film, which you're passionate about, but you work as a part-time sales clerk instead. Do you know how many friends I have that pounded the pavement to do something in the arts, and reluctantly took jobs as waiters and bartenders because they couldn't make anything happen? And you don't even know if you have to because you never even tried to pursue the one thing you actually care about. What is that?"

Shocked, she jumped up and shouted, "You're not my fucking family."

"Yes, yes I am. I'm your family right now. Me, Jason, even Pen, we are your family in every way that matters. They might be willing to let you float by for now, but not forever. That's not anger, so don't warp it in your mind. It's love. But you can't handle love, right?"

"You're talking out of your ass. My life is just the way I want it to be."

"I doubt that. You have some bullshit idea about who you are so you created a persona to match it, but it's all crap."

"Just get the fuck out."

"I must be getting close to something real, is that it?"

"You don't know what you're talking about," she insisted.

"Let's take your big obsession with the eighties, for example."

"I like the movies. So what?"

"Look a little deeper. It was all about big hair, big shoulder pads, and McMansions. But all of those big things covered up big lies. AIDS, racial injustice, sexism, all of it. Sometimes I think you're like the eighties. The quarterback shoulder pads don't fool me. What's behind all the lip gloss?"

"You're seeing things that aren't there. I like to party so I keep things simple."

Aidan shook his head. "I'll never get through to you."

"Just go. We're done."

As she heard the words come out of her mouth she gasped a little. She looked at Aidan to see what he would do.

"You hurt me tonight. Do you get that?" he asked softly.

She didn't know what to say, so she said nothing.

"I would let it go if I wasn't convinced it will happen again. Until you confront your demons, I know I'm only ever going to get glimpses of the real Tash, the one that hides in the MoMA film room and befriends a homeless man. The other version of you, what you show everyone else, she's just a shadow. I'm not willing to chase a shadow anymore."

Tash looked down.

Aidan pulled a copy of *Looking for Alaska* off of her dresser. "I know you've read this half a dozen times," he said, waving it around. "But you missed the point. Smoking to die isn't cool. It didn't make the character fun and mysterious. It's sad. Not romantic sad, just pathetic sad."

Tash looked perplexed.

Aidan put the book down and walked over to her, kneeling on the floor in front of her. "Listen to me. I love you as you really are, but you can't sit on the sidelines anymore."

She shook her head and turned away.

"You live at the edge of living, terrified to go after anything you actually want. Or even to figure out what you want. Why don't you think you're worth taking a chance on? If I do, why don't you?"

She looked him directly in the eyes, and said, "Stop your psychobabble and get out my apartment. We're over."

He stood up and looked at her, giving her a chance to take back her words.

"I never loved you. Get out."

He turned and left the room, gently shutting the door behind him.

A few minutes later, Jason knocked on her bedroom door.

He let himself in and Tash said, "I'm so sorry; did we wake you up?"

"Don't worry about it. What happened?"

"It's over. I told Coconut Boy to leave."

"Sweetie, I know you're upset, but don't call him that. His name is Aidan."

Chapter 7

Penelope opened her eyes at the crack of dawn. *This comforter is like a cloud,* she thought, knowing it would be the last time she'd wake up there. She quietly shimmied out of bed and got dressed. As she grabbed her backpack and started walking to the door, a voice called behind her, "You're sneaking out?"

Pausing at the door, she turned around and said, "I meant what I said. I can't do this anymore. It's not who I am. Please don't contact me again."

"But…"

"But nothing. You're married and you know it's much worse than that."

"You know my marriage isn't real. As for the rest of it…"

"Please, I never should have let this continue once I learned everything. We both know it's well past time."

"Look, I know we weren't meant to last forever. But I'm concerned about what I have brought to your life. If I had known. I feel like I put you in an impossible situation and that wasn't my intention."

"You didn't."

"Penelope, please don't regret anything. You're very special and I'm grateful that you reminded me of what I was missing. I care deeply about you."

She tilted her face shyly downward. "I'm grateful to you too. You'll always be my first, well, my first everything. But I need to move on and do what makes sense. Goodbye, Richard."

As Penelope left the hotel, she noticed the gardeners watering the bright red flowers that flanked the entrance. She was overcome by memories of the flowers at her father's bed and breakfast. On her way home, she thought back to that first day and everything that had happened since, like a film playing in her mind. She hoped that by remembering it all she could achieve closure.

It all began with a dreaded trip nearly one year ago during her summer break. Penelope was visiting her father for a week in Stowe, Vermont. As she pulled into the driveway of the large, refurbished Victorian, she wondered how she would survive a full week. While it was a magical place for those seeking a romantic getaway, for Penelope's father, it was a hideaway.

Throughout college and graduate school, she never scheduled Friday classes. This allowed her to visit for at least one long weekend each month, but full weeks were harder to bear. As she sat in her parked car, dragging her feet on going inside, she thought about how fatigued she felt after those long weekends. Tash once suggested that she "stop going so much because it's too far away and lame."

Penelope had responded, "He needs me. Since my mom, you know?"

Tash never mentioned it again. As Penelope sat there, she wondered if things would be different had she confided in Tash about how hard things really were. Lost in her thoughts, she didn't notice her father until he tapped on the car window, startling her. After catching her breath, she smiled at him and popped her trunk.

"Hey, Dad," she said as she emerged from her car.

Already leaning into the trunk to collect her luggage, he mumbled, "Hi, honey."

As they walked into the house, her father remarked, "You seemed deep in thought."

"Just a long drive."

"Well, come on in and have a snack. I just put the afternoon refreshments out in the library."

"Okay. I'll unpack and come down."

"Here," her father said, handing her a key. "I had to put you on the third floor this time. It's a full house all week."

Penelope nodded as she took the key. She followed her father up the dark mahogany staircase, smiling politely while passing an elderly couple on their way down. As she entered the small room that featured a rickety canopy bed and flowered wallpaper, she felt envious of her friends who were returning home for the summer to their own bedrooms.

"I'll just put these here," her father said, placing her suitcase and backpack on a bench at the end of the bed. "This one is heavy," he remarked, gesturing at the backpack.

"I have a lot of reading to do for school."

"Aren't classes over for the semester?"

"It's for my thesis. I'm supposed to present a proposal to the committee in the fall."

"Ah. Well, get settled in and I'll see you in a bit."

As he closed the door, she had two thoughts. *He forgot to hug me. This room is stuffy.*

Half an hour later, Penelope sat in the library sipping a glass of lemonade. Guests roamed about, occasionally stopping in to pick up a cool drink or a maple scone that paled in comparison to her mother's. Soon her father found her.

"Let's sit down and catch up," he said.

"Sure. Do you want to go sit outside on the porch swing?"

"Okay."

Penelope followed her father outside, glass of lemonade in hand.

As they sat on the swing it swayed, as if mimicking the unease they felt, but it soon steadied with their weight.

"So, the business is going well?" Penelope asked.

"We've been booked solid every weekend since the season began, and we're quite busy during the weeks as well. There was a lull between the end of the ski season and the start of summer, but that's normal."

"Uh huh," she said, in an attempt to show she was paying attention.

"I've been toying with the idea of doing some kitchen renovations. We'll see. How's that lemonade? I squeezed it myself."

"Oh, it's good," she replied, taking a sip of the overly tart beverage.

"So, how are things in New York?"

"Pretty good."

"The apartment?"

"It's great. I spend a lot of time hanging out with my roommates. You remember that Tash is a big film buff so we have a lot of movie nights. Kind of reminds me of when I was little."

"I still wish you would've gotten the other apartment, in the building with the doorman. New York isn't safe and you shouldn't get complacent."

"It's fine, Dad, really. You shouldn't worry."

"What about school?"

"Everything's good. I just have to finalize my thesis topic and get it approved. Some people don't realize how creative scholarship can be. I want to do something special. I've narrowed it down to representations of the Greek goddesses in contemporary art, but it's still too broad. Tash thinks I should focus on Persephone because she's kind of a rebel, but I'm leaning more towards Demeter, her mother, the goddess of the earth and harvest. Do you know the story about how she made the land desolate and barren each winter out of grief? She…"

"Honey, I have to run inside and check on the laundry machine. A guest needed it earlier, and, well, it doesn't matter. You stay here and enjoy the fresh air. I'll see you at dinner."

As he jumped up, the swing again swayed, this time taking longer to steady.

Penelope went to her room, where she napped and read before joining her father for a late dinner after he was done attending to his guests for the day. The dining room was only used to serve breakfast, and Ted avoided sullying the table linens by eating in the outdated kitchen instead, even when Penelope visited. He was able to fake his way through a couple of breakfast classics for his guests, but he was such a poor cook that after a year of eating frozen dinners he hired a local woman to deliver homemade, family-style meals once a week. This week it was roast beef, something neither he nor Penelope particularly enjoyed.

"Her roast turkey is top notch. The sides too. I should have asked her to make that for your visit," Ted said, noticing Penelope moving the food around on her plate.

"It's fine, Dad. I'm just not very hungry."

Although he was making an effort, Penelope was preoccupied with her greatest fear: she would have to accept her father as he now was, a man she hardly knew in a place she hardly belonged.

The next four days passed, each undifferentiated from the ones before. Penelope woke up at five o'clock to help her father prepare breakfast for the guests, which they served from six to nine, followed by an hour of cleaning. Then she read, drank afternoon lemonade, napped, read some more, and ate roast beef with her father, which, like their strained conversation, became increasingly difficult to digest. On the fifth day, everything changed.

The howling winds the night before forced her to shut her window, so Penelope was scarcely able to sleep at all in her stuffy room. She dragged herself down to the kitchen at five o'clock to find her father desperately searching in the cabinet under the sink.

"Morning, Dad. What are you looking for?" she asked sleepily.

"Flashlights. I can't find enough for all the guests."

"What? Why do we need flashlights?"

"The forecast changed overnight and the storm they thought was going to miss us is heading this way in full force. Hurricane winds, torrential downpours, and lightning are expected to start mid-afternoon," he said as he moved on to the pantry.

Penelope poured herself a cup of coffee, unbothered. "We probably won't lose power, Dad."

"I just want to be prepared. Check the freezer for batteries."

"The freezer?"

"They last longer there."

After locating the needed flashlights and batteries, Penelope and her father proceeded to make, serve, and clear breakfast. Penelope created emergency kits with flashlights and bottled water for each hotel guest, just in case. Concerned that the quickly dropping temperatures would make the place unseasonably chilly, Ted built a fire in the library fireplace. Penelope set out a platter of marshmallows and skewers to make the storm fun for the guests. From that point on, Penelope's day was no different from the days before, except the comfort she felt listening to the teeming rain outside. The conversation with her father was limited to weather reports he was reading on his phone.

Claiming he was exhausted from the long day, Ted retired immediately after dinner. Penelope washed the dishes and then searched the freezer for something sweet. She found a carton of Neapolitan ice cream tucked away in the back and opened it to discover the chocolate was gone. *It figures*, she thought. There was a frost-covered block of strawberry and vanilla left. After scraping away the freezer burn on the top, she put the rest in a bowl, grabbed her book, and went to curl up in the armchair by the fireplace. She was taking her last bite of ice cream when the bells on the front door rang out. She walked to the opening of the room and saw a well-dressed, middle-aged man standing in the entryway, dripping from head to toe.

"Can I help you?" she asked.

"I hope so. I have a vacation house about two miles away and we lost power. My back-up generator died after an hour. I usually only come up here during ski season and must have neglected to have the tank filled. I need a room for the night," he explained, as she noticed the puddle he was creating.

"Uh, my dad said all the rooms are filled but I can go wake him up and ask," she said.

"I wouldn't want you to do that. I'll find someplace else."

As he started to leave, sloshing with each step, Penelope said, "It's too dangerous to drive. Please come in and I'll get you some towels to dry off and a cup of tea or something. You can sit by the fire. I can fix the couch for you if that would be okay for the night."

"I wouldn't want to put you out."

"No, it's fine. Just stay put and I'll be back in a jiffy."

She returned a few minutes later with a stack of towels and some bedding. "Here, take off your coat and dry off with these." As she fitted the couch with sheets she said, "You'll be toasty in here by the fire. Can I get you some tea or coffee?"

"Tea would be lovely if it isn't too much trouble."

"No trouble. Are you hungry? We have some leftover roast beef, which I have to confess isn't very good. There are also some scones and muffins."

"Just the tea. Thank you."

Penelope returned ten minutes later holding a silver tray with a full tea service and a small plate of chocolate chip cookies.

"I found these in the cookie jar, in case you changed your mind and wanted a snack."

"Thank you. Do people really have cookie jars?" he asked.

"I guess people in Vermont do."

"I sense you're not from here?"

"No. I'm originally from Boston but I go to graduate school in New York City, at NYU. I come up here to visit my father from time to time."

"I live in the city as well. Normally, I only come up here with my son during the winter to ski."

"What brings you here now?" she asked as she poured him a cup of tea.

"Truthfully, the short version is that I'm unhappy at home and wanted a change of scenery."

Pleasantly surprised by his candor, she asked, "What would the long version be?"

"An earful."

"I have time," she said. "Uh, that is if you want to talk. I'm sorry, I'm being horribly rude. I've forgotten my manners altogether," she stammered, jumping up.

"Not at all."

"I should let you warm up and get some rest."

"Please, stay. Here, join me for a cup of tea," he said, lifting the teapot.

She smiled and sat down.

"Do you take sugar or milk?" he asked.

She shook her head.

"What's your name?" he asked as he handed her the teacup.

"Penelope. And yours?"

"Richard."

Penelope took a sip of tea and said, "I don't want to pry, but you mentioned…"

"That I'm unhappy at home."

She nodded. "I'm a good listener, that's all."

"Well," he said with a sigh, "where to begin?"

Over the next hour, Richard told Penelope that his twenty-year marriage was a sham. He revealed that he went out on a few dates with his wife because he was "never a ladies man and lacked the experience to know that indifference was a red flag." When she became pregnant and insistent on having the child, he felt marrying her was the right thing to do.

He explained, "I look back and see that I had other choices, but shall we say, appearances are very important in my family. At the time, it seemed easier to marry her and try to create a life together. Foolish."

Penelope listened sympathetically, thinking how lonely he must be, and how in her own way she could relate. She realized that she hadn't felt this connected to anyone in a long time.

"Have you ever thought about ending the marriage?" she asked.

He nodded. "I could never bring myself to do it though. I used to justify staying because I focused on my son and trying to keep his home together. The truth is that I feel sorry for my wife. We don't have any relationship to speak of, not even a friendship, but she's had a troubled life. The shell of the marriage is somehow important to her."

"And for you?"

He chuckled and shook his head. "I'm not used to people asking how I feel. Well, for me the shell is just what a shell is: empty."

"I'm sorry," Penelope said, unsure of herself.

"Please, don't feel sorry for me. My life has mainly been about my career and there's no one to blame for that but myself. The truth is that I'm probably not an emotionally giving person. Maybe the real reason I stayed all these years is because there is a part of me that is more comfortable with the façade. I don't know if I'd be any good at the real thing."

"Don't you want to find out though?" He smiled but before he could respond, she said, "Oh God, I'm sorry. That was inappropriate."

"No, don't be sorry. It's a thought I've had myself. That's really why I'm up here. I needed to escape to somewhere other than my office for a few days. You're remarkably easy to talk to. Believe it or not, I'm usually quite reserved."

She smiled. "Me too. I'm a good listener though."

"You also sound like quite a romantic. Is there someone special back in New York?"

"Oh, no, not at all. I mean no to both. I'm not seeing anyone and I'm not much of a romantic. I mean, I just never prioritized that stuff, but…"

"But?"

"My parents were very much in love, so maybe there's a part of me that at least believes that kind of movie love is possible. But it's not for me."

"Why not?"

She paused and set her teacup on the silver tray. "Would you like something stronger than tea? I think there's a bottle of brandy around here somewhere."

"Yes. Thank you."

Penelope returned a few minutes later with two brandy snifters.

"Cheers," they said as they clinked glasses.

"That's good," Richard said as he took a sip. "You know, the amber color is a bit like your eyes."

She blushed.

"I'm sorry. I don't mean to make you uncomfortable."

"You didn't. I'm not used to people noticing things like that. Most people just see my glasses and don't even know what color my eyes are."

"You're very beautiful. I'd imagine there are guys your age lined up for you."

"Hardly," she said as she took a swig. "I'm sort of invisible to most guys, which suits me just fine."

"You were saying that before, that you're not a romantic."

"My mother died when I was in high school and it destroyed my father."

"I'm sorry. Was she ill?"

"No, it was a car accident – some reckless person, texting. My dad became a different person overnight. A shell of who he used to be. I guess I don't want to open myself up for that kind of hurt."

"Take it from me: avoiding love doesn't spare you from pain. At a minimum, it creates a slow but persistent numbing that might be worse than actual pain."

Penelope took another sip of her drink. "I've been focusing on my studies anyway."

"That's right; you said you're in graduate school. Why did you pick New York?"

"I wanted to change my life I guess. Take more chances. But I haven't really changed like I hoped."

"Change is hard. What are you studying?"

"Art history."

They talked for hours about art, literature, and mythology. Richard was well-versed in every subject that came up, which he chalked up to "a good education." They batted around some of Penelope's thesis ideas and Richard suggested she read the work of Sarah Cohen, a feminist historian who has written about the goddesses in modernity. When Penelope asked how he was familiar with her work, he hesitated a bit before saying, "My wife has taken me to some book events."

"Oh," she mumbled, unable to conceal her irrational disappointment. After a moment passed, she said, "It must be really late."

Richard looked at his watch. "God, it's after two. I shouldn't have kept you so long."

Penelope stood up. "I should let you get some rest. I have to be up in a few hours to help my dad with breakfast. Please join us whenever you wake up."

He stood up and put his hand out.

She extended her arm in anticipation of a handshake, but instead he took her hand and clasped it in his. They stood for a moment, the only noise the last crackles from the dying embers of the fire.

"Well, good night," she said.

"Good night." It seemed as though he wanted to say more, but he didn't.

Penelope went to her room where she lay wide-eyed, wondering what had just happened and trying to understand what she was feeling. *He's so average looking and he's old; why am I thinking about him? He's obviously having a midlife crisis. But he has kind eyes, and he seemed to get me – really get me – and I think I got him. What was that?*

After a sleepless night, she rolled out of bed at five o'clock and headed down to the kitchen. *Dad must have slept in. Wonder what he'll say about Richard sleeping on our couch*, she thought as she started the coffee pot. She noticed that the two brandy glasses had been cleaned and placed in the drying rack, so she walked into the library to check on Richard. He was gone. The bedding was folded neatly, and atop it, she found a note.

Thank you for your hospitality and for listening. Forgive me for overstepping, but my failures have opened my eyes and so I want to offer you some advice. Open your heart to somebody, someday. They will be very lucky. You deserve all life has to offer. Richard.

She smiled as she held the paper, the faint smell of last night's fire still in the air.

"Penelope, there you are," her father said from the doorway. "I saw you started the coffee. You look tired. Did you get any sleep or did the wind keep you up too?"

"Uh, no. I didn't get much sleep."

Two months later, Penelope was crouching on the floor of the Fifth Avenue Barnes & Noble looking at Moleskine notebooks when she heard, "Penelope?"

She looked up to see Richard. She smiled as he reached his hand out to pull her up, her skin sparking when it touched his.

"Hi, Richard."

"Buying a notebook?" he asked.

"Oh, yeah. It's a start-of-the-semester ritual. I pick a different color each time."

"It's reassuring to know people still buy non-electronic notebooks."

"What about you?" she asked, sheepishly.

"I just left a meeting nearby and stopped in to get a birthday card for my sister."

She smiled softly. "I wondered if I'd ever see you again. Every time I visit my father and someone walks through the front door, I look to see if it's you, which I know is stupid because you have a house down the road and..."

"It's not stupid. I've wondered if I would see you again too."

"You left in the middle of the night. Was your power restored?"

"Actually, I drove back to the city."

"In that awful storm?"

"I wanted to do it before I lost my nerve."

"Do what?" she asked.

"Change my life."

She paused before asking, "And did you?"

He looked down and shook his head. "My wife lost her job. If you asked her, she would say that she made a career change, but that's par for the course. Her career was all she had. We're two of a kind that way. It wasn't the right time."

"I'm sorry."

"Don't be. You helped me more than you know."

She smiled. After an awkward moment, she said, "Well, I guess I should buy my notebook."

"Are you in a hurry? Maybe you'd like to get a drink or a bite to eat. I owe you for the tea and brandy."

"Oh, well, uh..." she stuttered.

"It's all right if you'd rather not. I hope this doesn't sound strange but I felt a connection with you that I haven't felt before, so seeing you again is remarkable."

"I felt the same way."

"Shall we then?"

"Yes. Let's," she said without hesitation.

Penelope helped Richard find a suitable birthday card, after which he insisted on buying her new midnight blue notebook. As they stepped onto a bustling Fifth Avenue, Penelope asked, "Where should we go?"

"We're a few blocks from The Plaza. The Rose Club has a great wine list. Have you been there?"

She shook her head. "Would it be pathetic to say that I was obsessed with the *Eloise* books as a child? I've always hoped for an excuse to go there."

He smiled. "The Plaza it is."

They lifted their champagne flutes, and said, "Cheers!"

"So, what do you think? Does it live up to your expectations?" he asked.

"It's just like the movies, especially the lobby. Although my fantasy was more hot chocolate than champagne."

He laughed. "Well then, since we're writing our own script anyway, shall I order us a bite to eat?"

"Sure."

"It's a special day. How about caviar?"

She nodded.

After Richard ordered, Penelope asked, "Why is it a special day?"

"Because I saw you again."

She blushed and looked down, hiding behind her long curls.

"And it's your first time at The Plaza."

She smiled.

For the next hour, they talked about their favorite books and films set in New York. Both workaholics, neither spent much time taking advantage of all the city has to offer. They vowed to push each other to work less and play more. Then Penelope came up with an idea.

"What if we meet up once in a while to see the places from our favorite books and movies? It could be a way to explore the city with new eyes. Since you brought me here, I feel like I should return the favor."

Richard smiled. "Your plan reminds me of something I might have seen in a movie."

"*Breakfast at Tiffany's.* They explore the city by taking turns doing things one of them has never done before. My idea is a spin on that."

"It's a deal."

The waiter came to remove their empty champagne bottle and Richard said, "I should probably take care of the check and get you a cab."

"Okay."

As they stood at the cabstand, Penelope felt morose. *Will I really see him again? What is this? Is there something between us? Does he feel it too?* She contemplated asking him but couldn't bring herself to be so direct. She took a deep breath to say goodbye when Richard said, "It feels like fate running into you today. I hope I can see you again. Another landmark from the movies, as you suggested?"

"Sure," she said softly.

"Should we exchange numbers?"

She nodded.

A moment later, a cab pulled up. They both seemed unsure of what to do so Richard hugged her and she gave him a peck on the cheek. On the way home she mused, *Was it really fate? Do I even believe in that?* When those thoughts faded, the warmth of their embrace lingered.

For the next three days, she checked her phone incessantly, something she had never done before. Disappointed with each confirmation that there was no missed call or text, she eventually decided, *I'm being impractical. He's older. He's married. He was just being nice. Let it go.* On the fourth day, she received a text message:

It was wonderful to see you the other day. I can't stop thinking about it. There's a showing of Breakfast at Tiffany's at The Paris a week from tonight at 7. It's not exactly a landmark but it does seem like fate. Would you like to go? Maybe we could go for a hot chocolate after. R.

Penelope felt exhilarated as she texted back:

I'd love to.

She spent the next week consumed by anticipation and worry. *What have I gotten myself into?* When Friday came, she laid potential outfits all over her bed and tried on jeans with several different T-shirt and blazer combinations, overcome by disappointment each time she looked in the mirror. *If I want to be less serious and have more fun, I need to change it up. I just need to get outside of myself.* After spending an hour trying on everything in her closet, she settled on a simple white sundress, far more frivolous than her daily attire. On her way out the door, she panicked and grabbed a blue cardigan, rationalizing that she didn't want to be cold.

She arrived at The Paris and was relieved to see Richard waiting for her, tickets in hand.

"You look lovely," he said as he handed her a ticket.

"Oh, thank you," she replied, hoping he wouldn't notice her sweaty palms.

They stepped into the crowded line of moviegoers, slowly making their way into the sold-out theater. Penelope's heart raced; she wasn't sure if it was the crowd, Richard, or both. As the smell of buttered popcorn wafted into her nostrils, she stole a glance at Richard. *With just one change, the familiar can be made unfamiliar.*

"What about over there?" he asked, pointing to two seats in the dead center of the theater.

"Perfect." Other patrons stood up to let them wriggle into the row, so he took her hand and led her to their seats. After some small talk about their days, the lights went out. They sat in the glow of the screen, and Penelope made a conscious decision to let go and lose herself in the movie, something she wasn't accustomed to. By the end, she had a palpable lump in her throat. Unable to speak, she turned to face Richard and smiled, teary eyed. He gently rubbed her hand.

After they made their way outside Richard said, "The Plaza is right here. Should we go for that hot chocolate?"

She nodded. *Could he be what I was waiting for? Maybe this is my chance to change my life.*

They entered the grand lobby for the second time, and Richard took her hand.

He pointed and said, "I think the hot chocolate is over there."

"What if we get room service instead?" Penelope's words surprised even her. *Who am I? I can't believe I said that.*

He nodded. "Stay here for a minute."

He returned a few moments later with a room key. They held hands during the impossibly long elevator ride, each watching the changing numbers as if afraid to look at each other.

They entered the room in silence and stood next to the bed, still holding hands. Richard stroked Penelope's cheek, leaned in, and kissed her. He took her sweater off and the strap from her sundress slipped off her shoulder. He touched her shoulder and she felt a shiver. They made love that night.

When she awoke the next morning, she suddenly wondered, *Was that a one-night stand? My first time can't be a one-night stand in a hotel. I think I feel different. Everything feels kind of different. Or do I just want it to?*

Richard looked over and said, "Good morning. Did you sleep well?"

"Uh huh."

He caressed her face and she averted her eyes.

"What is it? What's wrong?"

"You're married. I'm just wondering if you do this kind of thing often."

He shook his head. "I promise, not once in all of these years. And I didn't mean for this to happen with us, but I'm glad it did. Are you?"

She nodded.

"How about I order some breakfast and we can decide what landmark we're going to visit next?"

She was surprised that he'd thought of their plan.

"Remember? We said we'd see the sites from our favorite books and films."

"I remember," she replied.

Over the next several months, they visited the Empire State Building, Central Park, and Times Square. Penelope particularly enjoyed going to museums together so she could teach Richard about the origins of the paintings and their historical significance. They saw *The Woman in Gold* at the Neue Galerie and Van Gogh's *The Starry Night* at the MoMA. While standing before Van Gogh's masterpiece, she realized it was the closest she had come to looking at the stars in years and she felt grateful. After their outings, they always returned to The Plaza, which had become "their place." Since Richard didn't appear to have any worries about going out with her in public, she chose to forget that he was married.

She spent increasingly less time with her roommates, who were busy with their own lives and didn't seem to notice. Her schoolwork suffered a little and her thesis proposal was past due, but as a lifelong overachiever, she felt entitled to a break.

Everything changed on Valentine's Day. Penelope was approaching her apartment after class, trying not to slip on the veneer of frost covering the sidewalk. To her surprise, she saw Richard standing outside of her building. He looked startled to see her.

"Penelope! What are you doing here?"

"You're not here to see me?" she asked, bewildered.

"No. Is this where you live?"

She nodded. "What are you doing here?"

"I'm taking my son Kyle out to dinner, but he wanted to stop by his cousin's place to drop off a present. She recently broke up with someone and he wanted to make sure someone gave her a Valentine's gift."

Oh my God. It can't be, she thought, trembling.

"That name never meant anything to me before, but…" she mumbled incoherently.

"What are you talking about, Penelope? Do you know Kyle?"

"What's your niece's name?" she asked with dread.

"Natashya."

"Oh my God."

"You know her?"

"Tash is my roommate and she's going to kill me."

Over the next few months, Penelope started to unravel. For the first time in her life, even when she hunkered down at the library, she was unable to concentrate. She was racked with guilt, exacerbated every time she saw Tash, who was more protective of Kyle than anyone. Terrified she would confess the affair and ruin everyone's lives, Penelope avoided Tash, which meant avoiding Jason as well. Their movie nights and roommate talks became a thing of the past. Worse, Tash and Jason didn't seem to miss her. Penelope felt utterly alone. Richard was the only person she could talk to, which made ending it with him seem impossible. Now afraid to be caught together in public, they saw each other less frequently and only at The Plaza.

It all came to a head as the spring slipped into summer. Richard insisted that it was time to tell his wife. "We can't go on like this. You're too afraid to go anywhere and this feels wrong."

"Please don't. If you do, Kyle will surely find out and then it's only a matter of time before Tash finds out. We haven't been terribly close recently, but she's probably still my best friend. If she hates me, Jason will too. I will lose everything."

"Kyle won't find out. My wife would never tell him and neither would I."

"You don't know that. Besides, I don't want to be the cause of a marriage ending, whether it's a good marriage or not."

"You're not the cause. I've wanted to do this for a long time, since before we met."

"We should split up, just end things. Then you can do what you want and it will have nothing to do with me."

Richard shook his head. He looked broken.

"I'm ashamed I didn't end this sooner," she said, unable to make eye contact.

"Listen to me. I won't do anything, and you don't either. Let's just take some time and sort things out. See where the chips fall. Please."

Emotionally drained, Penelope agreed. In the coming weeks, she tried to pull herself together and look at things rationally. She hoped to make progress on her thesis but was entirely too preoccupied. Then one day Richard texted to say that he wanted to see her. She knew when she left the library to meet him that she would end the relationship once and for all.

As the cab pulled up to her apartment building in the early morning light after her last night with Richard, she had one thought: *Should I tell Tash?*

Chapter 8

*O*h *shit*, Jason thought as he approached the Battery Park set and saw Sam at the makeup tent. *I wonder if he still thinks I'm a jerk. Tash would have a field day with this. I hope she's okay.*

"Hey," Sam said as he pulled out a folding chair for Jason.

"Hey, dude. Uh, I mean Sam. Hey, Sam."

Sam smiled as Jason silently berated himself. *What's wrong with me? He's just the makeup guy. Don't let him rattle you.*

"They want to get started as soon as possible in case we go long. So Tanya here is going to do your hair while I do your face. Your makeup! While I do your makeup," Sam said, looking flushed.

"Cool. Hi, Tanya," Jason said with a nod. *Hmm, Sam seems nervous. He remembers. I can almost hear Tash saying that he's probably worried I'm going to get him fired.*

Soon they were doing the first set-up. Distracted with thoughts of Tash, Jason had trouble finding his light. He required repeated direction from the photographer. Sam noticed and requested they stop the shoot for a moment, pretending he needed to fix a stray eyelash on Jason's face.

When he got close to Jason, he whispered, "You seem a little off. Are you okay?"

"My best friend is in crisis, broke up with her guy last night. I'm preoccupied, I guess."

"Remember, you're the star. Tune it all out."

"Thanks, Sam."

Jason regrouped and was soon in the zone. He was egged on as the crowd of bystanders grew, necessitating the crew to put up more barricades. At the command of the photographer, Sam ran on set to do touch-up work.

"You're on fire now!" he said to Jason.

"Thanks, and for earlier too."

Sam smiled. "People are standing around, waiting for your autograph."

"Really, dude? I figured people stopped to see if anything looks exciting and they don't even know what it is."

"I heard some of them say your name. They know you," Sam said excitedly.

Jason smiled, but then caught himself, afraid to appear arrogant.

"You're all set. I'm jumping out."

"Cool. Thanks, Sam."

After another hour of shooting, they broke for lunch.

Jason bypassed the catered food and headed straight to his makeup chair. The rest of the crew ate their lunch together. Noticing Jason alone, Sam put his half-eaten tuna sandwich down, grabbed two bottles of water, and headed over to Jason.

"Thanks," Jason said as he took the water Sam offered.

"I'm sorry about your friend. I hope she's okay."

"She's going through some stuff and kind of fucking up her life, but she needs to figure it out for herself."

"Hopefully she will. Maybe you can nudge her in the right direction."

"You know what's funny is that we watch movies together all the time. She's one of my roommates. We watched *Desperately Seeking*

Susan like a week ago. You know the old Madonna flick, back when people thought she'd always be ahead of the trends?"

Sam nodded.

"The big scenes all take place here in Battery Park, and now I'm here."

"Yeah, that's right. I watched it online a few years ago. What I remember most was Roberta, the desperate housewife, you know before there were desperate housewives. God, she was so lonely in her sad, orgasm-free suburban marriage."

Jason laughed. "At first it seemed like it's all about Madonna's fabulous lace bustiers and sequined boots, but then I wondered if each of us really has a person we would chase around the world, you know, like the Susan character. That one person you can't quite forget... Jeez, listen to me. Sorry. I guess I'm still thinking about my roommate."

Sam smiled. "So, are you one of those models who doesn't eat? They're going to call you back soon."

"Just not during shoots. Nerves."

Sam smirked.

"What?" Jason prodded.

"It always surprises me when guys like you get nervous."

"Guys like me?"

"Guys who've had it easy."

"Wow, that's a big assumption."

"I keep putting my foot in my mouth," Sam mumbled before backtracking. "I just meant that you seem like you have every reason to be confident."

"It's not like I've had any training for this. I never planned on becoming a model. Some guy approached me at a yoga studio. Turned out he worked for one of the biggest agents in the business. I didn't really know what I was in for."

"Is that regret? Seems like you have a pretty huge opportunity."

"No regret. I'm just saying I get nervous. Pretty sure one of these days, these people are gonna figure out that I don't belong here."

"I doubt it. You're a rising star."

"I'm a token, an experiment."

Sam looked perplexed.

"The only thing they like about me is my skin color. I'm just a trend that hasn't gone out of style yet, you know?"

"God, I feel like a jerk."

Jason chuckled. "I'm not saying you should feel sorry for me. I have a sweet gig and I'm enjoying it. But it is what it is, you know?"

Sam nodded. "I bet people underestimate you."

At that moment, the photographer's assistant came to the tent to fetch Jason. As he walked back to the set, Sam called after him.

"What you asked before, about each person having someone they can't quite shake – I think we do, if we're lucky."

Jason smiled.

The shoot moved to the South Street Seaport and eventually the Circle Line Ferry, continuing until dusk, when the photographer finally lamented that there was no more usable light. Jason was ready to leave when he noticed Sam packing up.

"Sam, thanks again for everything today."

"My pleasure. You smashed it. And I hope your friend is okay."

"Would you, uh, that is if you don't have plans, would you like to go grab a bite to eat?"

"Are you asking me out?"

"Yeah," Jason replied.

"Well, I usually don't date models. You know, models always hang all over the makeup guys," he said, before bursting out into laughter.

Jason sighed.

"I was just kidding. I'm sorry. My timing is seriously off. Yes, I would love to go out with you, if you still want to."

Jason nodded.

"You must be starving. What are you in the mood for?"

"Ever since we talked about that movie, I've been craving Chinese food. Remember the scene where they get wasted and eat takeout on the roof?"

Sam smiled. "Chinatown it is."

"Do they really say that?" Sam asked as he took his last sip of hot and sour soup.

"Oh yeah. Sometimes I even hear the crew gossiping about me and they always say 'That one, the Chinese one.' And I'm like, my mom is Japanese and my dad is Korean. On what planet does that make me Chinese?"

"That's awful. Maybe it's the price to pay for breaking the stereotype."

"Most of the time I feel like a huge sellout. I've never said that to anyone before. I know it's a bullshit job and I let them use me, but it's such an easy way to make serious bank. To be honest, I don't know what I would have done if this hadn't landed in my lap. Most of my friends are struggling to make ends meet. Some had to move back home, couldn't survive in the city."

"I hear that. I lay awake some nights wondering how I'm going to pay my bills. My apartment is three hundred square feet and I can't afford it. The interest on my debt from my cosmetology program keeps growing and it seems like I'll never get ahead of it. I keep waiting for it to get just a little easier, but it never does."

"Why do you stay in the city?"

"It's oxygen. Survival. I'd do anything to stay here. You have to understand, I'm from a small town in Missouri where you lived in fear if people even suspected you were gay. I walked down the street with people following behind me, saying that they hoped I died of AIDS."

Jason listened intently, not taking his eyes off of Sam.

Sam continued, "I dreamed of making my way here someday. Cliché, I know, but for me New York represented more than a safe place; it was an idea, a concept. You know, the way America is an idea as much as a place. New York represents possibility. That idea got me through a hell that others didn't survive. As soon as I could afford a ticket, I left all that shit behind. Beating after beating, threat after threat, I found a way to survive. But I think if I gave up on the idea of New York now, well, that's something I wouldn't survive."

Jason outstretched his arm and put his hand on Sam's. At that moment, the waiter delivered the bill.

"Let me get this," Jason said as he snatched it up.

"I didn't mean..."

"I invited you out," Jason insisted.

As they left the restaurant Sam asked, "So now what?"

"Now how about you take me home to your tiny apartment?"

The next morning Jason woke up to the smell of French vanilla.

"I made coffee," Sam said from the galley kitchen. "Are you hungry or are you in a hurry?"

Jason thought for a moment. "Not in a hurry at all. Now come here and give me a kiss."

Sam prepared omelets while Jason showered. Over brunch they talked about photographers they like, the benefits of work travel, and books, discovering they both have an interest in architecture and design. Before Jason left, he invited Sam to a club opening the following night. Although he seemed surprised by the invitation, Sam agreed to meet him there.

When Jason got home late that afternoon, he bumped into Penelope.

"Hey, Pen."

When she turned, he could see she had been crying.

"Are you okay?" he asked.

"I'm fine," she sighed before closing the bathroom door.

Jason redirected his focus on Tash and knocked on her door.

"Come in."

He opened the door and walked right over to the bed, sitting on the corner.

"Hey sweetie," he said.

"Hey."

"You might want to get out of bed and start the day."

"I called out of work. I'm tired."

"Do you want to talk about what happened with Aidan?"

"No."

"There's something wrong with Pen. She looks like she's been crying all night. Do you know what's going on?"

Tash shook her head.

"Weeeeelll, then we can talk about me. Do you want to hear about the shoot?"

Tash sat up, leaning against the wall. "Wasn't that yesterday? Are you just getting back?"

"Uh huh. Remember that guy I met? Sam?"

Tash thought for a minute. "Makeup Boy?"

"We went out last night after the shoot and I stayed at his place."

"And you're just getting back now? Did you take downers and sleep all day?"

"No, he made me brunch."

"You stayed for brunch? Wow, so does this mean ugly sex is as hot as they say? You know, because they like try harder or something?"

"He's not ugly. He has great eyes, among other things."

"Oh my God," she said, perking up. "You actually like him!"

Jason smiled brightly.

"That's great, honey. But just remember, we're all tomorrow's discards. I wouldn't get too heavy."

"Sweetie, you have to call Aidan."

PART THREE

Chapter 9

66 **S**ince you're actually on time this morning you can help me open the shop," Catherine said.

Fine, oh passive aggressive one, Tash thought. "What do you want me to do?" she asked from the customer couch she was slumped in.

"Clean the jewelry case. A customer's child got fingerprints all over it yesterday."

She rolled her eyes and sluggishly made her way to the backroom to get the cleaning supplies. Moving a cleanser-soaked paper towel in circles over the glass case, she was completely detached from herself. Lost in rote movements and absent of discernible thoughts, she didn't realize that she was wiping the same spot on the counter over and over again. When Catherine called, "Tash, I'm opening," she was jarred back into the moment. *Great, another thrilling day begins.*

Inundated with the morning rush, Tash immediately started assisting customers. She was good at sizing people up and when she was attentive, customers were captivated by her. To them, Tash was the living embodiment of the confident, effortless style they were hoping to buy. When a young woman in a miniskirt came in, Tash pointed out each skirt in the store, explaining how flattering the cut is. Once in the dressing room with a pile of skirts, Tash assembled mix-and-match outfits and suggested additional pieces. "You look hot in that," she said, her standard phrase of encouragement. Her skills and charisma landed her the considerable sale.

Catherine remarked, "You know, you're very good with customers when you make an effort. If you made a bigger commitment to the store, you could be assistant manager someday."

"Thanks," she said, halfheartedly. *Then I can be just like you. Holy shit. I didn't think I could feel worse today.*

Deflated from the prospect of turning into Catherine, she returned to assisting customers. She rang up sales, issued store credits, answered calls, and ran back and forth from the register to the dressing rooms to the storeroom and back again. It was an utterly normal day.

When Catherine left to pick up lunch, Tash wandered aimlessly around, looking for an outfit to rehang or a display in need of adjustment. She thought about rearranging the new arrivals up front but didn't want to spur a lecture from Catherine. So she meandered back to the counter, her usual place for slouching and counting the minutes. Normally engrossed in making plans for her evenings, time moved far slower now that she was spending her nights alone at home. *It can't only be 12:05*, she thought as she glanced at the clock. *The days are getting longer. I wish there was at least a window display to create.*

Just when Tash thought she couldn't be any more bored, customers walked in. Like a switch going off in her mind, the ring of the door chime propelled her into a fantasy. In her mind's eye, the store suddenly turned into the scene of a musical. Everything was transformed into technicolor and she envisioned herself screaming and then breaking out into dance and song. Customers became backup singers and mannequins swayed from side to side.

"Miss, do you have these pants in a smaller size?" a customer asked, instantly closing the curtain on her fantasy musical.

"Yes, ma'am. I'll go check in the back," she replied.

Fuck, what's wrong with me? It's like I'm in a Björk video. God, who directed that video? It was so different than… fuck, snap out of it, she thought as she shook her head.

She returned with the pants to find even more customers milling about. Soon Catherine returned and took charge, assisting the wealthiest-looking customers while Tash fetched different sizes from the back, cleaned out dressing rooms, and offered bottles of water to bored men waiting for their wives. The hours passed slowly.

She breathed a sigh of relief when it was finally time to clock out. On the walk home, she barely acknowledged the street vendors trying to catch her attention, too lethargic to offer a smile or even a sarcastic word. As she crossed over from SoHo into the Village, the city transitioned from work to play, with the sounds of friends meeting filling the air. The only thing Tash could concentrate on was crawling into bed and watching TV, her new nightly ritual that had taken the place of the club scene. As she approached Washington Square Park, she noticed Harold wrapping something around his ankle.

"Oh, hello Natashya."

"What's wrong with your ankle?" she asked, staring at the purple, swollen appendage.

"Had a little tussle," he replied with a wince as he tried to wrap it with an old navy-blue bandana.

"Did someone do this to you?" she asked in outrage.

He shook his head. "A lovely young lady like you shouldn't worry. I'm fine."

"You need to put ice on that. Hang on and I'll run to the store."

"You needn't…" he tried to call after her but she was already on her way.

When she returned, she sat on the bench next to him and opened a plastic bag to reveal ice, baby wipes, and an Ace bandage. She opened the container of wipes and held it out.

"I thought it would be smart to clean it first," she said.

"Thank you," he replied as he used one to wipe the dirt from his swollen ankle. "You didn't have to go to all this trouble. I can get by."

"I know," she said. "Do you remember the day we first met? I had twisted my ankle."

He nodded.

She opened a soda cup filled with ice. "It was the only way I could get some," she explained. "Don't worry; I got some napkins we can put the ice in."

He offered a close-mouthed smile.

As he held the makeshift ice pack against his injured ankle, Tash quietly said, "Harold, I don't want to pry, but…"

"The time has come?"

She looked at him, uncertain of herself.

"Yes, you can ask me. Go ahead."

"How did you end up here?"

"I wish I could tell you the story you want to hear: a fairy tale about the perfect life that unraveled because of one tricky bend in the path I didn't see coming. The career that toppled, the love of my life I lost, the children I miss. I long for that beautiful lie. But Miss Natashya, I have no such story."

"I'm sorry. I didn't mean to…"

He put his hand up. "I do not wish to be a cautionary tale for anyone. But if my story were told, it wouldn't be one of someone who lost it all, rather, someone who never wanted anything to lose."

Tash looked down and tried to make sense of what he was saying.

"I am quite content, most of the time," he assured her, returning his attention to his ankle.

She stood up and smiled. "Don't wrap the bandage too tightly. It should fit comfortably. You might want to save the rest of the wipes, you know, for whatever. There's a sandwich and a bottle of water in the bag."

"Thank you, Natashya," he said as he continued tending to his injury.

She took a few steps and considered saying something more, but decided against it and headed home. She dropped her bag inside her front door and dragged herself to the kitchen. She took a tub of Campbell's chicken noodle soup from the cabinet and stuck it in the microwave. As it cooked, she grabbed a diet cola and opened a jar of maraschino cherries, popping a couple directly into her mouth. She bit into the sweet bursts, releasing their sugary liquid, and thought about how much she'd always loved them. When the microwave beeped, she stuck her soda under one arm and retrieved her soup and a spoon.

Both of her roommates' doors were closed. *Jason must be out with Sam again, and Pen's probably locked in her room.* When she got to her room, the floor covered with dirty laundry, she made space to put her food down on her nightstand before changing into her sweats. She crawled into bed, searched the sheets for her remote control, flipped on the TV, and started eating.

Afraid of bumping into Aidan at a club and too depressed to go out with friends, this had become her new nightly ritual. Jason spent most nights out with Sam, and although he invited her to join them many times, she didn't want to be a third wheel. Without plugging into the city's energy at night, her days felt longer and increasingly monotonous.

When he was home, Jason sat on her bed while she got ready to go to work in the mornings. She lived vicariously through his stories.

"I took Sam to a film screening at the SoHo House last night."

"What film?" she asked, searching for a clean tank top.

"I don't know. Some docu-whatever about eating disorders. It was a charity thing and my agent put me on the list."

"Kind of sketchy to send models to promote eating disorder awareness or whatever."

"Yeah, I know. Aaaaanyway, Sam is great in those places. He can talk to anyone and a lot of A-listers know him from work."

"Uh huh."

"I know it's early…"

"In the morning? Yeah, it is!" she said with a snicker.

"No, early in the relationship, smart ass," he said, tossing a wet towel at her.

"Okay, jeez, I'm listening. Early in the relationship for what?" she asked, still searching for a top.

"To think it might be something. It's good for me to be with someone like him. Someone, um, down to earth."

"First of all, it's not early in the relationship by your slutty standards; it's shockingly far into it."

He laughed.

"Second, he's so lucky to have you. Seriously."

Jason smiled.

"Shit, now I'm gonna be late for work again. Help me find a shirt."

"Tash acts like she doesn't need anyone. Like nothing gets to her. She's always in and out of relationships. They never last, but she's sort of a love junkie in disguise," Jason explained.

"Or maybe a love seeker," Sam suggested.

"Yes! You nailed it," Jason agreed and took his hand as they walked into Minetta Tavern. Recognizing Jason, the hostess immediately showed them to a reserved section of the bar. "We have a nice semi-round in the dining room ready when your friends arrive."

"Thank you," Jason replied as he and Sam hopped on barstools.

"This place is cool," Sam remarked, looking around. "You'd never expect this when you walk in."

"They have the best high-end cheeseburgers in the city," Jason said.

"You eat burgers?" Sam asked skeptically.

"Once in a blue moon."

"You never finished telling me about your roommate and her relationship drama."

"Actually, what I wanted to tell you was more about me, well, us I guess," he said, putting his hand on Sam's thigh.

"I'm listening."

"This is the first time I've done the healthy relationship thing. It's amazing. *You're* amazing, Sam. You're good for me."

Sam put his hand over Jason's hand and smiled softly.

"Listen, we're having a great time, but it isn't too heavy, right? I mean, we're keeping it light?"

"Uh, yeah. Of course. We're just having fun," Jason stammered, trying to conceal his confusion.

"I mean, I'm not seeing anyone else. How could I? We're always together. But it's meant to be a good time. We're on the same page, right?"

"Definitely," Jason assured him.

Their friends arrived just in time to rescue Jason from the uncomfortable moment. Sam leapt off his stool to give them hugs while Jason sat thinking, *Not too heavy? Keep it light? What exactly does he mean?*

As the group settled in at their table, Jason excused himself to use the restroom. He splashed cold water on his face, wishing he could go back in time and wash the heart off his sleeve.

A few weeks later, Tash received a text from Kyle asking her to meet for lunch. She was reluctant because she didn't want to talk about Aidan, and Kyle could always tell when she was in a bad space. But it would be nice to see him, so she agreed to meet at their favorite diner the next day.

"Damn! I'm perfectly on time and was hoping to surprise you by beating you here for a change," Tash said as they hugged.

"You get credit for being on time," he said as they slid into the booth.

The waitress tried to hand them oversized laminated menus, but Kyle stopped her. "We actually know what we want: two coffees and a platter of blueberry blintzes to share, please."

As the waitress walked away, Tash said, "She's new, not like the other dinosaurs here. She looks like she's our age. God, that's depressing. Can you imagine working here?"

The waitress returned with their coffee and a plate of complimentary bagel chips. As they fixed their coffee, Tash asked, "What's been going on?"

"Summer kind of sucks. I'm living back at home, which is a major drag."

"That blows," Tash said as she searched for a cinnamon raisin bagel chip.

"Now that my mom is a literary agent, she's working for herself so she's always home."

"That totally sucks."

"Yup."

"Does she like being an agent at least? Being your own boss sounds cool."

"She was pretty stoked that she landed a big deal for one of her clients. Some unknown guy, Pete Rice. His book is called *The Lost Notebooks* and she got him a deal with Random House. I guess it's her first big score. We got Chinese food to celebrate, which was lame."

Tash giggled.

"There's definitely something up with my parents though."

"You said that last time I saw you."

"Being at home, I'm certain. It's obvious. I don't know what happened but they don't talk at all. I mean, not a word. It's creepy."

"No offense, but they've always been kinda messed up."

"Yeah, I know."

"So, you seeing anyone?" she asked.

He shook his head.

The waitress interrupted to deliver their blintzes with two small plates for sharing. They each took a blintz and a dollop of sour cream. Kyle asked, "What's been going on with you?"

"These look really hot," Tash said as she cut into a blintz and watched the creamy filling ooze out.

Kyle put his fork down and looked intently at Tash. "Okay, what's wrong?"

"Why do you think…"

He shook his head. "Just tell me."

"Aidan and I broke up."

"When?"

"A few weeks ago," she replied before taking a bite of her blintz.

"What happened?"

"It's a long story," she said with a full mouth.

Kyle continued staring at her, tilting his head slightly as a means of gently prodding her.

She eventually threw her fork down. "Fine. It was stupid. I drank a little too much and danced with some guy at a club and it caused all of this drama."

"Some guy?"

"Some club promoter Aidan was kind of interviewing with."

"Oh, Tash."

"Whaaat? Don't 'Oh, Tash' me. He totally overreacted and said all of this awful stuff to me."

"Like what?"

"Crap about how I hide behind a persona like I'm fake or something. And how I'm wasting my life and don't go after my dreams."

"Well?"

"Well what?" she snapped.

"Hey, I love you but it sounds like he's just calling you on your shit, right?"

She didn't respond.

"And getting drunk and dancing with the club promoter? Really?"

"Why are you judging me and taking his side?"

"I'm always on your side. You know that. But what you did at the club isn't who you are, so what's really going on?"

"What are you talking about? You know better than anyone how I am when I'm out having fun."

"That's how you used to be; it's not who you are now. And for the record, I never thought that was how you were when you were truly having fun. I always thought that's how you acted to look like you were having fun."

"Sometimes it's hard to tell the difference," she said softly.

"Listen, I remember the assholes you dated in college, and I remember how they treated you. Aidan seemed really different, like he gets you."

"Wait," she said with a laugh. "You never like the guys I date."

"Exactly."

As she walked home in the summer heat, the foul smell of garbage permeating the air, she replayed Kyle's words. *It's not who you are. Then who the hell am I?* she wondered. The rumble of the subway caused the ground beneath her feet to vibrate and she was reminded of the sound of film spinning in the old projection rooms she visited during college. She started to imagine her life, frame by frame, whirling in front of her. Lost in thought as she walked down Macdougal Street, she paused when she noticed the rare music store her old boyfriend Jacob worked at was out of business. With Kyle's words still ringing in her ears, she saw a new series of images from a horrible New Year's Eve years earlier.

Drunk and high on pot and ecstasy, she and her boyfriend passed out in his bedroom after a party. She awoke the next morning, naked and lying between him and his lecherous roommate, with no memory of what happened, nor any doubt. It was unfolding again before her eyes in a series of visceral flashes. Pulling the dirty sheets up to her chin to cover her cold body. The stale smell of pot and cigarettes in the air. Pretending to sleep while he lay there. Chills going up her body but feeling too afraid to move to get her clothes. Trying not to even breathe. The lump forming in her throat, moving into her chest, like a vice getting tighter and tighter. Exhaling when he finally woke up and left the room.

As the flashes came faster and faster, she quickened her pace, as if trying to outwalk the images. But she couldn't outpace them. She remembered frantically searching in her pocketbook for cab fare to get home, only to realize that he had also stolen from her. *He took whatever he wanted.* The intense humiliation. Wondering, *Why do I care about cab fare? What's wrong with me?* She shuddered as she remembered boasting to her friends about what a "killer party" it had been, too afraid to say the truth aloud. The physical hurt. The wretched soreness that worsened the next day. The unbearable fear that it would never get better. The worry of disease.

Deep in thoughts she was trying to escape, she approached Washington Square Park and didn't notice Harold until he spoke to her.

"Hello, Ms. Natashya," he said.

She stopped to chat, still breathing rapidly. "Oh, hi, Harold. How's your ankle?"

"Better. Haven't seen you in a few weeks," he replied.

"Been busy. I'll bring you coffee soon."

"Lovely. And your young man? Haven't seen him around here lately."

"Oh screw you!"

Chapter 10

Every day for the next week, Tash looked for Harold on the way to and from work, hoping to apologize. Twice she brought doughnuts but there was no sign of him. *He's been gone a long time. Even when they run him off, he's usually not gone this long. I wonder if he's okay*, she thought. *I shouldn't have been such a bitch.*

She gave up on finding him for the moment and went home. She tossed her bag toward the common room love seat and watched it land on the floor. She left it, intending to head to her room, but wound up standing in Jason's doorway. He was lying on his bed and watching old cartoons.

"What are you watching?" she asked with an attitude.

"*Rainbow Bright.* She's amazing, and she's totally gay!"

Tash smirked. "I think rainbows used to just be rainbows."

"No way. I'm telling you, totally gay. Anyway, I needed something upbeat."

"Well, you picked the right thing. Why? What's up?"

"Relationship stuff. I don't know. I may be misreading something. Trying not to think about it and just chill."

"I hear that," she commiserated.

"There's a new cable station that shows marathons of the old eighties cartoons. You would love it! Beats the crap out of the stuff they make now. This shit is seriously inspired."

She shook her head. "Whatever. I'm going to make popcorn and chill in my room. You want some?"

He shook his head.

Tash went to the kitchen for a diet cola and tub of microwave popcorn before going to her room. She changed into her most worn-in cotton pajamas and crawled into bed, propped up against pillows. She cycled through the channels, searching for something to watch, came across the end credits for *Rainbow Bright*, and was curious enough to stop. *Jason's a trip. Too funny*, she giggled. Before she could change the station, *Jem and the Holograms* came on, catching her attention.

The aesthetic is fantastic, she thought, instantly riveted. *What a dope look. Such great colors. God, imagine this aesthetic in a live-action suspense flick. It would be like pop noir. J was right. This stuff is inspired.* After acclimating to the fashion and vibe, Tash became immersed in the story. The idea that one woman had two distinct personas, the glamorous Jem and the responsible, orphan-raising Jerrica, resonated deeply. *They keep acting as though Jerrica is real and Jem is an illusion, but they're both real. That's why Rio loves them both. He's kind of a douche, cheating or whatever, but he can't help it. Together, Jem and Jerrica are like the perfect woman. No wonder their superhuman, cyborg savior is named Synergy. Brilliant.*

She watched the *Jem and the Holograms* marathon for hours, relating to the two-persona lead character more than any real person she had ever known. They shared a bond. All night her thoughts vacillated from Jem to her conversation with Kyle. She kept replaying his words, "It's not who you are. That's how you acted to look like you were having fun." Every time there was a scene with Rio, she transposed Aidan's face on his. Eventually she fell asleep, with the glow of the television beaming like a halo around her face.

The next morning, she woke up to find her popcorn spilled across her bed and onto the floor. The television was still on and playing the final scene of *The Last Unicorn*. As Tash wiped the sleep from her eyes, the mythical creature admitted how she now lives with regret because she had to give up the man she loved to save herself. Tash sighed, searched for the remote control, and turned the television off. As she rolled out of bed, she stepped on some popcorn, making a crunching sound. She grabbed her robe and walked out into the hallway, peeking into Jason's room, where he was asleep on top of the sheets.

"Hey, what's up?" he mumbled.

"Sorry. Didn't mean to wake you."

"It's fine," he replied as he rubbed his eyes. "You look tired. Come sit," he said, propping his pillows up and stretching his arms.

"I didn't get much sleep last night. Don't laugh, but I flipped on that cartoon station and they were running a marathon of *Jem and The Holograms*. I kind of binged on it."

"I wouldn't laugh. She's outrageous. Truly, truly outrageous," he said with hearty laughter.

Tash grabbed a pillow and smacked him in the face with it. "Can I tell you something that will make me sound crazy?"

"Always."

"I kinda related to Jem, a lot. It's like she has this fun persona that this guy is attracted to, but it's not the only thing she is. She's a totally different person too."

"Yeah," Jason prodded.

"It made me think about Aidan. He said I hide behind a persona and need to figure out who I really am. And Kyle said something like that too. I think, I think…"

"Do you remember when we watched *Desperately Seeking Susan*?"

"Yeah."

"Well Sam and I were talking about it and I had a realization. They were in their twenties. Roberta, the Rosanna Arquette character stuck in a bad suburban marriage, she was our age. It's just the shoulder pads and makeup back then that made everyone look forty."

"And?" Tash probed.

"The movie is really about her trying to figure out who she is, not who people say she is or who she thinks she's supposed to be. It got me thinking that there's this time in your twenties, you know after college or whatever, but before whatever is supposed to happen actually happens."

"Before you figure your shit out," she said.

"Before you figure out who you are and what you're doing. Nobody tells you what the hell to do after school. It just feels like being suspended in air or something."

"Totally."

"I think it's like a period of time you have to struggle through to get to where you want to go."

Tash smiled.

"What?" Jason asked.

"It's like our Blue Period. Your friend doesn't have to off themselves. We kill off parts of ourselves; we have to. It's not really about grief or sadness, just being sort of lost," she mused.

"But lost on the way to somewhere. Don't forget that. If we say goodbye to some version of who we are, it's only to become a better version."

"Jason, can I tell you something?"

"Anything."

"I fucked up. I miss Aidan."

"I know," he said, leaning over to hug her.

"I love him," she whispered in his ear.

"I know."

She pulled away and wiped tears from her eyes.

"Call him," Jason said.

"I will. But I think I need to do something for myself first. I may need to go out of town for a few days. Don't tell anyone, okay?"

He nodded. "But only if you text me every day so I know you're all good."

She smiled. "Love you."

"Love you back."

Chapter 11

As Jason was shaking the Lucky Charms box, hoping enough bits were stuck in the corners that when freed, he'd have enough for breakfast, Penelope came into the small kitchen. She opened the refrigerator and stared at the nearly bare shelves.

Jason put the cereal box down in defeat.

"Can you grab the milk?" he asked.

Penelope passed the milk cartoon, which contained a few last drops. He watched them drip into his crumb-lined bowl. He stood and ate the two bites of cereal before saying, "Pen, wasn't it your turn to go to the store?"

"I'm sorry. I forgot."

"That's not like you," he said, putting his empty bowl on the counter.

She shrugged.

"Pen?"

"I'll go to the store today. I'm really sorry."

"I don't care about the groceries. We can get takeout. I'm worried about you. What's going on? Whatever it is, you can tell me."

She took a deep breath and looked behind her to make sure they were alone.

"Tash isn't here. She had to go out of town for a few days," he assured her. "Pen, what is it?"

"Promise me you won't tell anyone."

"I promise."

"That includes Tash, especially Tash."

He nodded. "Okay, but why especially Tash?"

"I had an affair with a married man."

Jason's jaw dropped. "Holy shit!"

"Jason!"

"I'm sorry. But holy shit! That was literally the last thing I thought you were going to say."

"There's more."

His eyes widened.

"The man, the man I had a relationship with. I didn't know it at the time, but he's Tash's uncle, Kyle's dad."

"Holy shit!" he bellowed. He put his hand over his mouth and shook his head. "Sorry, oh God, I'm so sorry, Pen. It's just *that* is actually the last thing I thought you were going to say."

She looked down and shook her head.

He walked over and put his hand on her shoulder.

"Come on, let's make some coffee and sit down. You can tell me how this happened."

Soon Jason knew the entire story, from their initial meeting in Vermont to the "fateful" meeting months later, and everything that followed.

"I had no idea how hard your visits with your dad were. I'm so sorry. I feel like I got preoccupied with work and going out and wasn't paying attention. I guess I haven't been the best friend to you."

"It's not your fault. I never said anything. I think it made me too sad."

"Honestly, we both thought you were completely together, like a model citizen visiting your dad all the time and working so hard in school."

"I guess I kind of was for a while, but it was never easy," she confessed.

"Can I ask you something personal?"

She nodded.

"Were you in love?"

She shook her head. "I don't think so. I think I was just lonely more than anything and I wanted to change my life. It all just kind of happened. For a while, it felt comfortable. It makes what I did so much worse. I mean, if we weren't really in love there was no excuse."

"If you weren't in love, and you broke up, why are you struggling so much? I don't mean that in a judgmental way; I just mean I've noticed how upset you've been lately. Some days it looked like you were crying in your room. Are you crying over him?"

"No. I've been depressed and ashamed. Once it was over, letting him go didn't even hurt. It should have hurt, shouldn't it?"

"Isn't it better that it doesn't hurt?"

She shrugged. "I've been terrified that Tash will find out and hate me. On top of everything, I let school slide to be with him. Now, the one thing I was always good at is also a mess. I'm overwhelmed."

Jason leaned in and hugged her, gently rubbing her back. "It will be okay," he whispered.

"Thanks," she said as she pulled back.

"First of all, the school stuff will work out. You can get yourself back on track with some of those long library days you love. And as for Tash, I doubt she'll find out. But I do think you should tell her. It will make you feel better. Plus, I'm pretty sure she'll be glad to know you're human like the rest of us."

"You know how close she is with Kyle. I messed up his family."

"I doubt she'll see it that way. It's up to you. Tell her or don't, but either way you have to let it go and move on. I know this is new territory for you, but people fuck up all the time. You have to rebound."

"Once my classes ended, I think I was kind of in a free fall. After my mom died, I went to college and then straight to grad school. I did what I knew how to do: school. Being a student is so easy. There is always more you can study, more you can read, to pass the time. When my classes ended, I had to start figuring things out on my own. That's when I met Richard. I thought it was fate but he was really just something to fill my mind and my time. I needed somewhere to be, someone to meet, and something to focus on. I mean, why do you guys think I always handle all the household bills and everything?"

"Because you don't want the electric turned off and you're the only real grown-up here."

She smiled. "There is that. But I also need predictable ways to fill my days. I need a structure that I understand, which I realize makes me sound pathetic. But I mean, without classes to attend or a family to go home to, what am I supposed to do?"

"You're already home, and you're with your family. I'm your family. Tash is too, in her own, dysfunctional way."

"You don't have to say that."

"I mean it. I know we can be pretty self-absorbed, but that doesn't make us feel like family any less. Isn't that part of what life is? Creating your own place in the world, with your peeps, even if they're a mess."

She giggled. "Thanks. I guess I needed a reminder."

"How about we shake off this funk by going out? How does a movie sound?"

She nodded. "By the way, where's Tash?"

After canceling on him the day before to spend time with Penelope, Jason met Sam at an Italian restaurant in Tribeca, promising to "make it up to him." As he approached the restaurant, he saw Sam waiting outside.

"Do they have a table?"

"I was thinking we could sit at the bar for a drink," Sam replied.

"Sure."

They sat at the nearly empty bar and savored the smell of garlic bread wafting in the air.

"You won't believe all the drama going on right now," Jason said as he focused on the cocktail menu. "My roommates are both going through some seriously screwed up stuff with guys. I promised I wouldn't say anything, but..."

"Yeah, that's what your text said. Listen..."

"Do you want to share a carafe of the house red wine or should I just get a glass?"

"Jason, I need to talk to you," Sam said solemnly, placing his hand on the drink menu.

Jason put the menu down and swiveled his barstool to face him. "What's up?"

"You and I have had a fun time together, but..."

Jason's jaw dropped. "Oh my God, you're blowing me off."

"I wanted to tell you in person. I just don't see this going anywhere."

"I don't get it," Jason said, mystified.

"We talked before, you know, about keeping it airy. I was coming out of a relationship when we met. I was flattered when you asked me out and, well, I never thought it would go anywhere. I'm not looking for a serious thing right now."

"So you used me to get over someone else?" Jason asked, trying to process what was happening.

"Not intentionally. But yes, you helped me move past someone else and now I need to be on my own for a while," Sam explained, putting his hand on Jason's.

Jason was silent.

"Let me guess, no one has ever broken up with you before?" Sam asked.

"Ah, no. But I've never really done the exclusive thing before. It never occurred to me that if I wanted to be with someone, he might not want to be with me. God, that makes me sound like a jerk. I don't mean it that way."

Sam laughed. "I know you think that you were slumming it with me or doing some noble thing by dating someone so obviously beneath you."

"No, not at all. I thought we had a connection," Jason said, hurt. "Is that how little you think of me?"

"I'm sorry. That came out all wrong. I always trip over my words with you. Maybe I should go."

"Wait. Why did you make me come here to meet you? Why not just call?"

"Because I suspect that when you end things with someone, you just take off and leave them wondering. I wanted to show you it doesn't need to be that way. I don't mean to be condescending, but…"

"But what?"

Sam stood up. "I should go. Despite what you may think, I've enjoyed every minute with you. It was a lot of fun."

Fun? Is that all anyone thinks I'm good for?

Sam turned back to Jason. "For what it's worth, I wish you great success in figuring out how to use your platform to achieve what you really want."

As Jason watched Sam walk away, he thought, *Why is he so damn lovely? It would be so much easier to hate him if he were an asshole.*

When Jason got home, he headed straight for Penelope's room and tapped on the door.

"Yes?"

He opened the door and said, "I just got dumped. I'm inconsolable."

"Oh, no. Come sit. I'll get a carton of sorbet and you can tell me what happened."

"Can we skip the sorbet and order a pizza instead?" he asked as he flopped on her bed.

"Of course."

A couple of days later, Tash returned. She wheeled her suitcase past Jason's room, peeking in to find him watching talk shows.

"Hey."

"You're back!"

"Yeah. What did I miss?"

"Oh sweetie, we had our own drama for a change."

"What's wrong? Why the *Sally Jessy* reruns?"

"Sam broke up with me."

"Oh, honey. Let me go put my bag away and I'll be right back for cuddles. We can talk about what an ugly douche he is."

Jason smiled. "Glad you're back."

As Tash finished sending a text, she turned to find Penelope standing in her doorway.

"Oh, hey Pen. I was just going to go check on Jason. He's pretty upset."

"Yeah, I know all about Sam. Listen, I really need to talk to you. It's important."

Tash widened her eyes, waiting.

"I've been working myself up to this and I'm afraid if I don't..." She trailed off.

"Is this about the bills? I promise I'll get you my share."

She shook her head. "No. It's just that, well, I wasn't going to tell you but Jason thought I should and, well..."

"Pen, I was just on a plane for like six hours. What is it? Spit it out."

"You may want to sit down for this."

Tash sat on the edge of her bed and Penelope told her everything, avoiding unnecessary details.

"Ewww! Gross," Tash groaned, squeezing her eyes shut in disgust.

"I'm so sorry, Tash. I had no idea who he was. I would never do anything to hurt you or anyone you care about."

"I'm not mad at you," Tash said.

"You're not?"

"No. I'm shocked and grossed out, but not mad. You didn't know, and it's not like I've never slept with the wrong guy. At least now I see why Dick is short for Richard."

"Are you going to tell Kyle?"

"No way. Listen, his parents have a totally screwed up marriage anyway. You probably did them a favor. I mean, if he wasn't getting it for years, you gave him what he needed. Otherwise he'd probably leave my aunt. She's a total whack job."

Penelope took a deep breath. "I've been such a wreck, terrified you'd never forgive me."

"You worry too much. But what the fuck did you see in my uncle? He's so totally unappealing, except that he's rich, but you don't care about that stuff."

"He was nice to me. He listened to me. I guess it was sort of like a fantasy. I've always been good at reality but I wanted an escape so I let myself believe it was fate. I've been kind of lost, trying to figure out where I fit in."

Tash smiled knowingly. "Don't worry. I get it. It's your Blue Period."

"My what?"

Tash and Penelope joined Jason in his bed, sandwiching him in the middle.

"Cheer up, J. I mean, how long was it going to last with a makeup artist anyway? He knows all of your flaws," Tash said.

Jason sighed. "I know. I just can't believe he dumped me. And I ate pizza, like the really greasy delivery kind!"

"How could you let him eat that?" Tash scolded Penelope.

"He needed comfort. I didn't think a healthy fruit snack was going to do the trick."

Jason and Tash burst into laughter.

"Pen, you made a joke!" Tash exclaimed.

Penelope shook her head.

"Maybe all the sex with my nasty old uncle loosened you up!" Tash continued through laughter.

"Oh, shut up," Penelope said, burying her face in her hands.

"Seriously, Jason, can you believe our virtuous little roomie was going all around town screwing someone?"

Jason laughed. "She's not a girl anymore."

"Honestly Pen, we thought you'd be chaste forever. If it weren't for who you did it with, I'd be impressed!"

Penelope grabbed a pillow and hit Tash in the head.

Jason, now hysterical, chimed in with, "Well, this took my mind off Sam."

As the laughter subsided, Penelope said, "I really missed this. You know, hanging out together."

"Yeah, sorry I've been so wrapped up in my own shit," Tash said.

"We love you for that, honey," Jason said.

Penelope nodded. "Hey, so where were you anyway, Tash?"

"First I visited my parents for two days to beg for some money and then I flew to LA. Listen, guys. I have big news."

That afternoon there was a knock on Tash's bedroom door. She opened it and came face-to-face with Aidan.

"Jason let me in. I got your text."

Her eyes lit up. "Thanks for coming over. Come in," she said, closing the door behind him.

"Do you want to sit down?" she asked as she sat cross-legged on her bed.

"I'm good here," he replied, leaning against the door.

"You never called or texted, not even once," she said.

He raised his eyebrows.

She sighed. "I know, I know. It was on me."

He lowered his chin.

"Listen, I'm sorry about that night, how I acted."

"You really hurt me."

"I know. I wish I could take it all back."

"Tell me why. What was really going on?"

She took a long, slow breath. "I've never had a relationship where someone treated me well, until you. I guess I self-sabotaged. Maybe you were right and I don't believe I deserve good things."

"Did something happen that night?"

"Some guy in the bathroom basically called me a whore and then someone offered me ecstasy."

"Assholes."

"No, you don't understand. A few years ago, I probably would have screwed that guy, and I would have taken whatever crap I could get my hands on, to party. I was a mess and I didn't care."

"So it's good because it shows how you've evolved," Aidan said supportively.

"You don't understand. Back then I did a lot of bad stuff, and bad stuff happened to people, including me."

Aidan sat next to her on the bed. "We're not responsible for everything that happens to us."

"I feel like I brought bad shit on myself. It's hard to shake that," she said.

"Then don't shake it. Deal with it head on, and then let it go."

"Aidan…"

"Yeah?" he said as he took her hand.

"I missed you so much."

He smiled brightly. "That's all I was waiting for, beauty queen."

She looked down, blushing. "Harold is missing. I saw him a couple of weeks ago and I snapped at him. I was having a horrible day and now he's missing and the last thing I said to him was mean."

"I'm sorry. Maybe the cops chased him off and he'll come back."

"Maybe."

"So are you coming or going?" he asked, gesturing to the suitcase.

"Both, actually."

He knitted his brow.

"Aidan, you were right about so much. I was stuck, afraid to take a chance on myself. I don't want to be bored or restless. I want to go after things."

He smiled.

"But you weren't right about everything. I am a person who likes to have fun and to be carefree. That's not an act; it's a part of who I am. If you can't accept that…"

He squeezed her hand. "I love that about you. Always have. I mean, I'm a deejay for a reason. I like the lighter side too."

She leaned in and kissed him softly. He took the back of her head in his hand and returned her kiss with passion. "I love you. You know that, right?" he asked as he pulled back, centimeters from her face.

She nodded.

"So you never told me, what's with the suitcase?"

"One of my professors always promised to hook me up with an internship at Paramount Studios. I finally took him up on it and flew to LA for an interview. They hired me on the spot."

He smiled. "That's amazing."

"It's actually a pretty crappy job and I'll mostly be getting people coffee, but if I'm going to have a crappy job I figured it should be where I can meet people who can teach me."

"That's awesome," he said.

"My bigger plan is to go to grad school and get my MFA in cinematography. I want to make films or at least do something related to film. I missed the application deadline but I'm going to apply for next year. UCLA has a kickass program. Even if I don't get in, there are a bunch of schools in the area."

Aidan looked down. "That's really great. Truly," he said softly.

"I was thinking: I know you're established here, but if you could move from Chicago to New York, can't you go from New York to LA?"

He looked at her, grinning like a Cheshire cat.

"I mean, there's a huge deejay scene in LA, right? At the very least, there must be a Forever 21 or frat party you can spin at. What do you think?" she asked with a smirk.

"Well, they do have coconuts there."

She smiled.

"Do you remember?" he asked.

"I remember."

PART FOUR

3 Years Later

Chapter 12

Tash used her palm to wipe the steam off the bathroom mirror. *Damn the LA sun. Are my freckles actually getting bigger?* She began rubbing foundation on her face, followed by blush, highlighter, her signature black liquid eyeliner, and mascara. *My eyes look fierce*, she thought, staring at her reflection. *I wish I hadn't agreed to work for Monroe today. At least I can party tonight.* After curling the ends of her perfectly straightened, long hair, she headed to the bedroom to get dressed.

While rifling through her underwear drawer, she noticed her favorite Polaroid of her, Jason, and Penelope in their old New York apartment. *Jason was so funny with that old-school camera. I miss him. Both of them. I'm glad they're both doing well.* Never one to display her vulnerability, she tucked the photo safely back at the bottom of the drawer. From her closet, she selected black leggings, a light gray tunic with strategically placed cutouts, and black gladiator sandals. She got dressed and looked herself over, putting on small, gold hoop earrings. *Something's missing.* She surveyed her closet. *Aww, perfect. Haven't worn you in ages*, she thought as she snatched her favorite black fedora, bought on Macdougal Street in New York, when Aidan first said, "I love you." The hat always reminded her of that day. Running her fingers along the rim, she wondered why it had been so hard to say I love you in return. *I did love him*, she lamented, placing the hat on her head. She took a final glance in the mirror. *Now I'm ready.*

Grabbing her slouchy black leather bag, she searched for her sunglasses and car key. Finding neither, she scoured the dresser. *Shit. Where's the key? I hate that you can't get anywhere in LA without a car. Must be on the mail table.* As she approached the small table by the door, she spotted her sunglasses, car key, and latest rejection letter. She slipped the glasses on her head and stared at the folded paper. *Don't do it, Tash*, she warned herself, but it was too late. She picked up the letter and began reading. *Dear Ms. Daniels, We regret to inform you that you have not been chosen to receive our screen writing grant. With the highest submission rate we have ever received… blah, blah, blah. Same shit, different day. At least when these jerks reject me, they don't tell me everything that's wrong with my work, unlike those film festival scumbags. Whatever.* She crumpled the letter, tossed it in the trash, and headed out.

"Stop honking, you assholes," Tash grumbled. *Why does anyone think they can get anywhere quickly in this town? I hope Monroe isn't pissed if I'm late again. I still can't believe I came to LA and all I'm doing is this personal shopping crap. At least when I worked retail in New York I wasn't stuck in gridlock. Monroe's life is a trip though.* Tash remembered the day they met, over a year ago. She was rummaging through a post-holiday sale accessory table at a store on Rodeo Drive, searching for the perfect bangle bracelet. A striking woman with platinum hair, who Tash pegged for mid-forties although she looked much younger, came out of the dressing room wearing an ankle-length, ivory dress. The saleswoman scurried over.

"I'm just not sure it's flattering on me. What about the color?"

"It's very sophisticated," the saleswoman assured her.

Tash snorted.

The woman turned to her. "Excuse me, Miss. I don't want to bother you, but what do you think of this dress?"

"It's fine," Tash replied, returning her attention to a seventy-five percent off jewelry bin.

"Please, I usually shop with friends or my assistant, but she recently quit to get married. I need an honest opinion. It's for a dinner party."

Tash dropped a handful of earrings and turned toward the woman. "That color is horrible on you. You have flawless skin; I'd actually kill for your complexion, but that dress washes you out. And you're swallowed up in fabric. It makes you look matronly and you're obviously hot, like, really hot."

The woman blushed. "It's an upscale event."

"Unless that's code for old lady event, you should show some skin, tastefully. Hang on, I'll find you something," Tash said.

"I'm a size…"

"Six, I know. I worked retail for a couple of years."

A moment later, Tash returned with a knee-length black crepe dress with three-quarter length flouncy silk sleeves. She held it out and said, "Before we waste any time, do you have good legs?"

"Well, uh…" the woman stammered.

"Veins or no veins? Just be honest," Tash said.

"No veins. I have nice legs."

Tash handed her the garment. Minutes later, she emerged from the dressing room, beaming.

The saleswoman ran over. "Oh, that looks great on you too. You could wear anything."

Tash rolled her eyes. "That's much better. You look ten years younger. And it's on sale," she said, smirking at the saleswoman. "Well, enjoy your party," she added, returning her attention to the sale table.

The woman extended her hand. "My name is Monroe Preston."

"Nice to meet you. I'm Tash, Tash Daniels."

They shook hands and Monroe said, "Please give the salesgirl whatever you were looking at. My treat."

Tash laughed. "That's okay."

"Please, I insist," Monroe repeated.

A little later, as they were checking out, Monroe handed her a small bag with the three gold bangles Tash selected.

"Thanks for the bling."

"My pleasure. It was wonderfully refreshing to have someone tell me the truth."

"I get that," Tash replied.

"You mentioned you've worked in retail?"

"Yeah, but I haven't done that in a while. I moved to LA to work in film, well, whatever, it's a long story. I had an internship at a film studio, but quit when my boss tried to feel me up. It was kind of a regular thing, but I finally had enough."

"That's awful. You couldn't report him?"

"Who would care? He was someone. I was no one."

"I understand how it works," Monroe said, compassionately. "What are you doing now?"

"You know those studio tours?"

Monroe nodded.

"I drive one of those trams. It's beyond awful, but it's all I could get. I'm really a filmmaker, though, and a writer. Aspiring, anyway. I have a short film that's almost done. I'll be submitting it to festivals and stuff."

"If you could use a flexible part-time job, I'd like to hire you as my personal shopper."

"Oh, I don't know."

"I'll pay you extremely well. More than you earn now."

Tash bit her lip and gave Monroe the once-over. "You know what? I'll do it. If I have to drive that tram one more day so tourists can take pictures on the *Friends* couch, I might explode."

"Splendid! Do you have time right now? I have a couple of hours before my Kabbalah class and I need shoes. We could stop for lunch. This calls for a champagne toast," Monroe said.

Tash smiled. "I'm in."

The two got along smashingly from that day forward. Monroe was never short on money; Tash was never short on candor.

Miraculously, Tash arrived at Monroe's estate on time. She was immediately buzzed through the security gates. Although she detested Beverly Hills, she thought the Spanish-style mansion set behind palm trees on a perfectly landscaped property would be an ideal film location. It was impossibly Los Angeles and reeked of throwback Hollywood glamour. Some days Monroe opened the door herself, looking like a movie star from the 1940s or '50s. Her resemblance to Marilyn Monroe was uncanny, and like her idol, Tash learned that she had changed her name to fit the big life she imagined for herself. On this day, Henry, the butler, let her in.

"Hey there, H," Tash said.

"Hello, Miss Daniels. Mrs. Preston is in her dressing room."

"Thanks," Tash said, flying up the grand staircase.

Tash walked right into Monroe's bedroom and through to her dressing room. Monroe, wearing a white silk robe, was seated on a pink leather ottoman, looking through a stack of shoeboxes.

"Oh, hi Tash. I'm glad you're here. I want to donate some of these to charity, but I'm not sure what to hold on to. And the clothes you ordered have arrived. Also, I have three events this weekend to prepare for."

For the next two hours, they sorted shoes and Monroe tried on outfits while Tash styled them with accessories. As Monroe had come to expect, Tash wasn't shy about assessing each look or admonishing a store for sending pieces Tash hadn't preapproved. When Monroe tried on a gray silk halter dress, Tash abruptly said, "Uh, no. Just no. You're not going to a party at the Playboy mansion." Monroe giggled. No one spoke to her that way and she adored Tash for it.

By the time they were done, Monroe had all her looks for the weekend selected, two garment bags full of items for Tash to return, and several shoeboxes designated for charity. When Monroe told her to take any of the shoes she liked, Tash selected a pair of black Prada heels. Monroe was half a size larger, but for shoes like that, Tash would stuff them with cotton balls to make them work.

"Okay, so I'll take these with me. I know you want to start planning the gifts you need for next month as well as the hostess gifts for your garden lunch. Would you like me to stop by on Monday?" Tash asked.

"I'm having a little something done on Monday. Can you come at lunchtime on Tuesday? I'll have the cook prepare something for us. You can bring your swimsuit if you want to take a dip before you leave."

"Sounds good. And whatever you're doing Monday, just remember: less is more."

Monroe smiled. "You're such a sweetheart," she said, hugging her.

On her way out, Tash turned and said, "Don't forget, Band-Aids on the back of your heels Saturday night. Those shoes aren't broken in."

"I'll remember. Thank you, Tash."

Tash winked and headed out, carrying the garment bags and her new shoes.

After spending hours in traffic to return Monroe's unwanted garments on opposite sides of LA, Tash stopped at home for a quick bite and to get ready for the night. Decked out in a T-shirt style, black sequin mini-dress and her new Prada heels, she headed out again. She noticed her neighbor Darrell going into his apartment. He was carrying canvases under his arm, the white cloth stark against his dark skin. She waved and he nodded in return. *Quiet dude*, she thought.

She arrived at the club at ten o'clock, after easily finding a parking space.

"Yo, T," a bouncer called as she bypassed the long line.

"Hey, Jimmie," she replied as he unlatched the rope, letting her in.

She walked into the mammoth space, lit with blue lights. Electro house music was blaring and the whole room of beautiful people pulsed like an excited heartbeat. As she wiggled through the crowd on her way to the bar, Texas gently touched her arm, his shaggy, blonde hair brushing the front of her face. "Well hey there, Tash," he said in his southern drawl.

"Hey, Texas. I'm in desperate need of booze. Catch ya later, okay?"

"Sure thing," he replied with a tilt of his chin.

He's sweet and I don't mind the flirt, but I'm so not in the mood tonight. She approached the bar and without a word, Leo handed her a tequila sunrise.

"You're the best bartender in LA," she proclaimed, taking the drink. She took a sip while scanning the room. Lu, her best friend in LA, spotted her and was already sauntering over. Tall with short blonde hair and dripping with it-girl charisma, Lu stood out in the crowd. Tonight, she was wearing black leather pants and an old Depeche Mode tank top that showed off her toned arms. Tash watched as every lesbian and bi woman in the place checked her out.

"Hey, baby," Tash said.

"Hey, babe. This place is on tonight," Lu said.

"You're lookin' good. Very butch-chic."

"You know it. I'm digging your vibe, very Liza Minnelli meets pole dancer."

"Good one, baby. Prowling for some poor girl to hook up with?" Tash mused.

"My own personal Jesus," Lu replied with a laugh.

"You're a heartbreaker," Tash teased.

"Speaking of, your little southern admirer is here," Lu said, grabbing Tash's drink and taking a gulp.

"Oh yeah. He's already made his presence known."

Lu smiled.

"You working tonight?" Tash asked.

Lu nodded. "Yeah, I'll go take over for your boy so you can have some time. Give me another hit of that first."

She took another sip of Tash's drink and they both started walking toward the deejay platform.

"See ya later," Lu said.

Tash waved and looked up. With his headphones on and working his sound, Aidan had never been sexier. He looked straight at her, grinning from ear to ear.

She smiled and mouthed, "I love you."

Chapter 13

Lu's alarm sounded at eight o'clock in the morning. Too exhausted to open her eyes, she felt around for her phone and turned it off. *Damn. This schedule is killing me. I can't wait to sleep tomorrow. Better get my ass out of bed before I pass out again.* She slithered up to a sitting position and forced her eyes open, the crust in the corners acting like glue. She yawned, long and slow, and then shook her head, trying to wake up. *I'm cold,* she thought, grabbing a pullover hoodie off the floor and putting it on as she shuffled out of bed. "Damn!" she hollered, stubbing her toe on the laptop carelessly left on the floor, and then tripping on a pile of clothes as she tried to make her way to the galley kitchen of her studio apartment to set up the coffee pot.

As the coffee brewed, she leaned on the counter and shut her eyes. The alarm rang again, startling her. *Fuck. I must have hit snooze.* She noticed five unread texts: four from women she met the night before, each making sure she had their number, and one from Tash, promising to see her that night. She responded to Tash:

Thanks, babe. But dude, if you need tonight w/ your man, no worries.

When the coffee machine finally beeped, she filled a mug and her to-go tumbler. She placed the tumbler next to her sunglasses on her small, two-person table, so that she'd remember it. With the mug in hand, she headed to the bathroom, slurping the steaming coffee on the way. "Well, that's a look," she muttered upon seeing herself in the mirror, hair matted to one side and bags under her eyes. *Please let the hot water be working*, she prayed, flipping the shower on. *Fuck. It's ice cold again.*

Lu arrived at the juice bar to find the typical Saturday line out the door, and her two younger coworkers frantically trying to keep up.

"Oh Lu, we're so glad you're here! It's been like this since we opened. We're running low on prepped veggies," Amanda said.

Too tired to risk slicing off her finger, Lu responded, "I'll take over at the register and you can do prep." She made her way behind the counter and switched off with her coworker.

After three hours taking orders for kale and carrot smoothies, the morning and lunch rushes were over and one of Lu's coworkers clocked out. The juice bar had been quiet for ten minutes when Lu told Amanda, "It's cool if you take your break. I can handle it on my own for a bit."

Finally alone and still wiped out, she leaned on the counter and rested her eyes.

"Um, excuse me," a soft voice said.

Lu opened her eyes to see a woman in her early twenties standing before her. "Oh shit," she mumbled. "Sorry. I was really spent. It got so quiet I must have nodded off. Hope I wasn't drooling."

The woman smiled. "That's okay. I'm sorry I woke you. Late night?"

Lu noticed how inconspicuously beautiful she was: wavy auburn hair, green eyes, and a freckled, porcelain face. "Uh, yeah, late night. I'm a deejay and I was working. I got, like, four hours of sleep."

"Wow, a deejay. That's really cool. Too bad you can't do that full-time."

Lu grimaced. "Uh, yeah. Too bad for me."

The woman blushed. "That came out wrong. I'm so embarrassed. I always say the wrong thing," she said, biting her lip. "I just meant it must be hard having a day job and a night job."

"Yeah, it's hard, but who doesn't have it hard, right?" Lu replied.

She smiled awkwardly. "My name's Paisley."

"I'm Lu. Well, Paisley, you must have come in for a juice or smoothie. What can I make for you?"

"Oh sure, right. I wanted a smoothie – something sweet. What's good?"

"The Tropical, Mango Sunrise, and Strawberry Star are all sweet."

"I'll go with the strawberry one, please."

A few customers came in while Lu made the drink.

"Here you go," Lu said, handing her the pretty pink concoction.

Paisley unzipped her purse, but Lu stopped her. "It's on me, since you had to wake me up and all. Plus, I was a giant grump."

"Oh, that's okay..."

"It's no problem. Enjoy," Lu insisted.

"Well, thanks. Uh, I hope you can rest when you get off."

"No can do. I'm working at Club 47 in Hollywood tonight. I'll crash tomorrow."

Paisley started walking out, sidestepping her way to the door, looking at Lu.

"What can I get you?" Lu asked the next customer. She tried to focus on his order, but she couldn't help but glance over to watch Paisley leave.

Chapter 14

Tash slowly opened her eyes, squinting to avoid the bright sun. Aidan was already awake, smiling at her, his bleached hair in spikes. "Hey, beauty queen," he whispered.

She looked into his evergreen eyes and gently touched the piercing over his right eyebrow. "How long have you been up?"

"Just a few minutes. It's almost noon."

"Shit," she mumbled.

"Doesn't matter. We have the day to ourselves. Plenty of time," he said, cuddling closer to her.

"Don't forget we're going to that club in West Hollywood tonight. It's Lu's first time headlining there on a Saturday. It's a big deal for her."

"Tonight? Really?"

"Yes, really. I promised. We need to support her," she said.

"I work with her all the time. She won't care if we're there, trust me."

"You don't want her to think you're a jerk, abandoning her now that you're almost famous. Plus, it'll be fun."

"I thought we might do something quiet, just the two of us," he said.

"I don't do quiet."

He laughed. "Okay, you got me there. I'll make some coffee and breakfast and then we can figure out the day. Your choice. Maybe the Getty, or the beach. Soon it'll be too hot. Gotta say, I won't miss that."

Tash rolled to her side, sat on the edge of the bed, and slipped her robe on. "I'm just gonna have a yogurt, but coffee would be good."

Aidan leaned toward her, putting his hand on her back. "Hey…"

She leapt up. "The Getty Center," she called. "I'm jumping in the shower. Bring me coffee when it's ready, okay?"

"Yeah, sure."

Tash went into the bathroom, put her hands on the sink, and dropped her head forward. She looked up, confronting her reflection. *No, Tash. Don't be pathetic. You're fine.*

Tash and Aidan sat on the crowded tram heading up to the Getty Center. It was their favorite place in LA. They had taken this ride many times, but today she noticed people staring at them. Aidan had his headphones on, lost in the beats of his future. Tash looked out at a landscape that not long before they feared would be lost to a wild blaze. She looked at Aidan with thoughts of the past and the future, place and space, swirling in her mind. Aidan squeezed her hand, thrusting her into the present.

They disembarked hand in hand. As expected on a cloudless Saturday, the grounds were teeming with locals and tourists.

"We were lucky to get a spot in the garage," Aidan said.

"Uh huh. We always have good parking karma. I'm starving. Let's grab a bite."

"Actually, I made a reservation at the swanky restaurant," he replied, raising his eyebrows.

Tash contorted her face.

"I made it weeks ago, in case we wound up here today. When you were in the shower, I called to push it back. They're holding a window table for us, but we're about fifteen minutes late so we should hustle."

"We usually grab something to-go and sit on the lawn," she said.

"Yeah, but I thought this should be special. Besides, we can finally afford nicer things. We can walk around outside after. Cool?"

She shrugged. "Sure."

Soon they were sitting in the far corner of the dining room, windows on all sides, overlooking spectacular mountain views.

"Wow, they really gave us the best table in the place," Aidan remarked.

Tash smiled. "You should probably get used to that."

Aidan opened his mouth, but before he could respond, a waitress came over to take their drink orders.

"Could you do us a favor and take a photo of us?" he asked, handing over his phone. Returning his attention to Tash, he whispered, "I want to remember how beautiful you look today."

"You're such a cheeseball," she quipped.

After taking a few shots, the waitress returned his phone and said, "I don't want to bother you and come off all fangirl, but could we take a picture? I love your music."

Aidan blushed. "Thank you. Of course."

He stood up and the waitress retrieved her phone from her pocket and handed it to Tash. After taking a couple of pictures of them, Tash returned her phone, adding, "I'll have a glass of prosecco."

"A seltzer water for me, please," Aidan said.

As she walked away, Tash smirked at Aidan. "At least I can say I always knew you were hot shit, even back when your big gigs were an H&M store and keggers at NYU."

He looked down and laughed. "It's surreal. Whoever thought that someone like Calvin would happen to hear me and that it would snowball into all of this."

"Imagine what it'll be like when your record drops. Aside from your club groupies, most people have only heard your single and you're already a badass at the star table."

"Luckily, I'll be on tour when it streets, too busy to let it distract me. I still can't believe Calvin asked me to open on his US leg."

"I believe it. Your music is dope. I thought that even before I knew you could also sing and play like every freaking instrument." She paused to take a sip of water. "And you've got that *thing*, anyway. That thing people want to be around."

He reached across the table for her hand. "As long as you want to be around, I'm good."

"You're such a sap," she teased.

The waitress delivered their drinks and took their orders. After she left, Tash said, "It's great we're not totally busted anymore. Living in that dump in the boonies was super depressing. I'm way happier in Venice Beach. Using your advance for a down payment on the condo was genius, but now that money is gone. You're getting paid squat on tour if you can't sell your CDs, and like, who buys those anymore? And you won't be getting your regular club money."

"What are you saying?" he asked.

"We're not flush," she replied.

"Babe, it's just lunch. And you know I've never cared about money. I want to make music, live my life. I'm cool with having just enough to get by, always have been. You're the one who relentlessly wants more. The way I see it, we caught a huge break. Let's roll with it."

"*You* caught a huge break," she muttered.

"Hey," he said, reaching across the table again. "You're talented and passionate. It's going to happen. It just might not be how you expect. That's the trick: being open to whatever way it comes. And it's not like you haven't done anything these past three years in LA. You rocked all those classes and actually made your short film and it's the bomb. No one can take that away from you."

Before she could respond, their food was served.

Aidan focused on his plate, cutting into his chicken. After a long silence, he gently said, "You will make this happen, but you gotta find happiness in the work itself again. The rest doesn't matter as much."

"Easy for you to say," she quipped back, taking a bite of her beet salad.

"Hey, you know I've always felt that way. For me, it's all about making music. I'd be happy spinning at a college party like the old days. Everything else is sparkle, as you would say."

"It's different in film. You need money and connections. There's no frat house version. Without funding, it's impossible to keep going. I can't hit my folks up again. I've done everything I can but all I have to show for it is a pile of rejections."

Aidan's face twitched.

"What's that look about? What could I have done differently?"

"After the internship…"

"Don't even fucking start," she shrieked, dropping her fork. "You'll never know what it was like working for that perv."

"Babe, I know. He put you in a horrible position. I still want to smack the hell out of that guy. It infuriates me. Leaving was the right thing, I just wish you could have found something else in the industry."

"Like what? Like giving freaking studio tours? There was nothing else." She picked up her fork and took a bite of salad. "You know I ordered this with the dressing on the side. Our waitress must have been too preoccupied making eyes at you to hear me."

"Do you want me to get her and ask them to make you a new one?"

She shook her head. "It's fine."

They sat for a moment and Aidan started eating. Tash took a deep breath and looked directly at him. "I'm sorry. I don't want to ruin the day. It's just…"

"Tell me."

"It's really hard. I mean, I could barely fund *Pop Candy* and it's only seven minutes long. And it was rejected from every short film festival I submitted to. Getting into a festival would have helped with the screenwriting grants for the full-length version, but it doesn't look like that's happening either. And..."

"Yeah?"

"And you're leaving," she moaned.

"It's only for the summer. Just a couple of months. I asked you to come with me or meet me on the road."

"You know I can't. Monroe has that Magic Manor thing and I have to do a ton of shit for her. Summer is her big event season."

"This morning you said that you didn't want Lu to think I was abandoning her. You know I'm not abandoning you either, right?" he asked.

"Yeah, I know. It's fine. I'm good on my own. But I could kill you for planning a huge birthday bash for me and not showing up."

"If we didn't have a show that night, I would fly back for it. In a heartbeat."

She smiled. "Chill, it's cool. It's just that being dateless at your own birthday party is kinda sad. Plus, with the whole eighties theme we were supposed to go as Jem and Rio. It was gonna be rad."

"Don't worry. My buddies at the club are all over it. I've planned every detail and it's not going to be even a little sad. I'm pumped, actually," he said, smiling widely and laughing. "It's gonna be sooo you. Truly, truly, truly outrageous. You'll love it."

She smirked.

"It's gonna be sick, but the summer is more than one night. Try not to get too wrapped up in Monroe's stuff. Don't forget that you took that job to leave time for your film work."

She rolled her eyes. "Being rejected doesn't fill as much time as you'd think."

"Remember, be open to whatever form it comes in. That gallery was interested in showing your film. That could be another path."

"Yeah, but I blew them off. Fucking kills me now. At the time, I was so focused on festivals. Everyone in the classes I took said that's the way you do it, that I'd never get future backing for the longer version unless I went that route. But if you're not the professor's pet student, you don't get the support you need for that either."

"There's more than one gallery in town. For that matter, there's no reason you can't pitch to New York galleries, or Boston, Chicago, or a fishing village in Maine. Just saying."

Tash furrowed her brow.

"Okay, well New York at least. My point is that it's truly a piece of art. I mean, it's stylized, totally pop noir like you intended. The black and white with those eighties pops of color – I think it's brilliant. Films like that can do well on the art scene. You know that better than anyone. That's what you said years ago when you first had the idea, before the people here got in your head. Maybe you should let it be what it is and not worry about what it'll lead to. Carve your own path."

"Maybe. Sometimes I think I should just bag it all. I don't know if I want to put myself out there again."

"It's tough, I know, but I remember how happy you were working on it. Even when it wasn't going perfectly, and even during those brutal editing months, you were alive. Just do me a favor and promise you'll think about it."

"I'll think about it," she said, reaching her arm across the table. Aidan rubbed her hand.

"I love you," he said.

"I know."

Chapter 15

Aidan and Tash circled the block, looking for a parking space. "Man, everyone's out tonight. Our luck may have run out," Aidan lamented.

Tash lowered her visor to check her makeup in the mirror. "Just valet."

"It takes forever to get your car when you valet."

"Not for you. They'll totally get your car first and you know it."

"Yeah, I'm not into cutting in front of everyone."

Tash rolled her eyes, flipped the visor up, and turned to face him. "Don't be lame. Besides, you're on the list like everywhere we go. It's the same thing. Ever notice all the people standing in line?"

He laughed. "Can't argue with that. I'll double back around to the front."

"Ooh! You don't have to," she said, pointing to a car pulling out.

"Our lucky streak continues," he said.

Minutes later, they were walking toward the club. Tash was wearing black cigarette pants, a white sequin camisole, and black high heels, her long hair curled into large ringlets at the bottom and her lips stained red. Aidan was sporting tight, black leather pants and a white T-shirt with a peace sign. At six feet tall, he was hard to miss, and together, they were impossible to ignore. Tash grabbed his hand as they strolled past the long line of hopefuls waiting for entry. When the bouncer waved them in, Tash grinned and squeezed Aidan's hand. He looked down, smiling like a schoolboy.

They walked into the intimate, moody club. The venue boasted garnet red walls, a large, black, mirrored bar, a VIP room with black leather couches partly obscured by the bar, and to the right, the dance floor. They spotted a few casual friends they knew from the scene and made small talk. Everyone wanted to shake Aidan's hand or was smiling in his direction. The manager invited them for a drink in the VIP room, but they declined. Lu was on the deejay platform, spinning for the crowd on the dance floor. Aidan raised his hand to get her attention. She smiled and pointed at him and back at herself.

"I think she wants you to make a guest appearance," Tash said.

"This is her night. I'm here to be with you."

"Oh look, she just held up two hands. I think she wants you to join her in ten minutes."

Aidan gestured to Lu, and she nodded in confirmation.

"Told ya so," Tash said.

Aidan blushed. "Well, at least I can get you a drink before she puts me to work."

"Damn straight."

Tash leaned on the bar, sipping her fruity drink and watching Aidan join Lu on the platform. Lu took the mic and turned the music down. "Hey, I'm takin' a break because I've got a treat for you. Before he heads out on tour, our friend, the kickass A-A-Aidan, is gonna jump up here and do his thing."

There was thunderous applause as the music swelled and Aidan appeared on the stage. With a fist bump to Lu, he put on her headphones and they swapped places. "Glad to be here, LA! Let's do it," he shouted, to more applause.

Lu pushed through the crowd toward Tash when someone touched her shoulder. She turned to see Paisley.

"Uh, hey there," Lu stammered.

"Paisley, from earlier today."

"Yeah, I remember," Lu said.

"Your music is great."

"Uh, thanks. I'm surprised to see you here."

"Oh, well you mentioned you were working here tonight, and I'd never been, and I thought, well, I thought..."

"It's cool. So, what do you think of our little spot?" Lu asked.

"I like it. When I got here and saw the line, I didn't think I'd get in."

"Sorry about that. If I knew you were coming, I'd have put you on the list. Come to think of it, how did you get in?"

"I gave the bouncer a hundred bucks."

Lu's eyes widened. "Yup, that'll do it."

"So, that guy's your friend?" Paisley asked, gesturing toward Aidan.

"Yeah, you know his music?"

Paisley shook her head.

"Guess you're not into the club scene. He's kind of a superstar around here."

"I'm not really a late-night person," Paisley said, biting her lip.

"What are you into?" Lu asked.

"Theater. I teach drama at a private high school."

"Very cool."

Paisley smiled.

"Where's the school?"

"Malibu. It's right down the road from me. I actually went to school there so it's kind of like I never left high school, which probably sounds a little pathetic. I guess I never really left home either. I'm crashing in my parents' guesthouse."

"You're from Malibu?" Lu asked, her eyes wide again.

"Yeah, why?"

"No reason. Just never thought people were actually *from* Malibu. But hey, teaching drama is dope."

"Yeah, I'm off for the summer now."

"Sweet deal. Do you have a summer gig?"

"No, I try to keep it chill. I do a lot of hiking, I hang out on the beach quite a bit, and my friends and I see a ton of movies."

"That reminds me, I was actually heading to the bar to meet someone."

"Oh, uh…"

"My best friend. She's into film too. The dude deejaying is her BF. They came here to support me tonight and my only chance to connect is while he's covering for me."

"I totally understand. Of course you should go see your friend." Lu smiled. "You gonna hang?"

Paisley nodded.

"Cool. See ya," Lu said, brushing her hand as she walked away.

"So, my drink is almost empty. Did you get lost on the way?" Tash joked.

"There's this chick, Paisley…"

"Yeah, I totally saw. She's pretty."

Lu blushed.

"Ooh, you like her."

"She's probably psycho. I met her at the juice bar today and she just showed up here."

"How did she know where you'd be?"

"I kind of told her."

Tash rolled her eyes.

"It wasn't like that. I was making small talk."

"You're one of the most private people I know. Intel like that doesn't slip out, not from you. I call bullshit."

Lu scrunched her face. "You're such a bitch," she said before laughing.

"She's hot and she's into you. It's not complicated."

"But she's so girly. She ordered a strawberry smoothie. Who orders strawberry past the age of ten?"

"I eat maraschino cherries out of the jar," Tash replied.

"Yeah, I know. It's weird."

Tash made a face.

"I didn't want to have to tell you this, but she's from Malibu. Malibu! She's like a real goody-goody; it's written all over her. I'm not feeling that."

"She looks comfortable in your world tonight," Tash observed, nodding toward the other side of the club.

Lu whipped around to see Paisley dancing with abandon in the middle of a group of vinyl-clad strangers. Her cheeks reddened.

"Aww… Lu likes a girl," Tash teased.

"Forget about me and the goody-goody girl. What about you and your guy? Why the hell are you here tonight? Shouldn't you be spending this time alone together?"

Tash's face fell.

"Babe, it's only like two and a half months. He'll be back before you know it."

"I know. Just didn't want to do the dramatic last-night thing. It's such a downer."

Lu rubbed Tash's arm. "Try to have a good night. This club has one of the sickest vibes in the city."

"I always think this place is so un-LA. It's missing the sanitized, canned happy thing."

"Funny, that's why I think it's the *most* LA of all the clubs I play; it's the underbelly, you know?"

Tash shrugged.

"Well, I'm gonna run for a bathroom break and then relieve your man. Get another drink and try to have fun."

"Yup, I'm the party girl," she said sarcastically.

"I'm off tomorrow if you want to hang after he leaves. Just need some shut-eye first. Text me."

Tash nodded.

"See ya, babe."

"Bye, baby."

Tash and Aidan got home at two o'clock in the morning. Tash kicked off her heels and announced, "I'm gonna get ready for bed."

"I'm starving. You want eggs or something?" Aidan asked, grabbing a fistful of Lucky Charms cereal.

"Sure. Sunnyside."

Tash shut the bathroom door and stood still for a moment, breathing deeply. She changed into her robe, put her hair in a ponytail, and washed her face. When she emerged from the bathroom, Aidan called, "Food's up."

She plopped down opposite him, crossed her legs on the chair, and sprinkled a little salt on her eggs. She dunked a piece of toast in the yolk, watching it ooze around her plate.

"You're gonna miss my late-night meals," Aidan said, crunching into a piece of buttered toast.

"I'll manage."

"Try to eat something more than cereal and soup from a can," he said with a laugh.

"Hey, I can survive on potato chips and cheese doodles if I have to," Tash joked.

He smiled. "I know you can take care of yourself. I guess I'm just really gonna miss taking care of you too."

After eating and brushing their teeth, they got into bed and turned off the lights. Aidan lay behind Tash, wrapping his arms around her. "It's really late," she whispered. "You don't want to miss your flight tomorrow."

"Okay, beauty queen. Sweet dreams."

"Good night."

Lu unlocked the door to her apartment and let Paisley in. "It's a mess. I wasn't expecting company."

"That's okay. Your place is really cute," she said, looking around. "I like your posters."

"Thanks. Got them all from indie music stores back in the day. Most of them are limited edition promo posters that I begged them to give me when they were done with them. They actually toss most of those."

"That's cool," Paisley said, inspecting an old Cocteau Twins poster.

"Thanks for sticking around the club all night. I hope you weren't bored out of your mind."

"I had a great time. I liked watching you work. You get really intense."

"Speaking of, I'm kind of sweaty and gross. I'm gonna take a quick shower, okay? Help yourself to a beer or water or something."

Paisley smiled.

Lu closed the bathroom door behind her, quickly taking her clothes off and tossing them in the corner. She flipped the shower on. *Please, let it be hot. Ah, yes!* She jumped in and let the water beat on her head, streaming down her body. Her eyes were shut when she felt hands slip around her waist. She opened her eyes to find Paisley in the shower with her. Lu gently touched her face and leaned in to kiss her.

Just before dawn, Tash rolled around in bed. When she turned to face Aidan, he put his hand on the back of her head.

"Hey, you," he whispered.

"Hey."

They stared into each other's eyes for a long moment. Tash moved closer to him, gently caressing his forehead. He pulled her head to him and they began passionately kissing. Soon they were making love, with eyes wide open. After, Tash nestled into him. "You smell good," she whispered, before falling asleep cradled in his arms.

A couple of hours later, the alarm woke them both.

"Shit, I gotta get moving," Aidan mumbled.

"Do you want me to make coffee?" Tash asked.

"Nah, I'll grab some at LAX. I'm gonna hop in the shower."

He leapt up and headed to the bathroom. Tash scrunched up the sheet, pulling it to her chest, and closed her eyes.

The next time she awoke, Aidan was sitting on the edge of the bed, softly saying, "My ride's gonna be here in five."

She groaned. "I'll throw on sweats."

"Stay in bed."

"No. Hang on," she insisted.

Aidan got up and retrieved a pair of sweatpants and an old NYU sweatshirt. Tash dragged herself out of bed and slipped them on.

"Okay, let's roll," he said, grabbing his supersized duffel bag and backpack. "Oh, don't forget your keys."

Tash scooped up her keys from the mail table and followed him out. His friend was already waiting for him at the curb. He loaded up the car and turned to Tash.

"You should've let me drive you," she said.

"It would be a waste of your time. Enjoy the day and having the car to yourself this summer. I'll text or FaceTime you when I get there."

"Have a good flight."

"I'll miss you so much."

"Yeah, me too. This is really a big deal for you; have the time of your life. Don't worry about me."

"You're gonna have a great summer too. Keep working on your film stuff. And stay out of trouble."

She rolled her eyes.

"I love you," he said.

She smiled, tilting her chin forward; a silent me too.

Aidan got in the car and looked out the window. Tash stood there and watched the vehicle disappear down the street.

As she walked back toward the apartment complex, she saw Darrell leaving his apartment, pulling a wagon loaded with paintings. She waved and he nodded in acknowledgment.

Shoulders slumped, she entered her quiet apartment, dropped her keys on the table, and shuffled into the bedroom. She took off her sweatpants and crawled into bed, pulling the covers up. She inhaled deeply. *It still smells like him.*

Chapter 16

Lu's eyelids flitted open and closed, like a butterfly scrambling to take flight. She saw flickers of Paisley, bathed in sunlight.

"You passed out. You must have been really wiped," Paisley said.

"Yeah, I slept hard," Lu muttered through a yawn. "What time is it?"

"It's almost two."

"Damn," Lu mumbled, stretching her arms and pulling herself up to a sitting position. "I'm sorry if you felt kept hostage. You could have bailed."

"That's okay. I snagged one of your books about the East Village in the 1970s and '80s."

"Cool stuff, eh?"

"Totally. I'll have to maybe borrow it to finish, if that's okay."

"Sure. You must be starving," she said, her own stomach growling.

"I had a granola bar. I hope you don't mind. I wanted to make you something to eat, but..."

"Yeah, haven't been to the store in a while."

"If you're busy and you want me to go..."

"No, not at all," Lu assured her, reaching for a shirt on the floor. "Maybe we can grab a bite. There's an all-day breakfast place nearby."

"Breakfast every hour, it could save the world," Paisley said.

Lu furrowed her brow.

"It's the lyric of a song."

"Ah, yeah. Old Tori Amos, right?"

"Uh huh."

"Cool. I like the musical free association."

Paisley smiled.

"So, you up for some chow?"

Paisley nodded.

"I'm gonna run to the bathroom. Hang tight."

When Lu re-emerged, her hair was damp and she was humming.

"Well, you're bright and shiny," Paisley remarked, seated on the edge of the bed with the book open on her lap.

"Yeah. My mind's been all blocked up for days and it finally feels clear."

Paisley stood up as Lu walked over, the book falling to the floor. Lu took her hand and said, "And last night…"

"Yeah, last night," Paisley said softly, biting her lip. They stared at each other before Paisley took a deep breath and continued, "Well, I guess you must be hungry."

Lu touched the side of her face. "Food can wait."

Paisley was still scouring the laminated menu when the waitress came over.

Lu leaned in. "Do you know what you want?"

"You go first," Paisley replied.

"I'll have the sausage breakfast sandwich and a coffee," Lu said. "The sausage here is homemade. It's awesome," she said to Paisley.

"Uh, can I please have an egg white omelet with spinach, no dairy, with fruit and coffee?"

"Toast and home fries? Comes with," the waitress queried.

"No, thank you."

"I'll have hers," Lu said, handing her both menus. She then turned her attention to Paisley. "I'm starving."

Paisley giggled and coyly tilted her head. "Well, I guess I'm kinda to blame for that."

Lu smiled. "You're blushing."

Paisley looked down, her cheeks getting redder by the second.

"This place is kind of great, huh? Totally kitsch."

"Uh huh," Paisley responded, still blushing.

Lu reached her hand across the table, but before she made contact the waitress delivered two cups of coffee. "Ah, thank you!" Lu said, immediately dumping cream into her cup. She held out the creamer.

"Oh, no thanks. I drink it black."

Lu gulped her coffee. "Lactose intolerant? I noticed you asked for no dairy in your omelet."

"I used to be vegan. I still try to keep as close to vegan as I can, but I do eat eggs sometimes. I know it's such an LA cliché. It's my mom; she's a total 'paint with all the colors of the wind' hippie and raised me that way."

"Is it totally gross to you that I ordered sausage?"

"Not at all. I'm not like that."

Lu sipped her coffee again. "So, your mom is a hippie living in a Malibu estate. How'd that happen?"

"She was in the music business, a producer, big in the nineties. She got in early on a lot of things and developed really nurturing relationships with a bunch of musicians. They were loyal to her. Grunge, hip-hop, the folk singer renaissance, she had a hand in everything. She spends most of her time now doing yoga and gardening."

"Wow," Lu said, her eyebrows raised. "That's dope."

"My mom's great, really supportive. We're close. I know it's sorta lame, but she's my best friend. She's from Newport Beach and grew up in this very white-bread, corporate kind of family. Not super rich, but upper-middle class. She was like this Bohemian chick that didn't quite fit in. My dad is a hippie at heart, but he's a computer geek and hit it big in tech. They're two of the mellowest people you could ever meet, but they've had these massive careers in intense industries. That's how they ended up in Malibu."

The waitress delivered their food, with the toast and home fries on a separate plate. Lu picked up her sandwich and took a bite. She moaned as she chewed. "Sorry, this is so good."

Paisley smiled, taking a bite of her cantaloupe. "What about you?"

"What about me?" Lu asked, taking another bite.

"You're not from LA. I'm guessing you came here for the music scene."

She nodded as she took a forkful of home fries.

"Where are you from? Where else have you lived?"

Lu chugged her water. "I'm from the Midwest, which felt like the middle of nowhere. Lived in Seattle before I came here. It was pretty cool."

"How'd you end up in Seattle?"

"My girlfriend at the time, Jenna. She was a couple of years older than me and was moving to the Pacific Northwest. Totally granola. She wanted to go to Portland to live on a commune or some shit, but I convinced her to go to Seattle instead. I figured it would be easier to get into music there."

"Was it?" Paisley asked, taking a bite of her omelet.

Lu shook her head. "I worked in a coffee shop. I was just buying time before I could make it here."

"What about Jenna? She didn't want to come?"

"We broke up. I left her, actually."

"Oh," Paisley said, taking a sip of coffee.

"I was never serious about her like she was about me. Don't get me wrong – she was a beautiful person." She paused and then added, "Honestly, she was a getaway car."

"What were you trying to get away from?"

"Everything," Lu replied, picking up her sandwich and taking a hearty bite.

Tash looked at her newly organized closet and shook her head. *I should have some outfits ready to go for days that I'm running late.* For the third time that afternoon, she removed every hanger from her closet, piling clothes on her bed. This time, she paired some pants and tops together on a single hanger. She then rifled through her jewelry drawer, taking out necklaces and bracelets to hold up against each outfit. After a long process of trying each piece of jewelry with each outfit, she wrapped the selected jewelry around the hook of each hanger, and rehung everything in her closet, beginning with outfits on one end and single items on the other. After reviewing her work, she made a few final adjustments, grouping similar colors and similarly weighted clothes. She felt proud of herself but then inadvertently glanced at Aidan's side of the closet and sighed. *I should start on my dresser.*

Half an hour into organizing her underwear drawer, her phone beeped with a message from Lu.

Hey. Slept half the day. Wanted to check in. What are you up to?

Color coding my bras

Fuck. I'm coming over. You have food there?

A little

Booze?

Yeah

See you in an hour

Lu showed up at Tash's with a grocery bag in one hand and a glittery cardboard tiara in the other. She held out the tiara.

Tash smiled as she put it on.

"I figured you could use a little sparkle," Lu said, walking past her toward the kitchen.

"I'm really fine," Tash said.

"Great, then you can help me make dinner."

Tash followed Lu into the kitchen and watched her unload spaghetti, crushed tomatoes, garlic, broccoli, maraschino cherries, and mini marshmallows.

Tash grabbed the jar of cherries and simpered. "But what's up with the marshmallows?"

"They're my thing. I usually indulge in private. I'll be weird with you."

Tash smiled.

"Oh, totally random, but I saw your neighbor, that painter dude, on the pier a few days ago."

"Darrell. Yeah, he sells his art there sometimes, 'til the cops chase him away. I saw him this morning with a wagon full of paintings, probably heading there."

"His stuff is pretty haunting. The eyes in the faces, like *wow*. What's his story?"

"I don't really know. He's kind of a loner."

"Hey, I need a large pot with a lid and a sauté pan," Lu said, poking through cabinets.

"Down there," Tash instructed, pointing.

"Great," Lu said and retrieved the items. "Do you have a colander to drain the pasta? And where do you keep olive oil and spices?"

"Oil and spices are over there," Tash said, pointing again.

She perused the selection of spices and dried herbs. "Nice spread, all organic."

"Aidan's kinda into cooking," Tash replied, as she grabbed the colander from an upper cabinet.

"You heard from him?" Lu asked.

"Got a text when he landed. He sent me a cheesy picture we took at the Getty yesterday."

"Cool. Open a bottle of wine and then you can help me peel garlic."

Tash swirled the spaghetti around her fork, using a spoon. "This smells so good," she said, before taking a big bite.

"It's one of the few recipes I've mastered," Lu said, sipping her Merlot.

"It's got a kick. You're such a badass, even in the kitchen. It's really good," Tash gushed, dragging a piece of broccoli through the extra sauce on her plate.

"Chili flakes. You know me, I like a surprise," Lu said.

"Oh hey, speaking of surprises, what happened with that chick last night, the goody-goody girl?"

Lu's face turned red.

"Ooh, you can't even speak," Tash teased.

"I'm chewing," Lu said, covering her full mouth with her hand. Tash shook her head. "Come on, give me the dirt."

"She came home with me and..."

"And?" Tash prodded.

"I jumped in the shower because I was gross from work..."

"Oh my God, she surprised you naked in the shower?" Tash asked, her eyes like saucers. "I told you she looked at home in your world. Not such a goody-goody, huh?"

Lu laughed. "Uh, yeah, she did," she said, looking down and smiling. "It was amazing. We just clicked, you know? We had this intense chemistry. And then today, again..."

"You are beet red!"

"I didn't expect to like her so much. She's such a sweetheart, really soft, you know? She's into art and she loves the outdoors.

It's been a while since I've felt this, if ever, really. Caught me off guard."

Tash smiled.

"We went to Mandy's for a late breakfast and…"

"Yeah?"

"I don't know. She wanted to do the whole 'tell me your life' thing. No surprise, her life has been all shades of rosy. Like seriously freaking perfect. It's just not me. Plus, I mentioned Jenna and probably scared her."

"You never tell anyone about Jenna."

"It was nothing. She asked me where I lived before, that's all. I have her number, but I'm not sure. I don't have time for a big thing. She's definitely not the casual type."

Tash dropped her fork, rested her chin in her hand, and stared at her friend.

"What?" Lu asked, taking a sip of wine.

"Look, I get it. I do, more than you know. But she's hot and you have a connection. Let go of your shit and see what happens."

Lu shrugged. "Speaking of letting go of shit, what's with the spring cleaning?"

"Slept late after he left. Felt like staying home. At least I got something done."

"Fair enough. You working tomorrow?" Lu asked, before taking a bite of pasta.

"Monroe is having 'something done,' so she doesn't need me until Tuesday."

"Not what I mean. You working tomorrow?"

Tash poured more wine in both of their glasses.

Lu tilted her head, sympathetically. "Look, I get it. Maybe more than *you* know. Do you want to talk about what's really going on here?"

"No. Do you?"

Lu took a sip of wine.

Tash stood up. "I'm gonna get more sauce, it's really good."

Chapter 17

Tash usually sped through Monroe's neighborhood, but today as she drove down the palm tree lined streets of Beverly Hills, she slowed down to take stock of each home. *That one's a garish monstrosity. What are they trying to prove? You're rich, new money, we get it. Ew, the next one's even worse. Why do the super rich have such bad taste? Oh, that one's pretty sick. Great throwback vibe. I can imagine the kind of person that lives there. Probably someone from the industry, a director from back in the day or a once-upon-a-time red carpet darling. Being a washed up star must be a mindfuck. And they all fall or fade. To get something you've chased, to live the dream, knowing it won't last and then having that truth come to pass. Maybe it's not an industry suited to happiness, just the pursuit.* Her thoughts turned to her own pursuit of happiness. *Can't believe I lost all of yesterday vegging in bed. I should be making movies, not watching them. Aidan would give me so much shit. What's my problem? I'm sliding back into who I used to be. Didn't think I'd ever go back. Fuck. Snap out of it, T. Get back to it. Okay, a couple of hours with Monroe and then when I get home, I'll work. I just need to get into it again.*

Tash's thoughts settled as she pulled into Monroe's driveway. She hopped out into the blazing LA sunshine to see Henry standing outside, speaking with the gardener.

"Yo, H," Tash called.

"Good afternoon, Miss Daniels. You'll find Mrs. Preston by the pool."

Tash waved as she walked around to the back of the estate. She spotted Monroe in the distance on the upper terrace, dressed in a white sundress, large white hat, and black sunglasses. She was seated under an umbrella at one end of the long teak table, reading as usual.

Tash walked on the pathway along the pool's edge, past the red, yellow, and purple flower beds, and then up the stairs to the sprawling terrace that ran along the backside of the estate. As she approached, Monroe looked up from her book and smiled. Tash immediately noticed her lips were poutier than usual. *Ah, so that's what she did.*

"What are you reading, another Oprah pick?" Tash asked, as she took a seat.

"It's supposed to be one of those soul-enriching books. It's on the best seller list, but so far it's nothing more than clichés and empty platitudes, as far as I can tell at least."

Tash smiled, thinking that Monroe was much wiser than most people probably assumed.

"How was your weekend? Did the clothes work out for your events?" Tash asked.

"I received compliments all weekend, especially on that jumpsuit. I never would have chosen that without you, but you were right, it was so comfortable. You have such a good eye. I've always loved to dress up, but I never had a real knack for fashion."

"You're getting there," Tash assured her. "You could do this on your own."

"People keep asking who my stylist is. Is it terrible I don't want to share my secret?"

Tash laughed. "I'm all yours."

A member of the kitchen staff brought over a tray carrying their lunch: two pristine butter lettuce salads topped with avocado and crab and garnished with fish roe, a mineral water for Monroe, and a diet cola for Tash.

"Thank you," Monroe said. "I remembered how much you enjoyed the crab puffs the cook made. I thought this would be refreshing on a hot day."

"Looks great," Tash replied, taking a bite of the tarragon-laced crab.

"How was your weekend?" Monroe asked, sipping her water.

"Uh, it was all right. Aidan left to go on that tour, so…"

"That's right! It's exciting what's happening for him. He's really made it. I was talking with one of my girlfriends and she knew his music, her son is a fan. I may have to ask you for an autographed picture or something someday."

"Sure."

"I have to confess: I looked online and wow, he's gorgeous. What a jawline. He looks like he was born for this. He has that indescribable *thing*. Your lives must be changing so quickly."

Tash sighed.

"Oh dear, I'm sorry. You must miss him."

"Yeah, I miss him, but I'm cool with him doing what he needs to do." She paused before continuing, "It's really his life that's changing, not mine."

Monroe took a breath, looking at her sympathetically. "I've had to come to terms with some things about Bill's world over the years. When a studio head is in the room, no one else is. It's about power. They all want something from him."

Tash put her fork down. "Can I ask you a personal question?"

"Yes."

"You look like a star, truly, you're crazy beautiful. I always wondered if you came to LA to be an actress or something."

Monroe smiled ever so slightly. "I wanted a grand life, more than anything. Of course, it was just a fantasy, but I was headstrong about making it happen. When I was a teenager, I watched a lot of eighties nighttime soap operas. The fashion and opulence blew my mind. My mother and I argued about them; she didn't care for those shows and we only had one television."

Tash smiled. "That's so funny. I'm obsessed with eighties pop culture. Love it. It influences my work."

"Then you understand the allure. I also watched old movies and fell in love with the stars of the 1940s and '50s. I mean that in the truest sense. Deeply in love with them. I guess I developed an idea of old Hollywood meets contemporary glamour, or at least what was contemporary at the time. I knew I'd get myself here, come hell or high water, to the land of palm trees and silver screen dreams." With a giggle, she added, "Mind you, I had no real talent or even passion for acting, but I thought it would fall into place if I could only get here."

"Did it?" Tash asked.

"I was living with a bunch of girls, models who were all waitressing or doing odd jobs on the side. I modeled for a bit. I didn't have much luck because of my body type. Thin was in and I was too voluptuous. All I could book were lingerie shoots. It wasn't glamorous in the least. The adult industry was interested, but that wasn't for me. Eventually, I gave up and took a job as a hostess at a chichi industry restaurant. One night, a VIP came in with a large group. You could tell he was important because everyone fawned over him. It sounds naïve, but I was drawn to him because of his sweet eyes. The most powerful man in the room had the gentlest eyes. He was taken with me too. He asked for my number that night, but I said no."

"Why?"

"I was so young, only twenty at the time. He was twice my age. I thought he was out of my league and I didn't want to be his girl of the week. My mother had warned me about that sort of thing and that sort of man. But he pursued me for weeks and eventually I said yes. It was a whirlwind romance and we got married ten months later. No one thought it would last, which I can understand, but here we are a quarter of a century later. We had a connection. It was easy. He always says I bring him joy, which is strange to me," she said, her eyes distant.

Tash cocked her head. "In a way, that kind of reminds me of my relationship with Aidan. We both like the lighter side of life. We gel."

Monroe smiled, pensively.

Tash continued, "What about acting? Since he's in the film industry, did you ever ask him to get you a part or an audition or something?"

"Never. Because of him, I met everyone. When I was young, many offered me small parts or representation. I always said I wasn't interested. I was tempted once, in the very beginning. We were at a party and I met the man who owned Guess. He asked me to do a test shoot. He said I looked like a modern-day Marilyn Monroe and he wanted me to be their next model. Guess girls became very famous at that time. I admit getting a little swept up by the idea."

"You didn't pursue it?"

Monroe gazed down and then looked confidently at Tash. "Our lives were busy with professional commitments, and Bill thought I would enjoy charity work, which turned out to be mostly hosting parties. I took some classes too. Sculpture, watercolors, I even took theology and philosophy in a continuing education program." She stared into the distance for a moment before continuing. "And I was adjusting to all of it, which took time. This life, even though I wanted it, I suppose it isn't natural for me. I had never known a world like this. Just getting rid of my southern accent took ages, and it still creeps in a bit." She paused again for a moment before concluding, "Besides, I never had any real talent, just a dream for something glamorous."

Tash looked around at the house and grounds. "Seems like your dream came true."

"Hmm, I suppose it did. Funny how things are often different than we imagine. We never know what form our dreams will take."

"Yeah, I've actually been thinking about that a lot lately."

Monroe smiled and sipped her water. "What about your short film? I didn't realize it was influenced by the eighties."

"Yeah, it's black and white with eighties-inspired pops of color."

"You haven't mentioned it in ages. Did you screen it at festivals?"

She shook her head. "That didn't work out. I've been hoping to write a feature-length version, but..."

"I'd love to see it sometime, your short film," Monroe said.

"Sure. I'll bring it by. Well, should we start on the garden party gifts? I have some ideas I think you'll like."

Lu picked up the cutting board to wipe off the carrot peels. She dropped the carrots into the bin and then started on the beets. Amanda turned around from the register and hollered, "Strawberry Star and Tropical Blend up next."

Lu's heart raced. She turned to the counter, but it was just a couple of kids. She made the drinks and then tried to wash the stains off her hands before saying, "Hey, Amanda, we're low on kale. If you can handle it up here for a minute, I'll go back and clean some."

"Okay."

Lu made her way to the backroom, gathered a pile of kale from the refrigerator, and threw it on the counter. She grabbed her backpack and took out her phone. She shut her eyes, shook her head, and then texted Paisley:

Hey. Sorry I didn't call yesterday. Busy. I'm off tomorrow. Wanna go for a hike or hit the beach?

She slid her phone into her pocket and started cleaning the kale. Ten minutes later, her phone beeped.

Let's go for a hike. Should I pick you up at 10? I'll pack snacks.

Lu smiled. *Damn, she's too sweet.*

Tash got home at the end of the afternoon, threw her keys on the entry table, and walked into the kitchen. She opened the refrigerator and mindlessly scanned the contents. Not really hungry, she opened the maraschino cherry jar and popped one in her mouth. The sweet, squishy burst soothed her.

She went into her room and changed into sweats and a tank top. Her laptop was on her dresser, taunting her. *Get your shit together.* She climbed into bed with her computer. Waiting for it to boot up, she thought about Monroe. *She has everything people dream of, but there was something in her eyes, like she wonders what else she could have had, wonders where she'd be had she gone for that modeling job. Hard to imagine her life could be any better than it is. I guess we all have many lives: the one we live and the ones we might have lived.*

Staring at her desktop, she looked at her grant application folder, her writing folder, and the link to her film. She hovered the mouse over each one as a lump formed in her throat. *Fuck it*, she thought, slamming the laptop shut. She fetched the remote control from the nightstand, flicked on the television, and nestled under the comforter. *His smell is fading.*

PART FIVE

Chapter 18

Monroe Preston had slept peacefully virtually every night since her wedding day. It didn't matter whether her husband was traveling or lying beside her in one of their many homes, free from the anxieties and to-do lists that kept most people spinning in their own heads, she shut her eyes each night and quickly drifted off to sleep. Until tonight.

Monroe lay awake nearly all night, her silk nightgown soft against her one-thousand-count sateen sheets. Something indiscernible wasn't quite right, or perhaps, she feared, she wasn't quite right. Listening to Bill breathing, she stared at the ceiling thirty feet above. She remembered being a young girl, lying awake in bed and counting the glow-in-the-dark stars she stuck on her ceiling, dreaming of her big life and no longer being Jenny Anne Foster from the south of nowhere. Suddenly, the county talent show flashed before her eyes.

"Mama, do I look all right?" she asked, twirling in front of the mirror, examining her silver sequined dress.

"You look like tinsel sparkling under twinkly lights. Lucky thing I'm good with a needle and thread, isn't it, since you love to dress up? Come on now, grab your baton. They're gonna call you next."

Moments after her performance she ran backstage, where her mother was waiting with open arms. "Now I warned you to practice more." She sighed before continuing, "Don't feel too bad, Jenny Anne. Everyone drops the baton sometimes."

"I don't feel bad, Mama. Did you hear the applause? They loved the dress you made me. It sparkled even brighter under the stage lights."

"Well of course they loved it. Who doesn't like tinsel in twinkly lights, sweet girl?"

With a slight snore, Bill rolled over, interrupting her thoughts and flinging her into the present. When he was settled, she let her mind wander back to how it felt standing center stage, and then to her mother's words. "You look like tinsel sparkling under twinkly lights." *That's all I wanted, Mama, to sparkle in Tinseltown. And here I am. But nothing is quite as I imagined.*

Even when Bill was in town, Monroe rarely saw him in the morning. His car always picked him up hours before she'd rise. So, when he tried to slip out of bed, quietly as usual, he was surprised when she whispered, "Good morning."

"Did I wake you?"

"I've been up for ages." He started to walk toward their master bathroom when she said, "Did I tell you Tash's boyfriend got a record deal?"

"Wow. That's great."

"He's on tour," Monroe added, sitting up.

"Uh huh," Bill replied, walking into the bathroom.

"He might really make it. Isn't that something?"

"Uh huh."

"Bill, I was thinking about the funniest thing," she hollered.

"Come in here," he replied.

She slipped on her silk robe and sashayed to the bathroom doorway. Bill stood at the marble vanity, brushing his teeth.

"I was thinking about that offer I got to model for Guess. Do you remember that?"

He switched his electric toothbrush off and turned to face her.

"I remember. Seems like another lifetime. What made you think of that?"

"Oh, I don't know. Tash asked me if I'd wanted to be an actress. We were chatting about why I came to California."

"With regret or nostalgia?"

She blinked and shook her head. "Do you ever wonder what it would have been like if I modeled or acted?"

"You hated modeling. When we were dating, you told me such horror stories."

She shrugged. "I suppose that's true. Well, acting then. A lot of people offered me things when we were first married. Remember? You discouraged it."

He crinkled his face. "I remember the offers. You never seemed interested. You told me you'd never even been in a high school play."

"Yeah, I guess."

He put his toothbrush down and folded his arms. "What's going on? Do you wish you had…"

"I'm being silly. I didn't act, you're right. I was just wondering 'what if,' I guess."

He walked over and kissed the top of her head.

"I'll let you get ready for your day," she said, closing the bathroom door.

An hour later, alone again, Monroe looked in the bathroom mirror, inspecting her freshly washed skin. After spraying her face with hydrating mist and gently rubbing in SPF moisturizer, she examined her newly plumped lips, pouting and releasing several times before concluding they still appeared natural. She couldn't shake her conversation with Tash. *It's been years since I've thought about those early days in California. I do wonder how things would be different if I had gone to that test shoot, or taken one of those other roles. Bill is right, though. I didn't have any real interest after I met him, just a curiosity or fantasy. And now that I've seen the other side, what their lives are really like, celebrity has lost its luster. I hope Tash is all right. She must be afraid her boyfriend will leave her. Maybe she's afraid of having to choose between his dream and hers. Or that his dream will eclipse hers, slowly becoming her own, before she can notice. Our choices always have shadow sides. Like I told her, dreams never come to us quite the way we expect.* Fluffing her platinum hair with her fingers, she remembered the first time she and her best friend Lauren tried to dye it, at the age of fifteen.

"My mother's gonna kill me if I ruin the towels."

"I'll help you clean up. Jenny Anne, you're gonna look like a movie star. You're already the prettiest girl in school," Lauren said.

"Do you really think I could be a movie star?"

"Definitely!"

"Oh, I don't know, there are lots of pretty girls. But it sure would be exciting to be famous and have everything you ever could want. To have people admire you. Don't tell anyone, but I've been thinking about changing my name to something that stands out, just like Marilyn Monroe did."

"I bet you'll look just like her when your hair is done."

"Maybe I should call myself Monroe. You know, as my first name."

"That's so cool. You should do it. Change your name as soon as you're eighteen and then go to Hollywood. Maybe I can be your assistant or makeup artist or something, if we're still friends," Lauren said, adjusting her wire-rimmed glasses.

"Of course we'll still be friends!"

"Ooh, the timer! Let's wash your hair."

Twenty minutes later, as she finished blow drying her hair, disappointment set in. Lauren tried to console her. "It's not exactly what you wanted but it's not that bad. It's kind of auburn-ish."

"It's not blonde like the woman on the box at all. I don't know what we did wrong. It's still dark brown, but now it has a reddish glow. It's awful," she whined.

Lauren comforted her as best as she could, reminding her she was still the most beautiful girl she had ever seen in real life.

Months later, after saving every penny she earned from her new after-school job at a local grocery store, she went to the fanciest salon in three counties where she learned it wasn't simple to go from dark to light hair. Her wish would take time and money. After a few visits, she gazed into the salon mirror to finally see the hair of her dreams reflected back at her.

"Oh wow!" she exclaimed, catching her breath. "I look like *someone*, you know."

"Everybody is someone," the stylist replied flatly.

"Uh huh," she muttered, admiring her transformation.

She bounded home to show off her new coif. Her mother wasn't impressed.

"Jenny Anne, most girls would kill to look like you just the way you are. You don't need to keep doing these things to attract attention."

"Mama, I want to stand out, to be in the spotlight. Don't you ever imagine a glamorous life? That's what I'm going to have. My life will be grand, you'll see."

Her mother leaned closer and gently touched her hair, grimacing. "You're young. You'll have different priorities someday."

"Like sewing until my fingers bleed, just to scrape by? Like sitting alone night after night in a house with more paint chipped off than is left on?"

Her mother, who always had a quietness, looked at her sharply.

"I'm sorry, Mama. I didn't mean it like that. But was your dream really to sew hems and make dresses for other women? Don't you want a closet of dresses of your own, and fabulous parties to wear them to?"

Her mother softly said, "Fancy dresses and parties don't make people happy. Taking care of yourself by doing something simple and useful is nothing to feel ashamed about. You'll see that someday."

"Then why are you so lonely?"

"One thing's got nothing to do with the other," she muttered.

"You don't think I'll make it, that I'll get out of here and do something special."

Her mother shook her head. "You don't hear a word I say. Going, going, going to some big and glitzy life, that's all you ever think about. You don't even act or sing. All you've ever done is baton twirling, and that was only because you liked the costumes I made for you. You didn't even practice. Glamour alone isn't a goal. It isn't a life. You're already plenty special, but I wish you'd get your head out of the clouds, Jenny Anne. Life will disappoint you."

Defiantly, she replied, "Lauren's mom invited me for dinner. They want to see my new hair. I have to go or I'll be late."

"Wipe off some of that makeup first. I don't want her parents thinking I'm permissive. Besides, you're plenty pretty without it."

Monroe continued fluffing her hair, wondering whatever happened to Lauren. *Such a sweet girl. I feel bad that I never called after I moved.* She glanced at her vanity, covered with top-of-the-line cosmetics, and thought of her mother. She looked over at the small, framed photo beside her wedding photo. "Funny thing is, Mama, you were right. I bet you'd love that. When you go to bed at night, you wash it all off and have only yourself. I still wish you would have lived long enough to see my life. The thing is, my head was in the clouds because I wanted to be up there with the stars. Nothing wrong with dreaming, Mama. Only bad part of dreaming is waking up. The details start to slip away, and you can try to catch them, to remember, but eventually they fade to black."

As she did each morning, Monroe grabbed the book off her night-stand to take to breakfast. She was midway through Sarah Cohen's latest tome and was eager to keep reading. Although she had a full day planned, she uncharacteristically meandered around her house, admiring the exquisite art that lined the walls. She stopped in front of the Andy Warhol rendition of Marilyn Monroe. Bill had bought it at auction for her thirtieth birthday. It was the best present she had ever received. *He said everyone would be famous in the future. Wonder if he ever said anything about being near the famous. It's not quite the same thing, is it Mr. Warhol? And what about you, Marilyn? Poor, haunted Marilyn. It's not so easy to be two people, is it? It's like being no one at all. What did Hollywood do to you? Did fame help you escape Norma Jeane? I guess it wasn't as glamorous as you hoped. I do wonder, though, were you truly and deeply unhappy or did you just wake up one day feeling somehow outside of the moment and outside of yourself?* She ran her fingers along the frame and suddenly had a thought that was entirely new to her. *Could it be that I'm living the shadow side of my own life?*

With this question lingering in her mind, she strolled downstairs and into the sun-kissed breakfast room. The cook promptly served her usual breakfast: Italian roast coffee, fruit, and a soft-boiled egg.

"May I get you anything else, Mrs. Preston?"

"There are some fashion magazines by the pool. I'd like to flip through them before Tash arrives, if you don't mind. Thank you."

The cook set off to retrieve the magazines and Monroe picked up a sterling silver teaspoon and started tapping the top of her egg. As it cracked, her mind veered to her early days in LA and one particu-larly terrible modeling job. She and another model were in a small backroom the size of a closet. It reeked of bleach and she wondered if it had been the scene of a crime. Monroe leaned against the wall, changing into lingerie two sizes too small when the photographer started screaming for her. The other model warned, "He's impatient." She touched Monroe's shoulder, "He's feely. Watch yourself." Monroe's anxiety grew as she hurried to the set.

"Get on the bed," he snapped.

Anxious but afraid to be perceived as difficult, she sat on the edge of the bed.

"Lie on your side."

In a flash, he had her flat on her back. She stared at the cracks in the popcorn ceiling as he hovered over her, his body odor permeating the air.

"On your knees," he barked.

She lifted herself up and he put his camera down beside her.

"Your bosom doesn't look right," he said, placing his hands on the underwire of her bra and manually adjusting her breasts.

Humiliated and wondering why none of the others in the room – assistant, makeup artist, hair stylist – intervened on her behalf, she withstood the manhandling. The other model glanced at her, but quickly averted her eyes. At the end of the shoot, embarrassed and afraid to end up alone with him, she quickly changed and ran out of the building, tripping on the cement stairs and bloodying both knees. When she got home and told her roommates what happened, they just shrugged and insisted "that stuff happens all the time" and she was "lucky it didn't go further." One of the girls, who she suspected was jealous of her, suggested it wasn't surprising because she "looks like a Playboy model" and "only does lingerie jobs, which everyone knows is code for something else." After that experience and repeated pressure to pose nude, she quit modeling. Determined to make LA work if only to prove her mother wrong, she took a job as a cocktail waitress, until months later her friend helped her score a hostess position at a high-end restaurant. Within eight months, she met Bill. As she sat in the breakfast room of their estate, she remembered the moment they met, when he'd stumbled on his own name, unable to take his eyes off her. She smiled, still able to feel the warmth emanating from him. *He's such a kind and generous man. I've been bathed in his light nearly my whole adult life. I'm luckier than I ever imagined, aren't I?* Lost in thought, she was visibly startled when the cook returned with the magazines.

"I'm sorry, Mrs. Preston. I didn't mean to sneak up on you."

"Oh, that's okay. I don't know where my mind was."

The cook placed the magazines in front of her. "May I get you anything else?"

"I have everything I could want."

Chapter 19

"**F**uck," Tash grumbled, realizing she was out of coffee filters. *I need caffeine.* As she created a makeshift filter using a paper towel, she remembered her days in New York with Jason and Penelope. *Pen always got so annoyed when I forgot to pick stuff up. Never thought I'd miss her so much. And Jason, oh my God, Snapchat isn't enough. I gotta go to New York and visit him. At least I know they're happy. Hard to believe they're both finally in great, committed relationships and truly living their grown-up lives, worlds away from their blue period.* As the smell of coffee began to waft through the air, her thoughts turned to her New York college days. *God, I was with some sketchy dudes back then. I was so messed up. Funny thing, as gorgeous as he is, I probably wouldn't have given a guy like Aidan a real chance back then; he's too nice. I would have driven him away, not believing he was for real. Hell, I still almost did that. Can't get over that I thought that loser I dated in college was cool. What the fuck, Tash? Asshole thought he'd share me with his lowlife friends, whether I consented or not. Scumbags.* She shuddered, wanting to clear her mind, and snatched her phone for a distraction. There was a text from Aidan.

`Hey, beauty queen. I know you're sleeping, damn time zones. Wanted to say I miss you. FaceTime me tomorrow before 2 my time if you can.`

Yeah, I miss you too, she thought, before replying with smiley face emojis. The coffee maker beeped and she filled her mug. *Fuck, there are grounds in it. I used to be good at this.*

Tash arrived at Monroe's with a sample invitation from the calligrapher. Monroe held the invitation up to the light and said, "I love how they've made the lettering on the top look like it's disappearing."

"Yeah, it came out great," Tash replied.

"Did I tell you it was my idea?" Monroe asked.

Tash shook her head.

"So, I was hosting a small dinner party for a few of Bill's employees. They were all making suggestions for the studio's anniversary party, typical stuffy parties and tired red-carpet themes. Sometimes people in the industry side of the business forget what it's all about, what draws people here, why we're still mesmerized when we sit in dark theaters, watching larger-than-life people on the screen and imagining our own lives."

Tash smiled, knowingly. "What do you think it is?"

"Magic. And that's what I told them. It wasn't meant as a suggestion, I was just thinking out loud. I said it should be a celebration of movie magic. And what better place to do that than Magic Manor, to put a fun, childlike spin on it?"

"I love it," Tash said.

"It's going to be the social event of August, the whole year really, but very exclusive. We're inviting studio executives and a select few of the actors, writers, and directors from our biggest, award-winning films. I emailed the calligrapher the final guest list this morning."

"Sounds fantastic."

"The studio is handling most of it, but there are still details for us to work out, including the gift bags and, of course, my outfit. I want to get everything settled for the rest of the summer as well. I hate to impose, but can you work some extra hours over the next few weeks? Bill and I decided to spend a couple of weeks at the Santa Barbara ranch house, and I want to make sure everything is taken care of before we leave. You'll have two paid weeks off while I'm away. Possibly more if I can convince him to stay longer."

"No problem. I could use something to keep me busy anyway."

Monroe smiled compassionately. "Okay, let's get started. I clipped some magazine photos. What do you think about a black, strapless gown?"

They worked for a couple of hours before Monroe had to leave for her weekly appointment with an astrologer.

"It's a scorcher today. With your boyfriend away, if you're not in a rush, you should take a dip in the pool and relax before you go," Monroe said.

"Oh, thanks, that's okay."

"I insist. Someone should enjoy the pool. If you don't have a bathing suit, you know we keep a variety for guests. Everything is in the pool house."

"I actually have a suit in my car, but…"

"Splendid! Stay as long as you like. I'll see you the day after tomorrow, once you've picked up the samples for the gift bags."

"Sounds good. And if you really don't mind, maybe I'll take you up on your offer."

"Of course. Please do."

Monroe's safari-themed pool house featured bamboo floors, brown and green wallpaper, and chocolate-colored wicker furniture. Tash slipped into her apropos leopard-print bikini and gold aviator sunglasses. *Not bad*, she thought, posing in front of the free-standing, full-length mirror. "Wow, look at these suits and sarongs," she whispered, admiring the long rack of designer swimwear carefully arranged for guests. *Wonder how many celebrities have worn these*, she thought, brushing her hands across the garments. *Monroe has some life.* She sprayed sunscreen all over herself and headed outside. Henry was waiting.

"I took the liberty of placing towels on that chaise under the umbrella," he said, pointing. "There's a diet cola on the table and I put several floats in the pool. Please let me know if I can get you anything else."

"Thanks, H. You're the best," she said, patting his back as she passed by.

"You're quite welcome, Miss Daniels."

Tash sat on the edge of the pool, her feet soaking in the warm, aqua water, her eyes focused on the majestic estate. She imagined what it would be like to live there. She always felt for those born in America, there were two versions of the American dream: the worker's version and the dreamer's version. This was the dreamer's version. This was where improbability kissed reality, sparking like a firework and casting an iridescent film over everything it touched. The glistening estate was merely a grand symbol of a dream realized. Tash was captivated. She took her sunglasses off, slid into the pool, and waded over to the bright pink flamingo float. *This is the life*, she thought, hoisting herself up onto the hot plastic bird. *A tequila sunrise would make this moment perfect. I should hit the club tonight, get back into the swing. Maybe Lu's working.*

After floating around for twenty minutes, she was parched and disembarked from her flamingo with a head-first dive. Gently gliding underwater all the way to the stairs, her mind cleared. She sauntered over to the chaise, casually reclined, and sipped her soda. *Too bad I don't have my iPod. I'll just chill for a bit and then head out*, she thought, closing her eyes. *This is so relaxing*, she mused, as she drifted off to sleep.

Soon, Tash was dreaming that she was walking down Abbott Kinney Boulevard in Venice Beach. Although she knew the stores well, they all looked different. Two mannequins in a window slowly began moving their heads toward each other. "This is weird. It's like a Björk video. What's in the next window?" Grass was springing from the floor, working its way up the mannequins' legs. "That's strange." She walked on. There was a large television in the third window, projecting Aidan's face.

"What are you doing, beauty queen?"

"Aidan?" she asked.

"Look everyone, it's my muse," he bellowed.

"Wait, what are you saying?" she pleaded.

She pressed her hands and face against the glass.

"Love you, beauty queen. Gotta go."

"Wait, Aidan!"

Static.

Her heart racing, she continued walking, quickening her pace, but soon feared she was slipping through the ever-widening cracks beneath her feet. She slammed her body against the next store window and caught her breath. Turning her head, she saw her reflection, frightened and undone. There was a Help Wanted sign that read:

Wanted: beauty seekers
Positions to fill: countless
Hours: time is slipping by

"Time is slipping by?" As she said the words aloud, the crack in the cement below her feet widened more. She prepared to leap over it, and then took flight. In midair, her stomach dropped. Tash's body shook violently and she woke up like a bolt.

"Huh," she mumbled, trying to acclimate herself. She sipped her watery cola before noticing the position of the sun. *Shit. I must have been asleep for a while.*

Dazed from sitting in rush hour traffic and troubled by her peculiar dream, Tash didn't notice Darrell standing outside her building smoking a cigarette until he called to her.

"Hey there," he said.

"Oh, hey. Did you hit the pier today?" she hollered.

He shook his head. "There's a time to sell and a time to create."

She smiled.

"You know the time to sell, right?" he asked.

She shrugged.

"When the rent's due."

She laughed half-heartedly and waved goodbye.

There's a time to sell and a time to create. Hmm. Bet he never gets creatively blocked. Feeling down, she took a shower and then looked in the mirror, debating whether she had the energy to go clubbing. *I'm spent from the sun,* she concluded before changing into sweats and a tank top. Her laptop sat on her dresser, taunting her. She grabbed it and switched it on. The seconds it took to boot up felt impossibly longer than the seconds before. There was a slowness to time that recalled her dream. *My muse? Is that what he said?* By the time her desktop loaded, she decided that she was too tired to work and flipped it off. *I'm kinda hungry.* She scoured the kitchen for something to eat. Settling on a tub of Campbell's Chicken & Stars soup, she stuck it in the microwave. Soon she was carrying her soup and a diet cola to her bedroom where she turned the TV on and slid into bed. She flipped through the stations and landed on *Purple Rain. Ooh good, it just started.* She blew on her soup before eating a spoonful. *Wonder what'll be on after this.*

For the next few weeks, Tash followed the same routine: running errands, working with Monroe, who seemed increasingly tired, swimming and sunning, texting Aidan to avoid FaceTime, staring at her film files without opening them, contemplating going to the clubs, eating soup from a tub, and watching movies. Eventually, she stopped turning on her laptop altogether.

Lu and Paisley had become inseparable. They went hiking, spent lazy afternoons at the beach, and strolled around farmers' markets. Paisley hung out at clubs while Lu worked. Every night they went back to Lu's, and every morning they awoke entangled in each other's arms. Paisley invited Lu to meet her friends a couple of times, but Lu cited work as an excuse not to go. One Friday morning before they got out of bed, Paisley asked again.

"So, you're off tomorrow, right?"

"Yeah. What do you have in mind?" Lu asked, sliding her hands down Paisley's torso.

Paisley giggled. "Well, *that* of course, but I was thinking of you coming somewhere with me tomorrow night."

"Where?"

"To a midnight screening of *The Rocky Horror Picture Show* in West Hollywood. It's this thing my friends and I do the first Saturday of every month. It's my only night owl thing, well, before you came along."

"Seriously?" Lu asked.

"You're not a drama nerd or a film geek so you may not get it, but yeah, it's actually really fun. You've seen it before online or something, right?"

"No, never did."

"Seriously?!" Paisley exclaimed, leaning back to register her shock.

"Okay, now I feel lame."

"No, I'm just surprised, that's all. So, you up for it?"

"I guess, sure."

Paisley smiled brightly. "You can dress up, but you don't have to."

"Uh, okay."

"Could you meet me there? I always go early to see my friends and stuff."

"Sure. Maybe I'll ask Tash to come if that's cool. Since you've been occupying all my time, I haven't really talked to her. I feel bad about it. She's having a hard time with the whole Aidan thing, even if she won't admit it."

"Definitely. Bring her. It's about time I meet her. I'll leave tickets for you both at the box office. And I was thinking one more thing."

"Oh yeah, what's that?" Lu asked softly, touching the side of her face.

"Maybe after, you could come grab a bite with my friends."

Lu inhaled and looked into Paisley's eyes, her hand still on her face. "Yeah, I can do that."

Chapter 20

"It's usually not so tough to find a spot around here," Lu said. "I'm telling you, my parking karma is totally fucking shot," Tash moaned, as they drove down the same street for the third time.

"Go down a couple of blocks before you circle this time," Lu suggested.

"Look at how many homeless people there are. Those tents must be crazy hot this time of year," Tash remarked. "It's really depressing."

"Yeah, it's gotten a lot worse in the past few years."

"Did I ever tell you about Harold, the homeless dude I was kinda friends with in New York?" Tash asked.

"Don't think so."

"Like I brought him coffee and doughnuts sometimes and we'd talk. He hung out in Washington Square Park near my apartment. The NYU kids treated him like crap. Maybe I thought I was better than them. But I probably wasn't."

"What do you mean? What happened to him?" Lu asked.

Tash sighed. "Not sure. I was having a bad day once and I was kind of bitchy to him."

"Nah, not you!" Lu joked.

"Hardy har har. Anyway, I never saw him again. Suddenly, he wasn't there, like he vanished. It bothered me for a long time, wondering what happened to him. And then I started to think about how I called him my friend, but it's not like I invited him over or ever actually helped him get his life together. Maybe I was just nice to him to make myself feel better."

Lu was about to respond when she spotted a driver getting into their car. "Over there," she hollered. Tash pulled up, waiting with her blinker on. The driver of the other car seemed to be in no rush to leave.

"Hurry the fuck up," Tash grumbled.

"Chill, we have time," Lu assured her, as the car slowly moved out.

Tash pulled into the spot. They hopped out into the steamy night air and started walking toward the theater.

"Thanks for coming with me. I was sort of surprised you wanted to," Lu said.

"Uh, what do I love most in the world?"

"I don't know. Your hair?"

Tash smirked. "Very funny."

"Film. You love film."

"Yup. Besides, I haven't gone anywhere except work in weeks. Been hibernating. It's probably good you dragged my ass out." Then Tash looked more carefully at Lu. "What's with the blue jeans and button-down shirt? You look so cleaned up."

"Paisley said to dress up."

"Uh, dumbass, she meant to dress as one of the characters."

"What?"

"Oh my God, I still can't believe you've never seen this before. At a lot of screenings, people dress up like the characters in the film. They even act out certain parts, like jumping up in the aisles and doing this dance, 'The Time Warp.' It's like a whole thing."

Lu shook her head. "Christ."

"It's fun. You'll see."

"Am I too dressed up?" Lu asked.

"Yup, but it's fine. No one who goes to these things is judgmental. They're like a misfit cult or something."

"Be careful what you say. You were pretty into it when I invited you," Lu said with a laugh.

"I'm a film junkie and *Rocky Horror* has had the longest theatrical run in history. Of course I'm into it. Besides, I want to meet your girl."

"She's not my girl," Lu said, looking down at her feet. "Well, I guess she is, but don't say that kind of stuff in front of her, okay?"

"I thought you were really into her," Tash replied.

"I mean, she's amazing. She's such a good person. Too good, you know? I just don't know if I'm ready to do the whole relationship thing."

Tash chuckled. "I thought lesbians were all about the love at first sight, 'let's get a place together' thing."

"I'm not that kind of queer."

Before Tash could respond, they bumped into the end of a long line of people waiting to get into the theater. The line was wrapped around the corner, and most people were dressed in campy makeup, wigs, and costumes.

"This is so weird," Lu whispered.

"Chill, you'll see. But please tell me we're on the list or something," Tash said.

"Yeah, Paisley said to go straight to the box office window."

"I don't see her anywhere," Lu said, scanning the crowded theater.

"Relax and sit. We're dead center. She'll find us," Tash replied.

The red velvet seat creaked as Lu sat down. "Give me your purse so I can save the seat next to me." Tash handed over her bag and Lu placed it beside her. "So, you've been busy working for Monroe?"

"Yeah, but she's going out of town tomorrow. I'll have a couple of weeks off."

"Cool. Doesn't Aidan's record drop soon?"

Tash thought for a moment. "Wow. Yeah, midnight tomorrow, actually. I've been so preoccupied I lost track."

"Since your boss and your guy are both on the road, why don't you come to the club tomorrow night? Haven't seen you there in a while. The party isn't the same without you. Do it for LA."

Tash giggled. "I haven't really been in the mood, I guess."

"Get back out there. Put on one of your killer outfits and let loose. I'm working the late shift the next couple of nights."

"Damn, you're gonna be dragging."

"I'm almost used to it," Lu joked.

Suddenly, the lights went out. The audience started pounding their feet and cheering.

A woman asked Lu to move the purse so she could sit. When she said it was the last open seat in the theater, Lu begrudgingly gave in.

"I don't understand where Paisley is. It's not like her to flake."

"Don't worry. She must be here. She'll find us after," Tash whispered.

"Listen, think about what I said. You're a club chick. Be who you are. Maybe it feels like A's space, but it isn't."

Tash offered a half-hearted shrug and then whispered, "Yeah, thanks. Now focus. You're gonna love this."

Lu rolled her eyes.

The film began. As an image of red lips appeared on screen, reflecting light onto the faces of the faithful audience, Lu waited in anticipation. When the opening wedding scene began, a troupe of actors ran in from the wings and began acting out the scene in front of the screen.

Tash squeezed Lu's wrist and whispered, "This is the bomb. Some theaters have volunteer casts that act out the whole thing live. Never got to see that before."

Lu smiled and then noticed Paisley among the wedding guests. She was wearing a lavender skirt suit and white hat. In unison with the running film, she caught the wedding bouquet.

Lu whispered, "That's Paisley."

"Oh my God. She's Janet."

Lu furrowed her brow.

Tash leaned closer and whispered, "She's totally making fun of her goody-goody image. Brilliant. Just watch."

Enthralled by what was unfolding, Lu couldn't take her eyes off Paisley.

Soon, Brad and Janet were walking in the rain toward a mysterious castle. With a folded newspaper over her head, perfectly wide-eyed, Paisley mouthed along, "There's a light…"

A smile began to creep onto Lu's face.

When "The Time Warp" started to play, everyone in the theater jumped up to participate. Tash showed Lu how to follow along.

Before long, Paisley was stripped down to her white bra and slip, childlike barrettes still clipped in her hair. Lu's smile brightened. During the climactic sexual liberation scene, when Paisley began throwing her head back and mouthing, "Touch-a, touch-a, touch-a, touch me. I want to be dirty," Lu, utterly mesmerized, smiled so wide it morphed into laughter. In that moment, with the glow of the screen reflecting on her face, Lu gave in to her feelings. She looked at Paisley and the cinematic images projected behind her and had one clear thought: *Damn. I love this girl.*

The lights came on and people started making their way out of the theater. Lu checked her phone and saw a text from Paisley:

Need to change real quick. Will meet you in the lobby.

Lu and Tash waited as the rest of the audience filed out. Tash, captivated by the building, was looking all around.

"This place is dope. I love these old, restored theaters. There's so much history. This one's super gothic. Imagine the premieres that took place here back in the day. I bet it was raunchy in the eighties."

"Yeah, it's cool." Lu was visibly nervous.

"What's with you?"

"Paisley was really something, huh?"

Tash nodded. "She's hot. And she definitely has a good, ironic sense of herself. I dig her."

"Yeah, me too," Lu said.

Tash smiled. "Lean in."

"I'm kinda getting that message," Lu conceded.

Soon, Paisley and four of her castmates were skipping into the lobby on what one called "a post-show high." After introductions, they walked to a nearby all-night diner. Paisley explained it was their after-show tradition.

At the diner, everyone ordered eggs, pancakes, or pie, except for Lu, who opted for a meatloaf sandwich at everyone's urging. The group of vegetarians was oddly thrilled someone could finally honor Meatloaf's performance in the film. As she bit into the sandwich and gravy dripped on her hand, Lu said she was "glad to sacrifice for the group." After an hour and a half of lively conversation, raucous laughter, and comfort food, Lu sat with her arm around Paisley, her belly and heart both full.

"Thanks for driving us, Tash," Lu said as they pulled up to Lu's apartment building. Paisley leaned forward from the backseat to peck Tash on the cheek. "It was great to finally meet you," she said.

"You too," Tash replied.

"Maybe I'll see you at the club tomorrow night."

"Yeah, I'll try," Tash said.

Paisley and Lu hopped out of the car, but Lu leaned back into the open passenger window. "So, you'll come tomorrow night?"

"Probably."

"Okay. Thanks for tonight. It was actually really fun."

"Yeah, your girl is great."

Lu smiled. "Yeah, she is."

Chapter 21

"Monroe, is there anything you'd like me to put in the car?" Bill called from the bedroom.

Monroe stared in the bathroom mirror, wondering if the dark circles under her eyes were as pronounced as she feared, or if they were like her heartbeat, louder in her own mind. She took a deep breath before responding, "No thank you, darling. Henry already loaded my small travel bag and my books."

"I need to make a quick call. I'll meet you at the car."

"Be down in a minute."

Even that brief exchange depleted her energy, so she sat perfectly still, taking deep, purposeful breaths. She plucked a tube of concealer off the vanity, rubbed the porcelain-colored goop on her fingertip, and gently dabbed it under each eye. She sat for another moment, vacantly gazing at the mirror before sauntering into her bedroom to fetch her beige Hermès handbag and oversized, black Chanel sunglasses. At the last minute, she rifled through her nightstand and removed an unopened prescription for valium. With the bottle tucked safely in her handbag, Monroe headed out. She stopped at her beloved Warhol, almost involuntarily, and cocked her head as if trying to see the brightly colored image from a new perspective. *Marilyn, I read something you wrote, something about how you felt life coming closer. Had it been further? Had you been removed from your own life? Is that what Mr. Warhol saw? Is that what he was trying to show us?*

Her daydream was interrupted when Bill called from the bottom of the staircase. "We should get on the road before the traffic picks up."

She smiled ever so slightly at the painting, slipped on her sunglasses, and hollered, "Coming, darling."

Bill turned north onto the 101, flipping through the stations on the radio.

"Oh, leave that on," Monroe said, as Billie Holiday's voice oozed through the speakers.

"Looks like an easy ride today," he remarked.

"You should have taken the driver so you could relax."

"It's my only chance to drive. If I had my way, we'd be in one of the convertibles."

"Oh Bill, you know the wind and sun are too much for me."

"That's why I leave one of them at the ranch house. We can just do a short, local drive when we're there. It's an excuse for you to put your hair up in one of those silk scarves I bought you in Paris."

"Mmhmm," Monroe sighed.

"Maybe you should try to take a nap. It's been weeks since you've slept properly. I don't remember you suffering like this since before we got married, after your..." He trailed off.

"Yes, I know."

"Back then, your doctor prescribed something. Maybe..."

Monroe interrupted. "Yes, I already got something, just in case."

"Hopefully you won't need it. A change of scenery will do you good. Riding always knocks you out, and the horses will be happy to see you too."

She turned toward him and smiled faintly. "I think you're right, darling. Perhaps I'll close my eyes for a bit."

"When we get to Ventura, should I stop at that produce stand you like?" he asked. "We could get greens for your smoothies and maybe some melon for breakfast."

"All right," she muttered, her eyelids becoming heavier. As Billie Holiday warbled her last note, Monroe shut her eyes.

I should remember to get kale and spinach. Oh, and cucumbers. I always forget the cucumbers. Bill wants melon. Perhaps they'll have nice cantaloupe. He loves cantaloupe. Suspended somewhere between sleeping and waking, her thoughts drifted to the supermarket where she worked at as a teenager. She remembered the day she quit, at the age of sixteen, as if it had just happened.

Her twenty-two-year-old manager, Tom, a tall, skinny man with dark hair and sparse stubble on his short chin, called her over the store intercom.

"Jenny Anne to the stockroom."

She headed straight to the stockroom, glad to have a break from bagging groceries, a job that made time move slower than the little turtles Lauren raced with her brother. Tom was already in the small, dank room, holding a clipboard. A crate of honeydew melons sat atop a stack of boxes.

"These melons need to be shelved," he instructed.

"Sure thing," she replied, wriggling past him in the cramped space. She placed her hand on a melon when she heard the clipboard drop onto the small table beside them. Suddenly, she felt him standing behind her, not a centimeter separating them.

"Those melons should be ripe," he said, his voice lower than usual.

"Uh huh," she mumbled.

He placed his hand on the melon she was touching, his body now pressed against her.

"You've been here for almost a year, right?" he asked softly. "Feel that melon. When something's ripe, it starts to smell different. When you bite into it, the sweetness drips from your mouth."

Her heart thumping, she said, "I'm all set here. I got it on my own."

"You sure you don't need my help?" he whispered, still pressed firmly against her.

"I'm all set," she replied, trying to control her shaking.

He stepped back. "When you're done with those, you can go on your break."

She inhaled, holding her breath until she was certain he was gone. She shelved all the melons, collected her backpack from her locker, and walked out of the store as if she was taking her break. She never went back, not even to get her last paycheck.

By the time she got home, tears were streaming down her face. She cleaned herself up before her mother got home from work, not wanting to upset her after a long day and afraid she might blame her "attention-getting" appearance for the incident. At dinner, she casually announced she quit her job because it had nothing to do with what she wanted to do in life. For weeks, she and her mother argued about it, her mother insisting "life isn't just made up of things we like." Lauren was the only person she confided in. After that, whenever her mother sent her to the grocery store, she took two buses to go to the store two towns over.

Every night, as she lay in bed counting the Day-Glo shooting stars on her ceiling, she dreamt of a life far away from minimum wage, managers, and buses. Sometimes she'd picture herself on the cover of Vogue and she'd imagine Tom, old and ugly, bagging groceries and looking at stacks of magazines adorned with her face.

As they pulled away from the produce stand, Bill turned the radio back on. Sinatra came through the speakers. "Ah, this is perfect for the scenic part of the drive," Bill said.

Monroe smiled. "You're so old-fashioned. I do love that about you."

He laughed. "I've been blessed with good taste."

She giggled. "I love the coastal part of the trip." She gazed past Bill, the deep blue water of the Pacific glistening in the sun. "The water in California always sparkles," she said softly.

Bill turned the music up and Monroe watched the water as if it were a film where the past and present met. Her husband provided the soundtrack. Her eyelids once again became heavy, but she fought to keep them open.

It always sparkles, she thought. *I'll never forget the first time I saw the Pacific. Vast and glorious, just like I imagined my future would be.*

She landed in LA with less than a thousand dollars in the bank and everything she owned crammed into two suitcases. She had hustled, mailing her semi-professional headshots to various modeling and talent agencies, the latter offering no response. However, she had meetings arranged with three modeling agencies and was told if she was signed, they would help her get settled and send her on go-sees to clients right away. Confident that she could make big things happen for herself, she ignored her bank balance and hailed a cab at LAX. When the driver asked, "Where to?" she handed him a slip of paper with the address of a cheap motel she had booked. He warned her, "Be careful. That's a rough area."

"That's okay. I won't be there long. Oh, and sir, can you drive by the Pacific? I've never seen it before."

"It's out of your way and will cost you more."

"That's okay. Please take the longer route."

When the Prestons arrived at their home away from home, they were promptly greeted by their housekeeper, who ran outside to help them. Bill handed her the cardboard box overflowing with fresh produce.

"Oh my, these berries are beautiful," she remarked. "I'll get these into the house right away."

"Thank you," Bill said, as he retrieved Monroe's bag from the trunk. "Feeling better? You dozed off in the car."

"Yes, a bit better."

"Shall we head inside?"

Monroe nodded. "I think after we settle in, I'll go to the stables, see the horses. Perhaps I'll go for a short ride."

Monroe changed into her riding clothes in her bedroom. She noticed the small, framed photograph of her mother on her dresser. Her mother was young and uncharacteristically wearing a party dress. It was Monroe's favorite photo. She picked it up and smiled. "Oh Mama, you were beautiful. Strange how you spent your life making party dresses for other women, but never for yourself. You never did care much for fancy clothes or makeup, but you didn't need any of that. I'm sorry I thought you were plain or simple. You weren't, were you?"

She gently placed the frame back on the dresser and sat on the edge of the bed, thinking about the day she called her mother boasting she'd been signed to a modeling agency.

"Mama, I don't understand why you aren't more excited."

"I told you, I'm happy for you if this is what you want."

"They set me up with an apartment with a bunch of other girls. They think I'd be good at print work, and I have go-sees all week."

"Go...?"

"Go-sees, Mama. They're like auditions."

"The thought of you parading around for them and being judged – judged on your God-given body..."

Monroe rolled her eyes. "It's not like that, not really. Besides, if I book some jobs, I'll be able to take another stab at talent agencies, maybe try my hand at acting."

"I just don't know how anyone could be happy like that, being rejected all the time."

"Mama, did you ever think that some people just are happy, and even if they're not, they're trying to be?" After a long silence, Monroe changed the subject. "What about you, Mama?"

"Oh, well, I'm fine. I'm the same."

"How's work?"

"The same as always."

"Have you gone to play cards at Elaine's?"

"I've been too tired." She paused for a moment. "Jenny Anne, we should hang up. This call will be very expensive for you."

"Maybe someday we won't have to worry about that. I'll call you next week."

"Call after seven when it's less expensive."

"Yes, Mama."

"And Jenny Anne, if you're happy, *truly* happy, that's all a person can hope for, I suppose."

"I'll call next week. Wish me luck. Bye, Mama."

All these years later, Monroe could recall every detail of that conversation. *Was dressmaking in that small town really your ideal life? I remember the stacks of unpaid bills, and you, sitting alone every night, eating reheated casserole and watching game shows. Weekends spent cleaning the house or doing odd jobs. Oh, I wish I knew what your dreams had been. You must have had some, even if you held onto them tightly. Or was it that you let them go too easily?* Her thoughts shifted to her mother's words about happiness: "If you're happy, *truly* happy, that's all a person can hope for." She began to wonder about her tone. She tried to remember how she sounded. *Were you mournful? Was I too preoccupied to truly hear you? Oh Mama, were you ever happy? If you were, when did your happiness end? When did life slip farther away?*

Luke, the stablehand, had prepared Monroe's favorite horse, Captain, in case she wanted to go for a ride. As she mounted the beautiful animal, his coat the color of dark chocolate with creamy white splotches along his gait, she whispered, "Oh Captain, how I've missed you."

"I took him out for a walk so he's ready for whatever you have in mind. I'll be here when you get back," Luke said.

Monroe nodded and then gently pressed on her horse. He began walking. There was little that brought Monroe the peace and joy she felt with her horses. She'd spent twenty-five years searching for meaning in religion, spirituality, astrology, mythology, self-help, and countless fads that had quickly come and gone, but she felt most centered when she was riding. It cleared her mind. But today, she couldn't focus on the horse, the breeze, or the sunshine. She couldn't quiet her mind. She began to wonder why she felt out of sorts these past few weeks, unsettled, and outside of the moment.

Bill adores me. Our lives are perfect. I have more freedom and glamour than I ever could have envisioned. What's wrong with me? Her mother's words came barreling into her mind. *"Glamour alone isn't a goal. It isn't a life."* She remembered when she called her mother to announce her engagement and the argument that ensued.

"Why are you always so negative? You're never happy for me."

"That isn't true. I just don't want to see you throw your life away. You're too young, you barely know him, and my God, Jenny Anne, he's too old for you."

"Stop being so provincial. He's not old, he's accomplished."

"And what will you accomplish in your life?"

"Do you know how many girls would kill to marry someone like Bill? Do you know how lucky I am?"

"You need time to find out who you are and what you can do for yourself. There will always be men who want to take care of a girl as pretty as you."

"Then why were you alone your whole life?" she shrieked. "Working till your fingers were raw, sitting alone at home and crying at night. Don't you think I heard you, whimpering, crying yourself to sleep?"

No response. When what seemed like an eternity had passed, Monroe softened her voice. "I'm sorry, Mama. You know I'm grateful for everything you did for me. I just want you to be happy for me. We're different, that's all."

"Jenny Anne, I hope you find what you're looking for. Call me next week."

"Bill is gonna buy your airline ticket for the wedding. He'll take care of everything. Don't forget, it's just a couple of months away."

"I'll talk to you next week."

"Bye, Mama."

Embarrassed by what she had said and preoccupied with planning a whirlwind wedding, she didn't call her mother for three weeks. When they finally spoke, her mother was quieter than usual, distant. Things that would usually provoke an argument got no reaction at all. Her mother's response to everything was, "that's nice," which was how she always spoke to others, but never to Monroe. Feeling guilty, Monroe assumed her change in demeanor was because of the hurtful words she had spoken weeks earlier.

Three days later, a police officer called to inform her that her mother had been killed in a car accident. Her car veered off the road, slamming into a tree. Monroe was devastated. Instead of flying her mother out to California, Monroe and Bill flew in for the funeral. After the service, she hosted mourners in her mother's home. The next-door neighbor, Elaine, walked over and hugged Monroe tightly. Elaine and her mother sometimes stopped at each other's homes for coffee, to play cards, or with a bowl of soup if one or the other was sick.

"I'm just so sorry, Jenny Anne. I always knew of your mother's troubles, but if I had thought…"

Monroe's eyes widened. "What are you saying, Elaine? It was a car accident."

Elaine took Monroe's hands. "It was a clear night and there were no skid marks. No other cars. You've always been such a firecracker that you kept her going, kept the flicker of fight alive in her. But once you were grown… I'm sure you knew… she always had such a sadness about her. She…"

Monroe squeezed her hands and released. "Thank you for coming."

Monroe didn't sleep for weeks. Bill suggested postponing the wedding, but she refused, saying, "Life is too short." He couldn't argue.

As she rode her horse, the afternoon sun beating on her face, she thought about every word her mother spoke in those final phone calls, trying to compare them to all the words she had spoken before. The words were like an avalanche threatening to overtake her mind. She squeezed her calves and heels and her horse began to gallop. "*You need to find out who you are. Glamour alone isn't a goal. Fancy dresses and parties don't make people happy. Life will disappoint you. You look like tinsel sparkling under twinkly lights.*" Desperate to outrun the avalanche, she applied more pressure and screamed, "Go, Captain." He began galloping at full speed, the wind pushing against her skin, pushing against the words.

Chapter 22

Tash was walking home from her favorite neighborhood boutique, swinging her shopping bag back and forth, when her phone rang. She flipped her sunglasses onto the top of her head and smiled as Lu's name flashed on the screen.

"Hey baby, what's up?"

"Just checking to see if you're comin' tonight," Lu replied.

"As a matter of fact, I just bought the fiercest little dress."

Lu chuckled. "You go, girl."

"Since when did you get so formal? Why not text?" Tash queried.

"Didn't want you to dodge me."

"As iiiiiif," Tash said, exaggerating the word.

"Glad to hear you're back to your old smart ass, it-girl self."

"Well, someone has to save the LA club scene from the monotony of the reality star brigade and their Z-list groupies."

"That's the spirit!" Lu exclaimed.

"I'll see you tonight. Ciao, baby."

"Ciao."

With her favorite eighties playlist blaring and a towel wrapped around her freshly showered body, Tash applied a final coat of hot pink lipstick. She stepped back and puckered her lips, blowing her reflection a kiss. *I need some extra pizazz*, she mused, adding a streak of silver glitter eyeliner above her signature black liquid liner. She batted her long, false eyelashes. *I've still got it.*

The Smiths' "How Soon Is Now" swirled in the air as she strutted into her bedroom and plucked the last couple of pieces of popcorn from the microwave bag on her nightstand, eating them one by one. Her new, sparkling silver dress was hanging on the back of the door. She slipped the slinky mini on, placing the spaghetti straps on her freckled shoulders. *Where are my strappy silver heels?* she wondered, scouring her closet. "Ah, you were hiding! Guess I haven't worn you in a while."

Sitting on the edge of her bed to buckle her shoe straps, she glanced up and saw the picture she and Aidan took on their first day in LA. Hair in a ponytail and makeup-free, she had tried to shield her face, but Aidan insisted on capturing the start of their adventure together. It was the only picture she'd ever put in a frame. She paused to examine their goofy smiles, then grabbed her purse and headed out.

Tash's mood had plummeted by the fifth time she passed the club, searching for a parking space. Circling the block in larger and larger loops felt like a less-than-subtle metaphor for her life. She feared her luck had simply run out. What was once within reach felt further and further away. Everything had always fallen neatly into place, but now nothing quite fit. Even her shoes felt too tight. Lost in her own troubles, she barely noticed the people camping out merely blocks away from the club. When they eventually caught her eye, she realized they were getting closer each month: the truth encroaching on the lie. *Must be more of them. Fuck, it's sad. It's like the fires springing up in the canyons, getting harder to control, harder to keep at bay. They're warnings that there's no such place as paradise, because there's always a shadow side. People here like everything to be airbrushed. They like their pretty pictures. Everything is filtered.* As a yellow Aston Martin zoomed past her, likely carrying fellow club-goers, she was confronted with multiple realities. Her complicated relationship with LA blurred at the intersection of her waning dreams and the stark reality that her life was indeed privileged.

By the time she found a parking spot, she was vacillating between rage and despair, but no longer sure why. Determined to shake it off and have a fabulous night, she turned her attention forward, ignoring everything in the periphery.

Reinvigorated, she breezed past the line of beautiful people. The bouncer ushered her over and unlatched the rope. As she passed through, he called, "How's A? You think he'll ever come back?" Her body clenched, but she turned, smiled at him with a shrug, and then walked into the packed club.

Tash wriggled her way through the crowd, slowly making her way to the bar. She stood for a couple of minutes before Leo handed her a tequila sunrise.

"You're slipping! Your arm's usually out before I make it over," she hollered over the noise.

"I know. Epic fail. Wasn't expecting to see you; you've been MIA. We all figured you went on tour with A after all."

"Nope. Just been busy. But I'm back," she said.

"And hotter than ever, but don't tell your man I said that."

She winked at him and held up her glass. "Cheers," she said, taking a gulp.

Leaning against the bar and steadily sipping her drink, Tash surveyed the room. It was full of the usual suspects. Lu was on the deejay platform, flaunting her favorite vintage David Bowie T-shirt and black leather pants as she rocked her sound. Paisley was holding her own on the dance floor. They were exchanging looks. *Wow, never thought I'd see the day. Lu's totally in love. It's great.* Just then, Lu glanced over, smiled brightly, and cocked her head. Tash held up her arm to say hi in return. Several people asked her to dance and offered to buy her drinks. Despite relishing the attention, she declined, gesturing to the one in her hand. Paisley came over and they chatted for a while. As Tash was finishing her second drink, a tall guy with a chiseled face and midnight-black hair sidled up to her.

"You're the most drop-dead beautiful woman here tonight. You know that, right?" he asked in a sexy English accent.

"That's quite the line," she replied.

"Ah, I'm gutted," he said, grabbing his chest. "I did want to impress you, but I can tell that's no easy task."

The corners of her mouth turned up in an almost imperceptible smile.

"Take pity on me and have a dance?" he asked.

She gave him the once-over, took the last sip of her drink, and nodded. With electro-techno beats guiding the way, they made their way onto the dance floor. Tash danced freely, happily losing herself in the moment. After fifteen minutes, her dance partner leaned in and said, "By the way, my name is Liam."

"I'm Tash."

"Oh, I know who you are," he shouted over the music.

Puzzled, she leaned in closer. "What do you mean?"

"My friends told me you're A-A-Aidan's muse. Don't worry, I know you're taken. I'm a musician and I was just hoping some of that good luck might rub off on me."

Repelled, she stepped back. Bodies whirled all around her, but Tash was perfectly still.

"Oh, I'm sorry. I didn't mean to offend you," Liam said.

"No problem. I need a break. See ya," she said, as she walked away.

His muse? Just like that fucking dream. Is that how people fucking see me now? Her internal rant continued all the way to the restroom where she intended to regroup. She tried to calm down, but her mind was flooded with warring images of herself – those projected from others were indecipherable from her own. She wanted to be carefree and strong, but another part of her wanted to run home and crawl into bed. *Fuck that. And fuck Aidan for putting me in this situation. I should be able to have a good fucking time.*

Determined to "have fun" no matter what, she made a beeline for the bar and ordered a third drink. Halfway through her cocktail, Texas appeared.

"Hey there, pretty lady," he said, running his fingers through his shaggy blonde hair.

"Hey, Texas. How ya been?"

"Can't complain, can't complain. Missing you, of course. Where you been hiding out?"

"Not hiding, just busy."

"Well, I sure am glad you're here tonight. This place is stuffed to the gills with rich kids blowing their trust funds."

"Yeah, nothing stays cool around here for long," Tash groaned.

"I don't want your boyfriend to kick my ass, but I must say, holy smokes you're looking mighty fine."

"He's not around these days, so I wouldn't worry about it."

"In that case, you want to finally grace me with your presence on the dance floor?"

Just as she was about to respond, Lu announced another deejay was taking over while she took a short break.

"Sorry, Texas. My friend is coming over. Later, okay?"

"Sure thing, pretty lady. Find me."

Tash watched as he walked away. Lu leapt off the platform, said something to Paisley, and then made her way to the bar.

"Damn, girl! You weren't kidding. You look amazing," Lu said.

"Thanks, baby. You're looking like a total boss, as usual."

Lu shrugged sarcastically. "Well, you know, I gotta represent. You having a good time?"

"Trying," Tash replied. She inhaled deeply, but before she could elaborate, the deejay made an announcement, and they both turned to listen.

"Hey everyone! It's midnight, and that means our very own A-A-Aidan's album has dropped." He paused to thunderous applause, before continuing, "This is my mix of our boy's single. To your feet, LA!"

Aidan's music swelled and the club was electric. Lu slowly turned to Tash.

"Well, bottoms up, baby," Tash said, raising her drink and downing what was left.

"Hey, you. Take it easy or I'll have to carry you home. My place isn't big enough for three."

"Goddamn it," Tash muttered.

"I was just teasing," Lu said.

"No, it's not that. I'm so stupid, I fucking drove here. It was force of habit, I guess. I always drive and then Aidan drives us home. You know he's a straight edge."

"How many have you had?" Lu asked.

"A few," she replied, playing with the straw in her empty glass.

"Leave your car and Paisley and I will drive you. We'll get your car tomorrow."

"I don't wanna stay all night," Tash whined.

"So Uber it. Paisley will take you to get your car tomorrow."

"Yeah, I guess that will work. Thanks," Tash mumbled.

"Listen, I gotta go to the bathroom and see Paisley before I jump back up there. Promise you won't drive?"

"Scout's honor," Tash said, doing the sign of the cross over her chest.

"Uh, yeah, that's so not from the Scouts. Definitely don't drive."

Tash smiled. "I promise. Go have a good set. Big shoes to fill," she slurred.

Lu winced. "See ya, babe."

"Later."

Two hours and two more drinks later, Tash was dancing with Texas when she began to lose her balance, falling into him with increasing regularity.

"Well, there, pretty lady. Maybe you need a little break," he suggested.

"Yeah, maybe I do," she replied.

She tottered over to the bar, occasionally stumbling onto him. He lent a hand as needed. Paisley spotted Tash's inebriated stumbles and came over.

"Tash, do you want me to call an Uber for you?"

"I don't want to leave my car here. Can't get another ticket," she slurred.

"I only had one drink, hours ago. I can drive you in your car if you want," Texas offered.

"How will you get home?" Tash asked.

"Uber. No difference to me if it's from here or your place."

"Paisley, I'm gonna go with my good friend Texas, here. We go way back," she said, patting his chest.

"Okay, drink a glass of water and take something for your head when you get home," Paisley suggested.

Tash nodded, grabbed Texas by the arm, and they headed out into the night.

A few minutes later, Paisley was hanging out on the deejay platform. Lu leaned over and asked, "I saw Tash leave. Did you get her a car?"

"Her friend offered to drive her."

"What friend?"

"Some guy, Texas. She said they're good friends."

Lu shook her head. "He's just a dude that has a monster crush on her."

"Oh my God, is she unsafe?" Paisley asked in a panic.

"Probably only from herself. Oh Tash, what are you doing?" she mumbled.

The task of finding Tash's car wasn't made any easier by her poor memory or the fact that she was having trouble balancing in her heels. When they eventually got in the car, Texas asked for her address, which she was miraculously able to communicate along with directions. He opened the windows and she complained, "My hair's gonna get all messed up."

"I think the fresh air will do ya some good," he said. "How about some tunes?"

"Okay," she replied.

He turned the music on and the sounds of the eighties came storming through the speakers. He lowered the volume and said, "Dig the throwback tunes."

"Yeah, me too, or I used to," she mumbled.

"Something bothering you, pretty lady? I got the feeling you were maybe trying to escape a little tonight."

Tash sighed. "Let me ask you something, Texas. Why'd you come to LA?"

"Came to sunny Los Angeles to get away from my family. Woulda gone clear across the country, but I love the warm weather. The big ole Pacific beckoned. Figured I'd take up surfin'."

"You an actor or something?"

"No way. I work at a Mexican restaurant. Saving for a food truck with one of my buddies."

"Wow, Texas. You know, you may be the perfect guy. You're the only person I know who's not here for the bullshit."

"There's no bullshit about you either, I'd reckon."

"Ha! You'd be wrong."

"Havin' a dream don't make it bullshit. Like my food truck. It may not happen, but ain't nothin' wrong with working for it."

"Hmm. Yeah, I guess," she mumbled.

When they arrived at Tash's apartment building, Texas parked the car. They both got out and he handed her the keys.

"Thanks, Texas. You're a nice guy. Such a nice guy," she said, nearly falling onto him. "And you're so good looking. Have I told you that?" she asked.

He blushed and cocked his head. "Can you make it into your apartment?"

"You've been flirting with me for ages."

"Uh, yes I have. Pretty hard not to. You seen yourself?"

Tash smiled. "That's just what I mean. You always make me feel good. But…"

"But you're definitely drunk and I'm pretty sure you still have a boyfriend. So, if you're okay to make it in, I'm gonna keep on being a nice guy, even though I'll kick myself tomorrow."

She gave him a long look, smiled, and said, "See ya, Texas."

"See ya, pretty lady."

A few minutes later, Tash finally stumbled into her apartment. Dropping her keys on the floor beside the entry table, she made her way to her bedroom. She plopped onto her bed, unbuckled her shoes, and flicked them off. Her feet were throbbing. She took off her dress and slipped on a tank top she found on the floor. *I need to lie down, but if I fall asleep with all this crap on my face, I'll regret it.* Resisting the urge to fall over on the bed, she forced herself to the bathroom. *Music. I need music so I won't pass out.* She flipped her eighties playlist back on, and Duran Duran's "Save a Prayer" filled the room. She listened to the words, staring at her reflection, and thinking about how shamelessly she flirted with Texas. Smeared eyeliner, sweat marks on her face, and a pit in her stomach were all reminders that she had nearly fallen to a new low. She pulled off her false eyelashes and took a long, hard look in the mirror. *I can't believe I came home with Texas. What the fuck was I thinking? If he wasn't such a stand-up guy, what would have happened? I'm such an asshole sometimes. And Aidan. Fucking Aidan. He put up with so much shit with me when we first hooked up. He deserves better. I'm not good enough for him.* As she looked at herself with disdain, her eyes began to well up and tears flowed down her face. She just stood there, drunk and crying. Finally able to catch her breath, she washed her face and raised her gaze to the mirror, patting herself dry. Puffy eyes, freckled skin, and regret stared back at her. She dropped the towel on the floor, shuffled into her bedroom, and collapsed into the bed. She grabbed Aidan's pillow and clenched it tightly until she fell asleep.

Chapter 23

Tash woke up late morning, her mouth dry and head throbbing. She grumbled as she opened her eyes, the light piercing her brain. In desperate need of ibuprofen, she dragged herself out of bed and stumbled to the bathroom. Glimpsing herself in the mirror, she recoiled, all the night's foibles etched on her bloodshot eyes and puffy face. She opened the medicine cabinet, retrieved the bottle of ibuprofen, and popped four into her mouth. She turned on the faucet, cupped her hands to collect some water, and then threw back the pills in one gulp. With the medicine cabinet still flung open and pill bottle on the sink, she stumbled back to bed. *Sleep. Please let me fall back asleep until my headache is gone.* Despite the sharp pain emanating from her temples, deep exhaustion won out and she drifted back to sleep.

Tash opened her eyes again at noon, grateful to find that her headache had abated. She wanted to go back to sleep to avoid facing the day for as long as possible, but her stomach growled so she got out of bed and lumbered to the kitchen. Aidan's box of Lucky Charms was on the top of the refrigerator. She grabbed the box, stuck her hand in to scoop out some cereal, and hopped onto the counter. Munching on the sweet morsels, she pictured Aidan, standing in his boxers, pouring cereal into a bowl, and then grabbing a fistful to eat dry. Her eyes welled with tears. "No Tash, not again. Not now," she said, wiping her eyes. She finished the cereal, hopped down, and tossed the box in the recycling bin. "Pull yourself together and just do it for him," she whispered. "He can't see me like this. I can't fuck things up for him. Don't be selfish, Tash. Not to him."

She walked into the bedroom, sat on the edge of her bed, and reached for her phone on the nightstand. With the phone gripped tightly in her hands, she took a deep breath, and then, feeling together, called Aidan.

"Hey, beauty queen!" he said.

"Hey, superstar. Congratulations! I can't believe your record is out."

"Yeah, me neither."

"How do you feel?"

"Well, I'm trying to be chill about it with everyone else, but between us, I'm pretty pumped."

"You should be. It's freaking awesome," she said, pausing for a moment before adding, "I'm so proud of you. I really am." As the words left her mouth, she knew she meant them and felt a twinge of relief.

"Thanks. You know, it goes both ways."

His words hit her like a dagger to the heart. She slumped over and inhaled deeply, intent on holding it together. Eventually, Aidan filled the silence.

"I wish you would have FaceTimed so I could see your gorgeous face."

"Believe me, I'm sparing you. Partied a little too hard last night."

"Ah."

"They gave you a huge shout-out at the club. Everyone's really happy for you."

"That's sweet. Glad to hear you went out. From your texts, I get the feeling you've been laying low. You getting any work done?"

"Not really, but I will. You know how tricky inspiration can be."

"Sure do. That's why we can't wait for the muses to visit, we have to chase them."

Hearing those words, Tash couldn't keep the tears back any longer. She sniffled a bit and softly said, "Yeah, I know. I will."

"Are you okay?" he asked.

"Uh huh."

"Really? Because I have no interest in moving backward. We need to be open with each other."

She sighed. "You know I can't keep things from you. I did something kind of stupid last night and I feel like crap."

"How stupid?" he asked, his tone sharper. "Something that can't be undone?"

"No, I stopped myself because," she hesitated, searching for the words before concluding, "because that's not who I want to be."

"Then let it go. We all screw up, but we can't let our mistakes define who we are. Focus on who you are today. Today is what you have."

She smiled, wiping the tears from her cheeks.

"I'm pretty lucky to have you," she said.

"You are," he agreed with a laugh. "Get out in the LA sunshine today. Hit the Getty or the beach."

"Yeah, that's probably a good idea."

"So, how's everything else? Who was spinning at the club last night?"

"Lu, and oh my God, she's totally head over heels. Remember that chick, Paisley, I told you she was sleeping with? Well, they're going strong and I've never seen Lu like this before. I think this might be it for her, although she'd never admit it."

Tash and Aidan continued talking for ten minutes. After they hung up, Tash jumped in the shower, determined to wash away the last night, the last few weeks, and the last residue of who she used to be.

"Rise and shine," Lu said, gently stroking Paisley's arm. "I made you breakfast in bed."

"What?" Paisley mumbled, as she opened her eyes.

"I made you breakfast in bed," Lu repeated. "Well, I guess it's more like brunch in bed. It's almost one o'clock."

"Yeah, but the sun was up by the time we went to sleep," Paisley countered, slowly sitting up with a yawn. "How long have you been up?"

"Hours. Couldn't sleep," Lu said as she placed a tray in front of Paisley.

"Uh, yeah, I see that. I can't believe you made me breakfast."

"It's nothing fancy, just oatmeal with strawberries and coffee," Lu replied.

"It's perfect. Thank you," Paisley said, taking a sip of coffee.

Lu smiled.

"Why couldn't you sleep? Are you worried about Tash?"

"She's having a really tough time. That's what last night was about."

"Have you heard from her?" Paisley asked, taking a bite of oatmeal.

Lu shook her head. "She'll text me when she's ready. I don't want to push her. We have an unspoken understanding."

Paisley looked at Lu, wide-eyed. "Is it all about missing her boyfriend?"

"It's about her feeling like he's on a rocket to the stars and she's stuck on the ground. They actually moved here for her, so she could break into filmmaking. She's faced a lot of roadblocks, a lot of disappointments, and a lot of bullshit, you know? And suddenly, out of the blue, he's catapulted into the stratosphere and he wasn't even trying." She paused before adding, "And she feels guilty."

Paisley furrowed her brow.

"She feels guilty because she knows she should support him, but the truth is that a part of her resents his success."

"And what about you?" Paisley asked.

"What about me?" Lu replied.

"Is it hard for you?"

"I mean, if I'm really honest, yeah. Aidan is the nicest guy in the world, truly, and he's big time talented. Don't get me wrong – I'm happy for him. But I've been here a lot longer and it's frustrating because as a woman on the circuit, these things just don't happen. Like, *never*. Guys see talent in other guys. They see them as their buddies and they want to go on the road with them. There's no fairness in it, and that always gets to me. And it's not like that kind of success is even my dream; I really just love the music. But it's tough knowing it could never be me."

"I'm sorry," Paisley said.

"Don't be. It's all good. I've just gotta keep reminding myself that the music is what matters."

Just then, Lu's phone beeped. She grabbed it to see a message from Tash, which she read out loud.

`Hey. I'm fine. Texas was a perfect gentleman. Sorry if I worried you.`

"I'm so relieved. I would have felt awful if something happened to her," Paisley said.

"Me too."

Paisley ate a heaping spoonful of oatmeal with a slice of strawberry. "Mmm. This is so good. How come you're so sweet?"

"I'm not. I guess you bring out the best in me."

Tash walked along the beach, holding her flip flops as the water rushed across her feet. Looking across the vast cobalt sea, a sense of abundance began to take hold. Mesmerized by the water, she walked farther than planned and soon found herself at the Santa Monica Pier. *Well, why not*, she thought, deciding to take a stroll down the landmark.

Children holding soft-serve ice cream cones that melted down their arms walked past her, couples took photographs with selfie sticks, and the famous Ferris wheel slowly spun against the cloudless sky. Craving something sweet, she bought pink cotton candy, indulging in a few sugary bites before tossing it. After a caricaturist tried to convince her to have her portrait done, she decided she'd had enough of the boardwalk. She turned to leave and saw Darrell sitting on a stool with a small painting at his feet, his dreads pulled back in an elastic.

"Hey, Darrell. How's it going?"

"Can't complain."

Tash picked up the painting of a woman's face painted in shades of blue; her eyes were haunting. It was reminiscent of a Picasso and Modigliani hybrid. "Nice work."

"Thanks. Sold a few other small ones today. Funny how the same painting that sells for thousands in a gallery is only worth about sixty bucks on the street." He chuckled. "I'm thinking about calling it a day, it's pretty hot in the sun," he said, beads of sweat dripping down his face.

"Can I give you a ride? My car is a few blocks down."

"That would be great. Thank you."

Darrell folded the legs on his stool, picked up his painting, and they headed home. During the ride, he asked about her work and Tash told him about her short film. As a fellow artist, and one who'd been working at it a bit longer, she realized he might have valuable insights and could help her brainstorm.

"I think I got distracted by the Hollywood thing and how people play the game. Even when I was taking classes, if you didn't follow a certain path, the professors wouldn't throw their weight behind you and you couldn't get into the festivals. My work is artistic," she explained. "A gallery was interested in screening my film, but I blew them off. I was stupid."

"Which gallery?" he asked.

"Patty Price's gallery down on…"

He cut her off. "I know the place. Patty is cool. You should stop by and see if she's still interested."

"Yeah, maybe," Tash said. "You know of any other good galleries?"

"When I first came here, I checked them all out. The scene here didn't exactly welcome me. It was happening for me in New York; I was a part of two group shows in SoHo, and there was this art dealer who hooked me up with high-end clients. Hoped it would translate here, but LA is a fickle place."

"Tell me about it. Fuck. Why'd you leave New York? Sounds like you had it made."

Darrell laughed. "Life happens, you know? Choices have to be made. Come to my place and I'll show you my work."

"Sure," Tash said.

When they arrived at their building, Tash followed Darrell into his apartment, a spacious studio that smelled like turpentine and was overflowing with paintings. Every inch of wall space was covered, and stacks of canvases lined the perimeter of the room. Darrell's life clearly revolved around his art. Half the paintings were of the same subject: a forlorn, dark-haired woman with haunting eyes. Tash stood before one piece, studying it.

"That's Sara, my girlfriend," Darrell said.

"Oh, I didn't know…"

"She's the reason I'm in LA. We lived together in New York for three years. She's a poet. We had wonderful conversations about art, philosophy, religion, all the big ideas, while we worked. I did most of the talking, but she would listen to me, sometimes for hours, encouraging me to go on. She was always quiet, but then one day, her quietness seemed to take hold, like she retreated into herself. Soon she was completely mute and it was as if her beautiful eyes had filmed over."

"Oh my God," Tash mumbled.

"We tried different medications. Nothing worked. I think that shit made her worse. She was from California and I thought the warm weather might help."

"Did it?"

"When her parents saw how bad she was doing, they had her committed to an institution. I'm not even allowed to see her. They blame me for everything."

"That's awful. I'm so sorry," Tash said. "Can I ask why you didn't move back to New York, if it was better for your career?"

"When she's released, I need to be here. This was our last home together."

"How long has it been?"

"Five years. But she'll come back, one day, when she's ready. She'll come back to herself and back to me. I kinda think she's taking a time out from the noise and composing a really long poem. And I'm lucky – I have my art to keep me busy until she's ready to share her beautiful voice again."

Tash smiled.

They said goodbye and Tash headed to her apartment. She grabbed her laptop and plopped onto the bed. She hovered the mouse over the link to her film and clicked on it. For the first time in a long time, she watched her own film.

Chapter 24

The day after watching her film, Tash woke up with a fire in her belly. *Be fucking brave*, she told herself. She made a pot of coffee and began an online search for art galleries in Los Angeles, San Francisco, and New York. She decided to start with the local galleries. Adept at using her charisma as currency, she figured her chances were better if she could pitch her case in person.

She visited every gallery and artist cooperative on the list. Some gallerists shooed her off and said that they don't accept "unsolicited works," others said they weren't interested in film work, and some claimed their calendars were booked for years. A couple agreed to watch her film and "let her know." Tired but determined, she sat in her car outside of the last place on her LA list: the Patty Price Gallery. Tash started biting her nails, desperately trying to muster the courage to face Patty, the one gallerist who had loved *Pop Candy*, and the one who Tash had naively blown off. *Be brave. Be fucking brave*, she told herself as she hopped out of the car.

She walked into the gallery. It was her favorite space in LA, with dark wood floors, high ceilings with exposed pipes, and white walls meticulously displaying large, abstract artworks. Tash felt it was the only gallery in LA that had the "it factor" that the New York scene possessed in spades. A young woman with short brown hair was sitting at the desk. Tash walked right over, shoulders back and head high.

"Hi. My name is Tash Daniels and I met with Ms. Price about a year ago. She was interested in showing my short film. I was hoping she might consider it again. Can I leave a message for her?" she asked, handing her a one-page resume.

A voice from behind called, "That won't be necessary."

Tash turned to see none other than Patty Price walking toward her, with her signature dark-rimmed glasses, red lipstick, and perfectly pin-straight, brown bob.

"Patty, it's wonderful to see you. I don't know if you remember me, but my name is Tash Daniels and..."

Patty cut her off. "I remember. You had a film. Seems like forever ago. You know how quickly the art world moves."

"Uh, yes, I do. Listen Patty, I want to apologize for not taking you up on your generous offer to screen the film. At the time..."

Patty put her hand up. "No need to explain. It wasn't right for you. It's your art. I get it."

"Well, that's the thing. I've reconsidered and I was wondering if you might be willing to give me another chance. If you'd just watch it again..."

"I'm booked solid for the next two years. We have your information on file. Thanks for stopping by." Patty abruptly turned to her assistant and began talking.

Tash quietly said, "Thank you," and left.

Although disappointed, Tash kept her spirits up. *Nothing ventured, nothing gained. Be brave.* She also knew that while many people could open or close doors, she was the architect of her own life. Her art and her happiness were in her hands. The weight of that responsibility finally felt like something she could handle, and for the first time, she embraced it.

The next day, she called all the out-of-town galleries on her list. Monroe texted that she decided to extend her trip, so Tash spent the next three weeks making lists of galleries in other cities, researching funding opportunities, and writing. Not quite ready to write her full-length script, she played with ideas. It was thrilling to be back in the creative zone, both planning and experimenting, finally working toward something. Most days she'd forget to eat until her stomach started grumbling in the late afternoon.

The day before Tash's birthday, Monroe returned. Tash stopped by to review final details for the upcoming studio anniversary party. When Tash met her poolside, she noticed Monroe looked run down. They discussed party details, but as their meeting wrapped up, Tash felt compelled to express her concern.

"Are you feeling okay? You look a little tired," Tash remarked.

"Oh, you're sweet to ask. I haven't been sleeping well, but I'm fine."

Monroe quickly changed the subject, giving Tash a pair of gold earrings from Tiffany's and the next two days off to celebrate her birthday. Tash beamed at the sight of the earrings, thanking her profusely.

"It's my pleasure. Wear them well."

"If that's all," Tash said, standing up.

Monroe smiled. "Oh, before you go, I wanted to remind you to pick up the silver pens from the engraver by the end of the day, for the studio party gift bags."

"No problem. I'm heading home to do a few things, but I'll get there before they close."

Tash picked up her Tiffany's gift bag and turned back to Monroe. "Are you sure you're okay?"

"Nothing a little sunshine and sleep can't fix," Monroe replied. "Maybe I'll do a face mask. That always helps."

Tash smiled. "Go for it."

Running late to make it to the engravers, Tash was frantically search-ing for her keys when her phone rang. "Fuck, I don't have time for this," she grumbled, but looked to see who was calling anyway. It was a local number that she didn't recognize. Thinking it might be the engraver or one of the other vendors for Monroe's upcoming party, she answered.

"Hello, this is Tash."

"Tash, Patty Price here."

"Oh, hi Patty," Tash said, her heart racing.

"Listen, I'll cut to it. You've probably seen that story on the news about the English video artist arrested for child porn."

"Uh..."

"Well, he was supposed to be a part of a group show starting in two weeks. Apparently, his love for video production was more var-ied than any of us knew."

"Wow, Patty. That's awful."

"Yeah, well it worked out for you. We were going to show one of his short films in our media room. Now there's a slot open. I know I wasn't that receptive when you came by, but your work would fit right in. Truth is, I love your film, have since you first showed it to me. Talent is what matters. And you had the chutzpah to come back here. I figure women like us should stick together."

"Thank you. I don't know what to say."

"Say yes. I'm in a rush, dealing with the nightmare of redoing all the signage, flyers, and media announcements."

"Yes. Of course. Thank you."

"My assistant will email you the details. Make sure you're on time for setup, I don't want any problems. And spread the word about the show."

"Okay. And Patty, really, thank you for this."

Tash hung up the phone and jumped up and down. *Did that just happen?* She leaned against the wall and inhaled deeply, wanting to savor this moment, the culmination of many small, unspoken acts of bravery.

Chapter 25

After yet another restless night, Monroe crawled out of bed and dragged herself to the bathroom. She stood in front of the mirror, examining the ever-darker circles under her eyes. Her arms felt heavy and her movements were lethargic, but she reached for her toothbrush anyway. Robotically brushing her teeth and washing her face, her only thought was how desperately she longed to sleep. Too exhausted to read, she left her book on her nightstand and headed down for breakfast. She stopped in front of her Warhol, captivated by Marilyn's expression. *Hmm. Today is August fifth, Tash's birthday. Isn't that the day they found your body, Marilyn? How your death must have shattered the myth people cling to, that a perfect life exists. But it wasn't about them, it was about you. I do wonder what happened. Perhaps you were you just so tired, tired of all of it, that you decided to sleep forever. Maybe it was subconscious. We'll never know, and yet, I feel I understand somehow.* She stood for a moment, blankly staring at the painting. *I should wish Tash a happy birthday.*

After spending the day watching her favorite films, a birthday tradition, Tash treated herself to Chinese takeout in bed. She maneuvered some lo mein out of the box, tipped her head back, and sucked down the noodles. There was something comforting about the feel of chopsticks between her fingers and a takeout container on her lap. It reminded her of late nights in New York watching TV in bed with Jason and Penelope. She smiled, grateful that her life was no longer about forgetting but remembering. Before long, she had finished the last spring roll and it was time to get ready for her party.

Thinking it would be a downer to dress up like Jem when Aidan wasn't there to be Rio, she had decided to go as Susan, the title character from *Desperately Seeking Susan*. She put her favorite playlist on shuffle, laughing when Foreigner's "Urgent" came on. Opting to go big or go home, she gave her makeup an eighties vibe with heavily shadowed eyes, rosy cheeks, and rouge-stained lips. She styled her hair in large ringlets at the ends, admiring herself before getting dressed. Decked out in black pants, a black bustier, sparkle boots, and several strands of rhinestones and faux pearls, she looked like she stepped right out of the film. As she admired herself in the full-length mirror, her phone beeped. The driver Aidan hired was waiting outside. *Time to get into the groove,* she thought, winking at herself before grabbing her purse and heading out the door.

Tash arrived at the club to see a line around the corner and many people dressed up in eighties attire. There were two signs outside that said, "Come Party '80s Style," and a third directing birthday party guests to the VIP entrance. Tash headed to the VIP door where she was given a wristband for drinks. "Happy Birthday! Have a blast," the bouncer said. She smiled and walked inside. Immediately, her group of friends and the club regulars cheered. Tash blushed. The entire place was decorated with neon twinkly lights and streamers. The bar was running a special on "Tash's Tequila Sunrise," and a half-naked male model was passing out feather boas. Tash smiled hard. *Oh, Aidan. I can't believe you remembered that night in New York.*

As she made her way through the crowd, friends wished her a happy birthday, and soon, strangers did too. Texas was among the well-wishers. He tipped his head and said, "Happy Birthday!" She tipped her head in return, put her hands on her heart, and said, "Thank you. Really, thank you." He smiled and walked off. Tash continued to the bar, where she was promptly handed a cocktail. As she was chatting with the bartender, someone tapped her shoulder. She put her drink down and turned around to see Jason. Her eyes lit up, her jaw dropped, and she started screaming, "Oh my God! I can't believe you're here! I can't believe you flew in from New York! Oh my God!"

Jason laughed and pulled her to him. They hugged each other tightly for so long it was as if time stopped. When they finally released, Tash had tears in her eyes.

"I could fucking kill you," she said, smacking his chest. "My makeup is gonna be a mess."

He laughed. "That's the price you pay for my presence. But get your shit together, we don't want to make a scene."

"I can't believe you're here. I'm so happy!" As Tash sniffled, trying to pull herself together, she got a better look at Jason. He was wearing a shiny purple blazer and had matching purple spray layered over his black hair. "What's with the purple?"

"Aidan said you were coming as Jem. I'm your Rio. But I see you're doing the Madonna thing instead," he said, taking her hand and twirling her around. "I dig it."

"Aidan told you?" she asked, searching her purse for a tissue.

"He called me as soon as he found out he had to miss your party. He bought me a plane ticket and put me up in a hotel so I could surprise you."

"I can't believe he did that," Tash said, dabbing her eyes, careful not to smudge her makeup.

"Yes, you can."

She looked down, smiling. "Yeah, he's the best."

"So, I need a drink and then we dance."

Tash nodded. She wiped her nose, stuffed the tissue in her pocket, and got Jason's drink. They clinked glasses.

"To you being more fabulous than ever!" he exclaimed.

"And to you being here," she added.

"Cheers and Happy Birthday, T," he said.

"Cheers."

A-ha's "Take on Me" came on and everyone in the club cheered. Tash patted Jason's chest. "Oh my God. I love this song so much. Too perfect."

"Yeah. Aidan really outdid himself," Jason observed, scanning the room.

"Speak of the devil," Tash said, retrieving her vibrating phone from her pocket. "He's calling."

"Hey there," she said loudly over the music, pressing her fingers to her free ear to block out the sound.

"Did my present arrive?"

"He's here. I can't believe you did this. I was so surprised."

"That was the plan, beauty queen."

"It's the best present I ever got."

"Aw, shucks," Aidan said, with a laugh. "So, tell me, how are you?"

Tash inhaled deeply. "Slowly learning that life is okay."

He laughed. "That's my girl. Get back to your party. Tell Jason he's the man."

"Yeah, I will." She paused before saying, "And Aidan, thank you."

After Tash hung up, Jason took her hand and led her to the dance floor. They danced for twenty minutes before taking a break to get some water. Engrossed in conversation, they were startled when Lu and Paisley joined them. Lu was dressed in black leather pants and a white T-shirt. She claimed to be an eighties singer but Tash heckled her for looking practically the same as she always does. In contrast, Paisley went all out. She was dressed as Rainbow Brite, complete with rainbows painted on her cheeks, arms, and legs. Jason took one look at her and said, "See, Tash? I told you Rainbow Brite was gay!" They all laughed.

They spent hours drinking, dancing, and laughing. At one point, someone put a white feather boa around Tash's shoulders. She stood in the middle of the dance floor, surrounded by her friends and hundreds of bodies in motion, feathers flying in the air and lightness in her heart.

Monroe slipped on her favorite gray silk nightgown and matching robe, and tied the sash around her waist. She opened her nightstand drawer and retrieved the unopened prescription bottle. Sitting on the edge of her bed and rolling the bottle in her hand, it occurred to her that she felt no emotion whatsoever. No sadness, or despair, or grief held her hand. Exhaustion was her only companion. She was done. After moving the bottle from one hand to the other, over and over again, she tucked it into her pocket. She got up and wandered through her house until she found Bill in his office, hunched over the desk.

"It's so late, darling. Why don't you come to bed?" she asked.

"I'll be there soon enough. I have to get through these papers first," he replied, gesturing to the stack on his desk.

"Good night, Bill. I love you. Truly, I do," Monroe said, before gently shutting the door behind her.

She bumped into Henry on her way back to her bedroom.

"Good night, Henry," she said softly.

"Good night, Mrs. Preston. Oh, I forgot to tell you that Miss Daniels left her short film here yesterday. She said you had asked to see it."

"Oh, that's right. I did promise her," she mumbled to herself. Then she refocused on Henry. "Maybe I'll watch it now. I know it's late, but would you mind putting it on for me in the screening room?"

"Certainly, ma'am," he replied.

Monroe settled into one of the raspberry-colored velvet seats in their lavish private screening room. Henry switched the lights off as the film began. Light from the screen flickered on Monroe's face as the opening credits rolled. Shot in black and white, the camera zoomed in on two young people on a city rooftop in the middle of the night. They were laughing and running across the roof, bits of paper swept up in the breeze. A burst of hot pink leapt off the screen, followed by eruptions of turquoise and purple. Monroe leaned closer. The corners of her mouth trembled and a smile began to crawl across her face. She leaned closer and let the glow from the screen wash over her. Her smile morphed into laughter and tears flooded her eyes. As her smile grew and her laughter became louder, the tears flowed harder. Her face was drenched by the time the closing credits rolled. She sat, soaking in a feeling she couldn't quite name, a feeling she knew was connected to life itself.

Henry returned and flipped the lights on. "Shall I close the room for you before I retire to bed?" he asked.

She wiped her face with her palms and turned to face him. "No. Henry, please get Bill right away. Tell him there's something he must see."

PART SIX

Chapter 26

Lu woke up to find Paisley's arm slung across her chest. Careful not to wake her, she gently maneuvered herself out of bed. As she searched the floor for a T-shirt to slip on, she noticed rainbow paint smeared across her chest and legs. Her hands were sticky, so she looked and discovered more paint. *I told her not to do the face paint*, she thought, although she couldn't help but laugh. *Definitely need strong coffee today.*

Still groggy, she shuffled to the kitchen. Given the demands of her day and night jobs, paired with an unpredictable sleep schedule, it was the smell of coffee that helped denote the start of a new day, whether at seven in the morning or two in the afternoon. So, she ignored the paint on her hands in favor of starting the coffee pot. After hitting the brew button, she went to the bathroom and got a look at herself in the mirror. Her hair was matted on one side and there was a multi-colored streak – red, orange, yellow, green, and blue – on her face. "Well, that's a new look," she mumbled.

She flipped the shower on, praying it would be hot by the time she finished brushing her teeth. She swished mouthwash around until her teeth gleamed. Stepping into the shower, she breathed a deep sigh of relief. The water was hot. She rubbed the bar of soap in her hands until it lathered, and then she scrubbed the rainbow splotches in a circular motion. The colors started to meld together, creating a light film of color all over her body. It dawned on her that she was quite literally covered in Paisley. Suddenly, the paint felt like more than an amusing annoyance. It was getting harder to tell where she ended and Paisley began. This made her uncomfortable. She didn't want to think about it, so as she had done for most of her life, she focused on the task at hand and pushed the distressing thoughts to the far edge of her mind. She took the bar of soap and vigorously rubbed it directly on her body, watching the colors trickle down until they circled the drain. When the water ran clear, she could breathe again.

Lu emerged from the bathroom, drying her hair with a towel.

"I just poured myself a cup of coffee. You want some?" Paisley called.

"Fuck," Lu grumbled, having just pulled a muscle in her neck at being startled.

"You okay?" Paisley called.

"Yeah, just a neck strain. It's fine."

"Coffee?" Paisley asked again.

"Yeah, please," Lu replied, tossing her towel in the corner. "I thought you'd still be asleep. Did I wake you?" she asked, before taking a seat at the small table.

"The smell did. You know there's paint on the handle of the coffee pot?" Paisley said as she took the milk out of the refrigerator to splash some in Lu's mug.

"Yeah, it pretty much got everywhere."

Paisley bit her lip. She handed Lu a mug of steaming coffee, taking the seat opposite her. "Uh, yeah. Sorry about that. Guess I kinda went overboard."

Lu smiled and blew on her coffee before taking a sip. "That's okay. It's sweet you went all out for Tash. Besides, it's a reminder of a fun night. Better than a hangover, eh?"

Paisley giggled. "I hope Tash had a great time. It seemed like she did."

"She definitely did. I think she spent most of the summer dreading her birthday. It's hard to celebrate when you feel low, but she's doing a lot better. I can tell. Having Jason there meant the world to her."

"I guess I was sort of dreading it too. I mean, not the party, per se, but just that it's a marker of time. I've been thinking about how the summer's almost over." Paisley looked down, as if searching for the words. "I start teaching again soon."

"That's right," Lu said. "I almost forgot."

"Yeah, well, the thing is I won't be able to be on your schedule anymore. I mean, I'll be working during the day, so I won't be able to go to clubs as much and you know always crash here."

Lu silently sipped her coffee and Paisley continued.

"I mean, I can come on the weekends, but…"

"Look, I get it. This summer has been amazing, but you need to get back to your life."

"Well, I wouldn't exactly put it that way. You're obviously a part of my life. A big part. But things will change." She looked at her feet, something obviously on her mind.

Lu slipped her hand into Paisley's hand and asked, "What is it?"

"Come to my place tomorrow. My folks invited us over for brunch. They've been dying to meet you."

Lu pulled her hand away and shifted back in her seat. "I'm not so great with parents. Never been into the whole family thing."

"They're not like that. You'll like each other; they're cool. My mom's really into music. And they're important to me, so I want you to know each other. Besides, if you met them, maybe you'd be more comfortable staying at my place sometimes. I'm sure you've avoided it because of the whole parents thing. You'll see that the guest house is actually really private. That way, when I'm teaching, we could maybe go back and forth."

Lu inhaled and took another sip of coffee.

"It's just brunch. I promise, you'll like them."

Lu looked down, squirming in her seat, and then looked up at Paisley. She noticed the flecks of aquamarine sparkling in her eyes, the brown freckle on the tip of her nose, and the soft pink indent at the edge of her upper lip: the beautiful rainbow of Paisley's face of which she never tired. "Yeah, okay. I'll come to brunch. I have to open the juice bar, but I can take off at eleven."

Paisley crinkled her face into a silly smile as her cheeks reddened. She put her mug down and leaned forward to kiss Lu. Then she jumped up and said, "I'm taking a shower."

Lu continued drinking her coffee, wondering what she had gotten herself into. Paisley was thinking about the future, and what's more, how their futures were tied together. Lu was fiercely independent, "an island," Tash always joked. She had never allowed herself to need another or to be needed. The idea of a family being more than a random group with whom meals and homes are forcibly and temporarily shared was foreign to her. She had no interest in spending time with family, including her own, whom she visited once a year on Thanksgiving out of obligation and spoke to on the phone only a few times more. Although she periodically flirted with feelings of guilt for her lack of interest in people she described as "good folks who did their best," those thoughts were few and far between. She rarely thought of them at all.

As she listened to the water from the shower, Lu wondered what she would tell Paisley's parents about herself. She hated answering questions about her upbringing. Her peers simply accepted her as Lu K, hot LA deejay, but older people always asked her "real" name. She never understood why people were so interested in something she felt had nothing to do with who she was. What a boring question.

Lucille Kowalski grew up in Cincinnati in a nuclear family hovering on the edge of the middle class. They were impossibly ordinary: her father, a sales clerk; her mother, a nurse; her older brother, a high school hockey player; and Lu, a misfit. To Lu, it seemed they were all dwelling in the same space without rhyme or reason, random cohabitants. The only real time they spent together, aside from holidays and annual back-to-school shopping, was at the dinner table. Lu's mother insisted they eat together every night, at six o'clock on the dot. Lu sat at the rectangular, Formica table each night to eat a dinner that didn't taste quite right and make small talk that didn't sound quite right.

For as long as she could remember, she had a passion for music, although for years there was little she could do about it. Her school offered music classes, but they were full of uninterested kids clanging away on bongos and tambourines. When she was twelve, her grandparents gave her a small, preprogrammed keyboard designed for kids. She played with it every day, finding ways to push it beyond its bounds. At the age of thirteen, her parents indulged her with weekly piano lessons, but without the ability to practice at home she never got far, and they eventually decided it wasn't worth the money. When she began high school, she realized how limited her exposure to music had been, mostly rock, pop, and classical. At fourteen, she discovered other kinds of music: electronica, trap, hip-hop, trip-hop, and techno. She loved anything with an interesting beat and became fascinated with creating and digitally altering music. When she attended her first high school party, some kid's older brother was deejaying. He wasn't merely playing existing music, but rather, creating his own mixes. A new world opened to her. She wanted to learn everything she could about music production and deejaying. She begged her parents for a laptop, deejay turntables, a mixer, and other basic equipment, but they said it was too extravagant. They always paid for her brother's sports equipment. It felt terribly unfair. Was it because she was a girl? Was it because her interest was somehow less valid? Did they not take her seriously? These questions haunted her. She concluded that a girl with a dream is on her own in the world. She spent the next year mowing lawns and babysitting, even though she was ill-suited for the latter. By the time she was fifteen, she had hobbled together the necessary equipment, all second-hand, and began the long road of self-education.

Lu studied her family during the long silences at dinner. She was taller than her mother, lankier than her father and brother, and looked as out of place as she felt. One night, as she swirled the tuna casserole around her plate, it dawned on her: *I must be adopted.* The thought brought instant relief. Suddenly, she had an explanation; she didn't feel like one of them because she wasn't. The next time she was home alone, she searched the cobweb-filled attic for some proof of her lineage: a baby blanket with another name, a stack of unopened mail from her birth mother, or her real birth certificate. When she didn't find anything, she crept into her parents' room and rifled through their drawers. The only noteworthy discoveries were a secret stash of Oreo cookies her father was hiding and a stack of poems tucked away in her mother's underwear drawer. The poems were in her mother's handwriting, although she had never known her to have the slightest interest in the arts. That was the first and only time she ever thought her mother's life may not have been as boring as it seemed.

After coming up empty on her search, the question of her origin festered. One night at dinner, after her father told her brother to rake the leaves that weekend, to which her brother merely grunted in response, Lu couldn't hold it in anymore. She looked around the table and blurted out, "So, am I adopted or something?"

Her mother casually replied, "What a strange thing to say."

"That's not an answer," Lu said, more convinced than ever.

Her brother laughed. "I wish you were adopted so we could send you back."

Lu ignored him and pressed her mother. "So, am I? It's okay, I just want to know."

"No, you're not adopted. Why on earth would you say that?" her mother replied.

"Because it's the only thing that would explain it, explain us. Haven't you noticed that we don't have anything in common? Not a single thing!"

"I don't understand. We're a family. Is this about that band you want to see?" her mother asked.

Her father sighed. "Not that again. It's past your curfew and that part of town isn't safe."

Lu shook her head. "I told you, it's not a band. It's an open mic night. I want to perform. If I'm gonna do something in art or music, I need experience."

"Maybe you could be an elementary school music teacher," her mother suggested.

"If she's going to be a teacher, she should teach math or history. That's more stable," her father added.

Lu sat in disbelief before shouting, "What are you talking about? I don't want to be a teacher!"

"Well, you don't need to decide now," her mother said.

Lu opened her mouth, but knew there was no adequate response. These people had no idea who she was and they never would. She looked around the table and silently screamed: *How the fuck can I be one of you?*

The next day, Lu stopped at the cheap salon in their local shopping center and got her hair cut very short, "edgy," as she instructed the stylist. That night at dinner, her brother said, "You look like a boy." She replied, "And you look like an idiot." Her parents never said a word, as if they hadn't noticed the loss of ten inches. Lu knew they were too uncomfortable to acknowledge it and so they ignored it. While she had never uttered the words out loud, Lu considered that to be the day she boldly and unapologetically came out, both about her sexuality and musical career path. From that moment on, she considered herself a free agent, free from the pretense of caring about other people's expectations.

Two weeks later, she snuck out to go to the open mic night after paying her brother twenty dollars to cover for her. When it was her turn on stage, she recited a spoken-word poem she had written for the occasion, set to music. The poem needed work, but her delivery and sense of musicality were compelling. Even at the age of fifteen, she possessed the charisma to command attention and was invited to come back. And so began her years of performing in coffee shops, bookstores, bars, and anywhere else that would give her a stage. She met older artists and musicians, some of whom were catty, which taught her to always watch her back. Others became friends "from the scene," although sensing there was somewhere bigger and better in her future, she tried not to get too attached. She frequently found herself in sticky situations. Some nights, drunk men heckled her, other nights they hit on her. These encounters forced her to learn how to negotiate personal safety. One night, a man followed her to the bus stop, making lewd comments. She eventually whirled around and said, "Look buddy, it's not happening. I like girls." He got right in her face and started screaming homophobic slurs, his spit hitting her cheeks. He threatened to "give it to her good," claiming that "a real man would fix you." She was terrified but did her best to hide it, jumping on the first bus that came by. She thought about asking the bus driver for help, but was unsure if she could trust him either. She concluded she was on her own and could no longer risk certainty about people. From that night on, Lu wore her distrust like armor, even when it was exhausting and lonely to do so. She learned to carry herself with attitude and confidence at all times. At the urging of a twenty-something gay man she befriended at a slam poetry event, she began seeking out LGBTQA-friendly venues. She felt an uncomfortable mixture of gratitude for these safer spaces and resentment at the need for them. They made her world at once bigger and smaller. Over time, she developed her persona as Lu K and built a small and loyal following.

When she was seventeen, her brother left for college and her mother began working the night shift. So ended family dinners. This worked well for Lu, who was busy living her authentic life, one her parents didn't care to know about. After a string of casual encounters with girls from school, she met Jenna at a club when she was eighteen. Lu cared for her but could never truly match Jenna's feelings, but when Jenna prepared to move across the country, Lu jumped at the chance to go with her. She left Cincinnati determined to find her people, even though she was equally determined not to need them.

This all came rushing back as she drank her coffee and thought about meeting Paisley's parents, and then as she thought about Paisley, her softness and goodness. Eventually, she heard the shower turn off. *Fuck, I need to get out of my head. Coffee, I need more coffee.* She slurped the last bit in her mug and got up for a refill, stretching her neck, still strained from earlier when Paisley startled her. *Damn,* she thought. She searched the cabinets for ipuprofen, but the bottle was empty so she settled for another cup of coffee. When she put the pot down, she noticed her hand was sticky again. She looked to see a rainbow splotch in the middle of her palm.

Chapter 27

Monroe's eyelashes were stuck together, with thick layers of crust in the corners. She wiped away the particles and slowly opened her eyes. *I can't remember the last time I felt so rested.* It was as if she had slept for days. She turned to look at the clock on her nightstand. It was almost noon. She stretched her arms, reached for her silk robe, and sauntered into the bathroom. She saw her reflection in the mirror and thought, *I know you.* Then she glanced at the small picture of her mother, picked it up, and whispered, "I think I know you too, Mama. Rest well." As she moved to put the photo down, she heard a slight rustling noise and realized she still had the pill bottle in the pocket of her robe. She retrieved the bottle and confidently tossed it in the trash. After freshening up, she grabbed the book on her nightstand and headed to the breakfast room. On her way, she bumped into Henry.

"Good morning, Mrs. Preston, or perhaps I should say good afternoon."

"I can't believe how well I slept, Henry. I feel marvelous."

"Shall I have the cook prepare your usual breakfast or would you prefer lunch?"

"Perhaps an egg white omelet and we'll call it brunch."

"Very good, Mrs. Preston. Shall I bring your book?"

"Thank you, Henry," she replied, handing him the book.

Henry hurried off to inform the cook. Monroe strolled through her home, absentmindedly humming. This time, when she stopped by her Warhol, she saw it with fresh eyes.

Oh Marilyn, thank you for helping me to see. I finally understand what you meant, about life slipping further away. Some of us use glamour as armor, or perhaps as a mask. Others of us prefer to dwell in isolation. No matter the path, we can never hide from ourselves. We can't stop the feelings in all shades of light and dark. She stood for a moment and then smiled, mischievously. *I'm glad Mr. Warhol captured this part of you, the smile just a bit too bright. He was clever. Rest well, dear Marilyn.* Monroe walked away knowing she had finally made peace with something that could not be named and knowing that the painting that had once captivated her would now take on a welcome ordinary quality.

She practically floated into the breakfast room. She poured herself a cup of coffee and picked up her book, left on the table for her. Before she could open it, the cook walked in and presented her meal.

"This looks delicious. Thank you," Monroe said.

"May I get you anything else?"

"My cell phone, please. I must have left it upstairs." *I need to get in touch with Tash right away.*

"Ooh, this is so Cali," Jason said, as he took his seat on the patio at Café Gratitude.

"Yeah, it's kind of hot today but I knew you'd want to sit outside. It's *the* it spot. I once saw Jennifer Lopez here."

"How'd she look?"

"Flawless, of course. She was wearing a short, gold, tunic-style dress, and I would have killed to know what brand of highlighter she was using. Her cheekbones, like *wow*."

"Forget the celebs. Look at the waiters. My oh my," Jason said, lifting his dark sunglasses to get a better look.

"You're such a slut," Tash joked.

"Uh huh," he ageed.

"I can't believe you're moving in with your boyfriend. That's so grown-up. But I can see you haven't lost your wandering eye," Tash said, as Jason strained his neck to look at the waiter.

"Looking is good. Keeps us healthy. It's like yoga for the libido."

She laughed. "I do have to admit the waiters here are seriously hot and they have this chill, Zen thing going on that makes 'em even hotter."

"Speaking of," he said softly as their waiter approached.

"My name is Brock and I'll be taking care of you today. Welcome to Café Gratitude. Have you dined with us before?" he asked as he filled their water glasses.

"I have," Tash said.

"It's my first time," Jason said coyly.

Tash rolled her eyes.

"Welcome. Would you like to hear today's question?"

"Absolutely," Jason replied.

"Today's question is: In what ways are you growing? I'll give you a few minutes with the menu and check back."

As he walked away, Tash shook her head. "You are positively shameless."

"Brock. His name is Brock. I mean, *hello*. He must be a porn star. God, I love LA."

Tash giggled. "I missed you so much."

"Me too."

"We're not really answering that lame question, are we?"

"Hell no. I just wanted the pretty man to stay at the table longer. Okay, so what's good here?" Jason asked, picking up his menu.

"It's totally vegan, but the food is amazing. They have great pressed juices and smoothies you'd love. They do breakfast 'til one on the weekends and I know how you adore brunch."

"Oh my God, I love the names of things."

"Yeah, when you order something, they'll compliment you based on the name they've given the food you select. Like if I order a muffin, he'll call me beautiful. It's so LA."

"Do you ever order based on what you want the hot waiter to say to you? I totally would," Jason mused.

Tash laughed. "I'm not as hard up for compliments as you are."

"Yes, you are."

She crinkled her face.

"The doughnut is called holy. That's adorbs," Jason remarked. "Isn't there some nineties song that goes something like 'you'll never gain weight from a doughnut hole?' Kind of heavy for brunch, huh?"

Tash shrugged.

Soon, Brock returned to take their order. "What can I get you, Miss?"

"I'll have an Arabica coffee and the superfood granola, please."

"You are courageous and powerful," Brock said.

Jason smirked.

"And for you?"

"I'll have the energy juice and the buckwheat flax pancakes, please."

"Would you like to add berries or cashew whipped cream?"

"Let's live a little. I'll add it all," Jason replied.

"You are succulent and open-hearted," Brock said.

Jason smiled. "Indeed I am."

Brock grabbed their menus and walked away. Tash shook her head. "You are so bad. And since when do you eat carbs?"

"I'm treating myself. I mean, cashew whipped cream. How could I pass that up? Damn, I love LA. I can't believe you don't."

"I never said that."

Jason took his sunglasses off and placed them on the table. "Oh, please. It's me."

Tash looked down.

"Tell me."

"I don't want to be a downer," she replied.

"Sweetie, I didn't come all this way for fake talk."

"It's been a really big adjustment. In the beginning it was great, but then…" She trailed off as Brock returned with their drinks.

Jason took a sip of his green juice. "Come on, how could you not love this?" he asked, holding up the glass.

"Gross. It looks like sludge."

Jason laughed, but then his expression turned more serious. "What happened? Was it the dead ends with your film? If they don't get it, screw them. You're ahead of your time."

"Not being able to make anything happen was depressing, but then… God, I feel like a piece of shit for even thinking it…"

"When Aidan got a break, it was hard as hell and you wanted to pull your hair out. Metaphorically, of course. Your hair is fab."

"You know how much I love him and how talented he is. I mean, if anyone deserves…"

Jason interrupted. "You don't have to do that with me. I get it. Aidan's awesome. We all love him. Not the point. You can want good things for him and still feel that it's not fair."

"Thanks. I guess I really needed to say it out loud to release it."

"What about Lu? Can't you talk to her about this?"

Tash raised her eyebrows. "Are you kidding me? She's been working the LA club scene way longer than Aidan. It's tough for her too. Tougher than she'd admit."

Jason took another sip of his juice. "How's the summer gone while he's been away?"

"Honestly, I wasted most of it. I just couldn't try anymore. I couldn't keep putting myself out there just to be rejected. But then I decided, *fuck it*. Regardless of what happens, I'm going to make art. That's how I got the show I have next week. I crawled my way back to myself."

"Which is freaking amazing," Jason said. "See? The waiter was right; you *are* courageous and powerful."

Tash blushed.

"I guess we answered that inane question-of-the-day after all. Sounds like you're growing in lots of ways."

"You too, sweetie. I mean, a full-time man and a full-time job. That's a big change! I'm so proud of you for starting your own interior design business. You're gonna crush it. Using your celeb platform from modeling to build something creative that you actually care about, well, that's awesome. And you never looked better."

Jason smiled. "And Pen! She was always a grown-up, but now that she's getting married, I mean, like wow. And he's so perfect for her. You'll see at the wedding next summer. He has an Indiana Jones thing going on. He's really nerdy and loves talking about dusty old history things, but he's buff and goes off on wild archeological digs. They're adorable together."

Tash smiled. "Just as long as she doesn't make me wear something awful at the wedding."

"Oh, honey, you're fucked for sure. I'm picturing pink taffeta, hopefully with lots of ruffles."

She shook her head and laughed. "You're such a shit. I can't believe you have to head back tomorrow."

"I know, the price of having an actual job. Modeling was so much better."

"Well, on the plus side, you never would have ordered pancakes when you were modeling, and I'm totally taking a bite."

"Oh, before I forget. I saw Harold, that homeless guy you used to talk to."

"You did?" she asked, her eyes wide.

He nodded. "At Chelsea Park. Seemed like that's where he hangs out now."

Tash smiled brightly, relieved to hear Harold was still around.

Just then, Brock delivered their food.

"This looks amazing," Jason gushed.

"You go ahead. I'm gonna check my phone quickly, to see if Aidan's tried to reach me."

Tash had received a text from Monroe.

Hi Tash. I'd like to invite you to the studio's
anniversary party. Please buy yourself a fabulous
gown and put it on my account. It's only a few days
away, so tell them any alterations need to be done
immediately. Use my name. I'm sorry for the last-
minute notice. I do hope you can come.

Tash was stunned. Monroe had never invited her to an event before.
She slipped her phone back in her purse and looked at Jason.

"What?" he asked, with a mouth full of pancakes.

"Uh, so how do you feel about spending the afternoon helping
me pick out a designer gown?"

Chapter 28

Lu pulled up to the estate, her heart racing from the stress of being nearly twenty minutes late. She cranked the air conditioning in her car, afraid she'd sweat through her shirt and have pit stains when she met Paisley's parents. The sight of the modern, oceanfront mansion did nothing to calm her nerves. As she sat in her car, berating herself for wearing a button-down shirt and trying to catch her breath, the front door to the house opened. Paisley flitted over, her white sundress blowing in the breeze. Lu jumped out of the car.

"I'm so sorry. The line was out the door today and my replacement was late. I changed as quickly as I could and motored, but the traffic was epic."

Paisley smiled. "Don't worry about it. You're not that late. And you look great, but you didn't need to dress up."

"Is it too much?" Lu asked nervously, as she made sure her shirt was tucked in.

"You're perfect. My folks are out back. Let's cut through the house to join them and then I can take you around to my place after we eat."

Lu nodded and followed her. They walked into an enormous entryway that opened to an even more enormous living space. Everything was white and airy. The far wall was made entirely of glass, offering an expansive view of the cobalt sea from the moment you entered the house. Even after years in LA, Lu believed that places like this only existed in movies.

"Holy shit," she muttered.

Paisley giggled. "The view is pretty rad, huh?"

"Uh, yeah. You could say that."

"Come on," Paisley said, taking her hand.

They walked to the other side of the room and stepped through the sliding glass door onto the patio. The back of the property boasted a long infinity pool overlooking the Pacific. There was a row of lounge chairs facing the pool, a firepit and bar to the left, and a large table to the right, where Paisley's parents were seated under umbrellas. They casually stood up as Lu and Paisley approached.

"Mom and Dad, this is Lu."

Lu stuck her hand out. "So nice to meet you, Mrs...."

Paisley's mother interrupted. "Please, call me Ivy."

"And I'm Paul," Paisley's father said, outstretching his hand.

Lu smiled. "I'm so sorry I'm late. I had trouble getting out of work and then the traffic was terrible."

"Don't worry about it. We're enjoying the beautiful day," Ivy assured her. Lu noticed how much Paisley resembled her. Ivy was taller and thinner, but they had the same coloring: hair, eyes, and complexion.

Paul was a slight man with light brown hair and glasses. "The traffic gets worse each year," he remarked, sitting down.

"Shall we?" Ivy said, indicating they should all take a seat. "You know, sometimes I think that when Paul retires, we should pack up and move to the mountains to get away from all the congestion here. Maybe Montana. It's beautiful there."

"She says that, but she could never leave the ocean," Paul said with a smile.

"He's probably right," Ivy conceded. "I've been spoiled. There's nothing like doing yoga on the beach. I don't know if I could give it up."

Lu smiled. "Your home is spectacular."

Just then, a staff member came over with carafes of freshly squeezed orange and grapefruit juice.

"Theresa, this is Lu," Paisley said.

"Nice to meet you," Lu said.

"Can I get you coffee or tea?"

"Coffee would be great, thank you."

"For me too, please, Theresa. Oh, and Lu takes milk," Paisley added.

Lu glanced at Paisley, thinking that no one had ever really known her well enough to remember her likes or dislikes before.

Ivy turned to Lu and said, "Please help yourself to some juice, if you'd like."

"I got it," Paisley said, picking up the pitcher of orange juice and pouring some for Lu and then for herself.

"Thanks," Lu said, taking a sip. "Wow, that's delicious. Sweeter than what we've had in the store lately."

"Paisley told us you have a part-time job at a juice bar," Ivy said. "I'm a big juicer. I do a detox at least once a month."

Lu smiled. "Yeah, I've been there for years. I'm the assistant manager. But honestly, it's just a way to pay the bills."

Ivy grinned. "Yes, we've heard you're a gifted deejay. I think it's admirable to do whatever it takes to live as an artist. I could tell you stories about famous musicians I've worked with who walked dogs, washed cars, and bussed tables to make ends meet. That's how you know the real artists: their willingness to work hard because they have to find a way for their art. It's just in their soul. It's a beautiful thing to be around that energy. That's what drew me to the music business."

"You'd be surprised, but it's the same in the tech world, at least for the real creatives who tinker in their parents' garages because they've got some wonderfully bonkers idea they can't let go of no matter how many times they fail. Some people breathe invention and they've just got to spend their lives discovering and creating," Paul said.

Lu smiled, nodding along. It hadn't been five minutes and she already felt that these people saw her, understood her, and what's more, they embraced what mattered most to her. She felt more at home with them than she ever did with her parents. She liked them.

Theresa and another staff member returned with coffee and brunch: an eggless vegetable frittata, fruit salad, and a mesclun salad with tahini dressing.

Once everyone was served, Lu said, "This looks great."

"Most of it came from my mom's vegetable garden, even the herbs."

Paul chuckled. "Be glad it doesn't come from Paisley. This one couldn't keep a cactus alive. She could kill weeds."

"Dad," Paisley whined.

"It's true," Paul insisted, taking a bite of salad.

Paisley turned deep crimson.

"You've always been wonderful with animals, but your dad's right. You didn't inherit my green thumb," Ivy added.

Paisley rolled her eyes. "At least I'm good with bunnies."

Ivy laughed. "You'll always have bunnies."

Lu loved the playful banter. It was clear they were all connected in a special way.

"So, tell me more about your music, Lu," Ivy said. "When did you begin developing your sound?"

They spent the next hour eating, talking about music, and gently teasing Paisley. Ivy was a fount of knowledge about music and Lu loved listening to her stories about the industry. She thought she'd never stop laughing when Ivy told her about a party at which two members of the Rolling Stones were almost thrown out because someone thought they were homeless people that wandered in off the street. Ivy also knew what the industry was like for women. She said, "It's always tougher for women. If there's ever anything I can do for you," but Lu quickly declined and moved the conversation forward. Paul was equally disarming, just as Paisley had described. In meeting them, she understood Paisley better. They all made sense together. As comfortable as Lu felt with them, there remained a small, nagging discomfort. She fit easily into their dynamic. Things never came easily. She didn't know how to trust it.

"You can see it's a lot cozier than the main house" Paisley said, waving her arms around.

"It's great," Lu replied. "It's kind of dope to have a two-room house."

"When I was in high school, I begged my folks to let me live here. They wouldn't let me, but my friends and I would sneak in here whenever it wasn't being used. Once I caught one of the guys from Aerosmith in here with a half-naked model. That's a funny story. I was banned from the guesthouse for months. I know I need to move eventually, but it's been great to finally be allowed to live here."

Lu smiled.

"Take a load off on the couch. I'm just gonna grab us some water," Paisley said.

Lu plopped down. She picked up an art book from the coffee table and started flipping through it.

"You should take my mom up on her offer, if there's ever anyone you want to meet or something," Paisley hollered.

"That's really nice of her and all, but there's no way I would ever ask her for a favor."

"She doesn't mind. She loves helping musicians. If you're too shy to ask, I could do it for you."

Lu put the book back on the coffee table. "No way. Please, don't."

Paisley walked over and handed her a glass of water before taking the seat next to her. "Okay, but I don't see what the big deal is."

"Can we just drop it?" Lu asked.

"Yeah, sure," Paisley said. She tilted her head toward the book Lu had been looking at. "Someone gave me that because the Hockney on the cover reminded them of this place. I don't really see it though. To me there's something unbelievable about his work. It's all surface."

"Yeah, I was never a huge fan, but I can see the resemblance. I mean, this place has a sort of hyper-real, picture-perfect quality."

Paisley giggled. "Yeah, it's kind of a postcard. But what's inside is real. Now that you've seen it and met my folks, can you picture yourself spending some time here?"

Lu squirmed. "The thing is, Malibu is way too far from work for me."

"Yeah, and your place is far from my work."

"Yeah, it's a drag. You know the crazy hours I work. I can't be on the road all the time."

Paisley huffed and shook her head. "I'm not suggesting we always stay here."

"I just don't see how I could ever really come this far."

"Of course you don't. That would mean you'd have to consider someone other than yourself."

"Excuse me?" Lu bellowed, leaping up.

Paisley took a deep breath, steadied her nerves, and then looked up at Lu. "You don't care if it works between us. You can take it or leave it."

"That's not fair," Lu said. "I'm here now."

"When I told you that school is starting soon and things would have to change, you assumed that meant we were over. And you didn't even care. I mean, that was your first thought. You made it pretty clear. And I..."

"What?" Lu asked.

"I can't do it anymore. We don't want the same things. I want to find a way to make it work, to make us work, and you don't even care if we break up. You won't meet me halfway and I can't keep doing it for both of us and hoping or pretending."

"If that's how you feel, maybe I should go."

"Yeah, I guess maybe you should."

Without hesitation, Lu walked out the door. Her heart was racing again, but this time with an overwhelming feeling of regret. Too proud or perhaps too afraid to deal with these uncomfortable feelings, she scurried to her car and headed home.

For the next three days, she focused on each task at hand, whether it was peeling carrots at the juice bar or spinning at the club. Yet no matter how hard she tried to push Paisley out of her mind, she kept slipping in.

Chapter 29

Tash finished washing off the green face mask she applied to make her skin luminous. She was patting her face dry when her phone beeped. There was a text message from Lu.

Hey. You're probably getting ready for that fab Hollywood thing, so no sweat if you don't have time. Just feeling meh. Text if you have a minute.

She immediately dialed Lu's number.

"Hey," Lu said. "You didn't have to call. I know it's a big night for you."

"The driver's not picking me up for two hours. What's going on?"

"Do you think I'm really screwed up?"

"Define *really*," Tash joked.

Lu let out a small laugh. "It's like I'm standing at a precipice and I want to take the leap, I really do, but I'm afraid of..."

"Of smashing to the ground and shattering into a million pieces?"

"Thanks for the vivid image! But seriously, what if I crash?"

"Yeah, that could happen. But what if you fly?"

Lu sighed.

"Listen, I get it. I do. You've gotta do what feels right for you. I just know from experience that being the invincible cool girl takes a toll. It's a lot easier when we have people who get us so we can let our guard down from time to time."

"It's gonna sound stupid, but I never thought I'd need someone, you know?"

"Needing someone isn't half as scary as being needed. Maybe that's what you're really afraid of. But it makes you rise. And push yourself. It's easy to get lazy in ways we don't even recognize."

Lu exhaled. "It probably doesn't matter anyway. I fucked it up."

"Oh please," Tash said. "You can fix it. You've just gotta decide what you really want."

"I want Paisley."

"Then why are you wasting time with me?"

"Promise me one thing," Lu said. "If it doesn't work out, we never had this conversation."

Tash giggled. "You know it. Good luck."

"Thanks. And have an amazing time tonight. You're probably gonna meet so many of your heroes."

"Totally. You should see the guest list. I still can't believe Monroe invited me. I wish Aidan was here to go with me."

"He'll be back soon, right?" Lu asked.

"Yeah, and I'll be busy 'til then anyway. I have work to do for Monroe, then Tuesday I have to go do the set-up at the gallery. He gets back Wednesday. Then the opening is Thursday night. You'll be there, right?"

"Wouldn't miss it."

"I better go get glamorous. Oh my God, you should see my gown. It looks like liquid gold and has this plunging neckline. It's a showstopper, if I do say so myself. I'm wearing my hair down on one side, with waves. Very old-school Hollywood. And of course, bright red lips."

Lu laughed. "You're gonna crush it. Have fun, babe."

"You too, baby."

After exchanging text messages with Paisley, Lu spent an hour pacing around her apartment, waiting for her to arrive. When she heard a gentle knock, she squeezed her eyes shut for a moment and then opened the door.

"Hey, come on in," she said, closing the door behind her. "Thanks for coming here. I would have come to your place if I wasn't working later tonight."

"It's okay," Paisley replied, taking a seat on the edge of Lu's bed. "I wanted to apologize to you anyway."

Lu furrowed her brow and sat down next to her. "*You* wanted to apologize?"

"I overreacted. I was going to reach out, but then you didn't try to get in touch with me, and…"

"I'm the one who should apologize," Lu said, taking a deep breath. "You were just calling me out on my shit. And in some ways, you were spot on. But it's not that I don't care or that I don't want to be with you."

Paisley took Lu's hand. "Then what is it?"

"I want to show you something." Lu jumped up and pulled a photograph out of her dresser drawer.

"What's that?" Paisley asked.

Lu plopped back down on the edge of the bed. "It's a picture of my family."

Paisley took the photo and then looked back at Lu.

"They're nothing like your family. I mean, you guys get each other. No one from my family has any clue about who I am. And they don't even try to learn."

"That must have been tough growing up," Paisley said.

"It made me rely on myself. If I wanted something, I had to find a way to make it happen. I could never count on anyone else to do anything for me. Don't get me wrong, they're not bad people. I don't have a horrible sob story." She looked down as if searching for the words. "When we started dating, you asked me why I moved to the West Coast. You asked what I was trying to get away from. See, the thing is, I wasn't really trying to flee *from* something, but rather *to* something."

Paisley smiled.

"And now I don't want to run at all. I just want to be. I've never felt that way before."

Paisley rubbed Lu's hand.

Lu smiled. "I love you and I want to be with you."

"I love you too," Paisley said.

Lu cupped Paisley's cheek and planted a soft kiss on her mouth. When she pulled back, Paisley said, "So I guess this means you'll be crashing at my place part of the time."

"Actually, what I said about Malibu being too far from work was true." Paisley looked down and bit her lip. Lu continued. "I was thinking, my lease is up soon. I know it's fast, but I was hoping we could get a place together, somewhere in the middle."

Paisley smiled brightly, grabbed Lu, and they fell onto the bed.

Tash stepped out of the limousine to a frenzy of flashing lightbulbs. Photographers clicked away as she slowly walked the carpet toward Magic Manor. Meryl and Goldie were walking ahead of her, and one of the directors she most admired was following behind her. *This is unbelievable, even if it is just one Cinderella night.*

She walked inside and was immediately handed a glass of champagne. Waiters milled around with trays of caviar blinis, mini salmon *en croute*, and artichoke hearts topped with mushroom duxelles. She was popping a blini into her mouth when a parlor magician started doing an illusion. People gathered around to watch. By the end of the trick, Tash was laughing and chatting with a few other guests, but they all turned to look when the Prestons arrived. Monroe looked stunning in a strapless, black satin gown, her ears and neck dripping with diamonds. Tash caught Monroe's eye and they both tilted their heads in acknowledgment of each other. Monroe held her finger up as if to say, please wait for me. Tash smiled and continued making small talk as Bill and Monroe greeted their guests. Soon, Tash saw Monroe whisper something to her husband. Then she sashayed across the room.

"Tash, you look gorgeous. I'm so glad you could make it."

"I can't thank you enough for the invitation and the gown. This is one of the most exciting nights of my life."

Monroe smiled.

"Oh, and you look beautiful too."

"Thank you. I feel wonderful. I had been suffering from terrible insomnia, but I finally started sleeping soundly again." She paused before adding, "It's the strangest thing and I'm a bit embarrassed to admit it, but it actually started after you told me about Aidan's tour. For some reason, I couldn't get it out of my mind."

Tash crinkled her face. "I guess it stirred something up for you too."

"There was just something about his fast success that took hold of my mind. I don't know if you remember, but we also spoke about why I came to Los Angeles. I hadn't thought about that in years and, well, it's not important why, but that got my head spinning. So yes, in a strange way, your boyfriend's tour was the impetus for some restless nights."

"I'm glad you're feeling better."

Monroe looked at her earnestly. "It was your film. I watched your film." She squeezed Tash's hand. "You had never told me what it was about."

Tash smiled. "That was one of my problems with the film festivals and grant proposals. I was terrible at describing it and I think people misunderstood it or wanted it to be something easier to define, something more Hollywood."

Monroe's eyes widened. "When it started with that couple, I thought it was going to be a love story. But that's not really what it is at all."

Tash shook her head. "No, it's not."

Monroe released Tash's hand and then held her hands up as if trying to animate what the film was about. "It's about that thing inside each of us. That thing, that feeling, you know? Possibilities. It's about possibilities."

Tash smiled. "Yes, that's exactly right. I should have had you help me explain it. People didn't get it."

"Well, I did. And Bill did too. I showed it to him and he thought it was brilliant. Hold on, let me get his attention. That's why I invited you; he wants to chat with you."

Tash was dumbfounded as she watched Monroe wave Bill over.

"Well, hello there," he said, extending his hand. "We've seen each other briefly at the house but I don't think we've properly met."

"It's nice to meet you, sir," Tash said, shaking his hand. "Thank you so much for having me."

"Monroe was quite taken with your film. I know you didn't ask her to show it to me; I hope you don't mind that she did. You can't imagine how many people have asked Monroe to show me their headshots, or scripts, or films. She never has before, not once, so I watched your film with deep curiosity. I can see why she was moved. You have a great sensibility. It showed tremendous promise."

Tash blushed and tried to keep her mouth from falling open. "Thank you. I'm extremely honored."

"Let me cut to the chase. A couple of years ago, we acquired several small production companies. One of them specializes in art films, producing pieces for museum theaters, supporting the shorts, and so on. We had the idea to turn it into something, maybe even work with streaming platforms, but the truth is, we haven't done much with it yet. We need to get some talent in there with vision to curate and develop content. Are you available to come in Monday for an interview and to meet the team?"

Tash's jaw dropped. "Uh, I don't even know what to say."

"Say yes."

"Yes, of course. I'll be there."

"Terrific. I'll have my assistant call you to confirm the details. It was wonderful talking with you, but I can see one of my snippiest screenwriters and snarkiest directors huddled together. They're giving me the eye. If I don't go say hello, they'll make my life hell."

Tash laughed. "Of course. Thank you again for the opportunity."

"I'll join you in a minute, darling," Monroe said.

As soon as Bill walked away, Tash's eyes became misty.

"Oh, don't cry dear, you'll ruin your eye makeup."

"Monroe, I don't know how to thank you. I can't believe you did this for me."

"There's no need to thank me. You're talented, truly talented. Tash, you have a passion. I envy that about you. It's something I always longed for."

Tash smiled.

"Just promise you'll meet me for lunch from time to time and you'll tell me if what I'm wearing belongs on the worst-dressed list."

"Of course," Tash replied, sniffling.

"I better join Bill before he thinks I defected. Enjoy yourself tonight. There should be quite a lot of magic."

"I will. Monroe, please know how grateful I am. I think you're extraordinary. And I bet you have more passion in you than you realize. It's never too late."

Monroe smiled and sauntered off.

Tash stood, glowing as brightly as her gown, taking in the feeling, the chatter, and the magic.

Chapter 30

Tash was standing in the back of the gallery's media room when Patty popped in to check on her.

"How's the system working?" Patty asked.

"It's great," Tash replied, turning to face her. "Projecting it on all three walls was an awesome idea, especially for the opening running scene. You feel like you're moving with them."

"Glad we could make it work. We were prepared for it from a show we did last year, but I always cross my fingers for anything tech."

Tash smiled. "I hear ya."

"I'm dashing out for a lunch meeting. I'll see you Thursday night."

"I'm just gonna run through it a couple more times to make sure there aren't any glitches with the thirty-second delay between showings. Then I'll set up the chairs and head out myself."

"Ellen's up front if you need anything. Make sure to use the white folding chairs. They're stacked in the back room."

"Okay. Thanks, Patty."

As Patty left, the film ended. Tash walked to the center of the dark, empty room, waiting for the film to restart. She was standing still, her mind quiet, when she heard someone step into the doorway and knock on the wall. Thinking Patty forgot something, she turned, just as the film began again. The light hit her face as her images popped up all around her. She gasped. It was Aidan. He was wearing black leather pants, a T-shirt, headphones slung around his shoulders, and the sexiest smile she had ever seen. "Hey there, beauty queen," he said, leaning against the doorframe.

She smiled as the light and images from her film bounced off her face. "Aidan," she said, as if confirming it was really him. "I thought you weren't coming home until tomorrow."

"Yeah, after you called yesterday with your incredible news, I decided to skip the big party. Hitched a ride with one of the crew who had to get back for his kid's birthday."

"How'd you know where to find me?"

"When I got home, I bumped into Darrell. He told me you'd be here."

She smiled.

"So, creative development for an artsy production company, a subsidiary of a major studio. I mean, wow. Holy smokes. That's amazing. Congratulations. I'm so proud of you."

"I still can't believe it. I'll be going through submissions and curating content with two other people, who I met and actually really like. I mean, it's not glamorous, but Aidan, can you believe it?"

He smiled, looked her up and down, and then said, "Yeah, I can believe it."

She blushed. "I might be able to pitch some of my own work too."

"I'd expect nothing less," he said, walking over. They stood inches apart, staring at each other as the light from the projector hit their faces.

"So, what have you been up to this summer?" she asked.

He slipped the headphones off his shoulders and put them on her ears. "This is something new I've been working on." He put his arms around her waist and hit play. She listened to his beats as her images swirled around them both. She remembered that day at the MoMA years earlier, sitting together in the film room, someone else's images floating around them. That night they made love for the first time, their eyes locked. Now her whole universe was filled with their art, and their love.

After a few minutes, she took off the headphones, leaned in, and kissed him.

"God, I missed you," he said.

"Me too. I love you. I'm sorry for how things were before you left. I had to work through some stuff."

"I know. It's all good."

"Oh, I never told you, Jason saw Harold in Chelsea."

Aidan smiled. "So, you said your new job starts November first. Did Monroe ask you for two months or something?"

"No. She's so amazing, she just let me go. I'm already done. I offered to help her find a replacement, but she said she could find someone. I actually think she's going to do it on her own for a bit. She texted me this morning that she's signing up for a class, either writing or fashion design. I think she's trying to figure out what's next for her. You know, find her bliss."

"That's cool."

"Yeah. And I'll still see her. She stops by the studio from time to time and made me promise to meet her for lunches."

"Why aren't you starting the new job right away?"

"I asked for two months. When I start, I want to give it my all and I really want to write my full-length screenplay first, while I have time. I know I should have done it this summer, but I was going through some stuff and…"

"You don't have to explain."

"I know nothing may come of it, but it's just something I need to see through. So, I'm taking two months off to write. With what we're both making now I figured we could swing it. Is that okay?"

"It's perfect, actually."

She raised an eyebrow.

"Calvin's two-week UK tour starts the week after next. We bonded, and as a thank you present, he invited us to come along for a vacation, all expenses paid."

Tash grinned.

"When we were in New York, you asked me if I could deejay in LA. Do you remember?"

"I remember."

"Well, can you write in London? I figured we could use the time together. You can write during the day and we can party at night. The clubs are supposed to be the bomb. We could even catch some theater if you need inspiration. So, what do you say, beauty queen? Are you in?"

She watched the images floating around them, and then looked into his eyes. "I'm all in."

Further Engagement for Book Clubs
or Class Use

Discussion Questions

1. *Film Blue* suggests we can all become different versions of ourselves. Explore this topic in relation to any of the central characters. What about with yourself or your friends?

2. The issue of coping with all forms of abuse comes up in different ways in the book, from Sam being harassed on the streets of his hometown, to Aidan being beaten up in high school, to Tash remembering her sexual assault, to Monroe and Lu remembering being harassed. How are these issues reflected in your community?

3. *Film Blue* suggests that the art we make and experience helps shape who we are. Explore this topic in relation to any of the main or supporting characters. What about with yourself or your friends?

4. The use of a fictional lens allows for the exploration of characters' pasts as well as their "inner worlds" through techniques

such as flashbacks and interior dialogue. Select an example from the book that shows how one of these techniques helped to illustrate the identity issues the character was struggling with.

5. Popular culture and art are referenced throughout the book. Select a few of these references to explore. How does it influence the character? What, if any, symbolism is evoked? What, if any, metaphors to do you see?

6. Sociologically, *Film Blue* explores the "front stage" and "back stage" of each main character. Find a few examples of scenes in which we can see how the back stage is influencing the front stage, or where there is a disjuncture between how a character presents publicly and the behind-the-scenes reality.

7. Issues related to privilege surface throughout the book, for example, in mentions of homelessness. Explore this topic using examples from the book and what you think about the characters and their perspectives.

Creative Activities

1. Select one of the characters and fast forward five years. Write a short story based on where you think they are now.

2. If *Film Blue* was a play instead of a novel, it would likely include monologues by the main characters. Select a character and write their pivotal monologue.

3. Write Tash's full-length screenplay, remembering that the short version is about "possibilities."

4. Write an alternative ending to *Film Blue*.

5. Create a visual or audio-visual version of *Pop Candy*, Tash's short film. You could use film or a visual arts media such as drawing, painting, or comics.

6. Respond artistically to *Film Blue*. Using any media – literary, visual, or performative – create an artistic response to a theme in the novel or illustrate how the novel made you feel. Write a brief artist's statement to accompany the work.

7. Create a piece of art, in any media, that could be a part of the group show at Patty Price's gallery. Think about how the piece complements or relates to Tash's short film. Title the piece.

About the Author

Patricia Leavy, Ph.D. is a bestselling author. She has published over forty books, earning commercial and critical success in both non-fiction and fiction, and her work has been translated into numerous languages. Over the course of her career, she has also served as series creator and editor for ten book series with Oxford University Press, Brill/Sense, and Guilford Press, and she is cofounder of *Art/Research International: A Transdisciplinary Journal*. She has received numerous accolades for her books. Recently, *Celestial Bodies: The Tess Lee and Jack Miller Novels* won the 2022 Firebird Book Award for Romance and the 2022 International Impact Book Awards for Romance and Women's Fiction, and her novel *Spark* won the 2021 National Indie Excellence Award for New Adult Fiction, the 2019 American Fiction Award for Inspirational Fiction, and the 2019 Living Now Book Award for Adventure Fiction. She has received career awards from the New England Sociological Association, the American Creativity Association, the American Educational Research Association, the International Congress of Qualitative Inquiry, and the National Art Education Association. In 2016, Mogul, a global women's empowerment network, named her an "Influencer." In 2018, the National Women's Hall of Fame honored her, and SUNY-New Paltz established the "Patricia Leavy Award for Art and Social Justice." In 2021, she founded Paper Stars Press. Please visit www.patricialeavy.com for more information or for links to her social media.

Made in the USA
Middletown, DE
05 October 2022